SABRINA'S
TEARDROP

Other books in the Inspector Chard Series

Fortuna's Deadly Shadow
Fatal Solution

SABRINA'S TEARDROP

LESLIE SCASE

SEREN

Seren is the book imprint of
Poetry Wales Press Ltd,
Suite 6, 4 Derwen Road, Bridgend, Wales, CF31 1LH

www.serenbooks.com
facebook.com/SerenBooks
Twitter: @SerenBooks

ISBN: 9781781726792
Ebook: 9781781726808

A CIP record for this title is available from the British Library.

The publisher acknowledges the financial assistance of the Books Council
of Wales.

Printed in Bembo by Severn, Gloucester.

To my son-in-law,
Neil
A Proud Salopian

Author's Note

This is a novel of the late nineteenth century. For authenticity, some characters may reflect attitudes of misogyny and other social prejudices prevalent at the time.

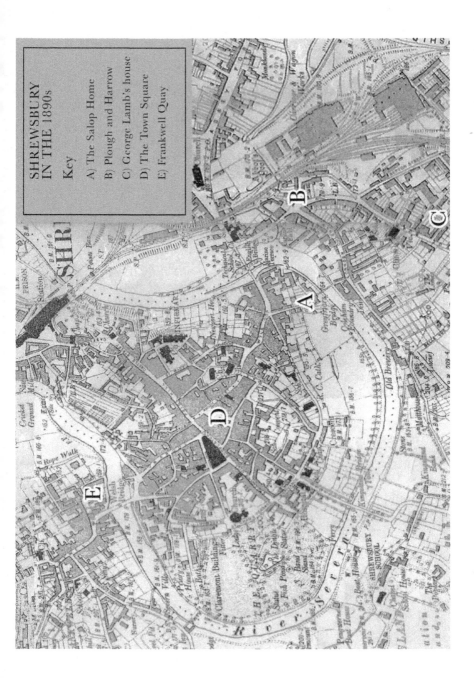

SHREWSBURY
IN THE 1890s

Key

A) The Salop Home
B) Plough and Harrow
C) George Lamb's house
D) The Town Square
E) Frankwell Quay

ONE

January 1895 - Shropshire

'Faster, damn you!' shouted the passenger of the hansom cab as it raced through the darkness towards the river bridge at Atcham. A whip cracked as the driver responded to the command.

'If only the blasted train had been on time at Crewe,' the passenger muttered, tapping the sill of the carriage door in agitation. This evening's event had taken weeks of preparation and everything rested on it. Yet now he was late, but hopefully not too late.

The hansom crossed the bridge and slowed, before turning sharply off the road and through the outer gate of Attingham Estate. Braziers had been lit at fifty-yard intervals to mark the private road across the vast grounds, but it was still necessary for the cab to proceed slowly. Lights from Lord Berwick's mansion could be seen in the distance and music sounded faintly on the breeze.

The cab's occupant stroked his moustache and continued to bemoan his bad luck. 'I should have been back hours ago. This has cost a fortune to set up and if it goes wrong, I'm ruined,'.

The hansom made its way to the front of the mansion and the passenger quickly alighted, embarrassed at having arrived at such a prestigious occasion in a cab rather than a carriage.

Hastily paying his fare, he ran up the steps to the main entrance and threw his hat and coat to a waiting footman.

'Where on earth have you been Charles?' demanded a short man wearing pince-nez spectacles. Bald apart from wispy strands of white hair that framed his pate, he used a handkerchief to pat sweat from his brow. Evidently, he was flustered.

'I had business in the north and my train was delayed. There was barely time to call at my house to change,' explained the late arrival.

'You are alone I take it?'

'Yes Leonard, I thought it best to leave her behind,' answered Charles.

'Good, very wise. Come into the dining room and I'll tell you how we've been getting along.'

Before they had chance to leave the marble-walled entrance hall, a tall, fair-haired, straight-backed figure strode up to them from the direction of the drawing room.

'Charles! There you are! What are you playing at? We've finished dining, the gentlemen have finished their port and cigars…'

Leonard Warren became flustered once more. 'Be discreet Stanmore,' he cautioned. 'Come into the dining room. Our guests seem happily entertained and won't miss us.'

Grunting his agreement, Jeremy Stanmore followed Warren and Charles Landell across the hall into the dining room.

'I'm glad we didn't have to pay for all that silver,' commented Warren to his two business partners.

'No, it's all Lord Berwick's, but we've paid for everything else. We've provided all the staff, the catering and even paid to decorate half a dozen guest rooms. You'd have thought the old bastard could have provided the staff at least,' replied Stanmore.

'That was likely, was it? He hardly ever comes here. It's only by chance he's back in the country and not swanning around the Mediterranean on his yacht. His funds are low and so I saw a chance for mutual benefit,' Charles explained. 'We desperately need to draw in new investors for our business dealings in South Africa. He's one of our existing investors and is hard up for cash. If we can get enough capital out of this evening, then I've promised we'll pay him a fee, less our expenses.'

'I am pleased to say that the evening appears to be a success. Most of the guests are very wealthy and seem to be willing to invest considerable sums,' said Warren.

'All of them *nouveau riche,* with the desire to impress their friends,' sneered Stanmore. 'The opportunity to dine with Lord Berwick and to boast that they've seen the mysterious Sabrina's Teardrop appears to have been too great to resist.'

'Yes Charles, we must thank you for getting Lady Deansmoor to attend, wearing the famous jewel,' added Warren.

'It wasn't difficult. We are related after all, albeit distantly. I think the mansion itself was quite a draw.'

Stanmore scoffed at Charles's remark. 'It's all show. Its timber framed for God's sake! The granite facing stones hide the fact.'

'But look at the lighting,' argued Warren. 'It's electricity. In every room. Every single room, even the servants' quarters,' he exclaimed. 'It's a miracle of modern technology.'

'I bet we're financing the fuel for the generator as well,' grumbled Stanmore. 'I had a quick look at the expenses for running this event earlier today. Quite substantial.'

Charles Landell held his breath, concerned about what might come next.

'Nevertheless,' continued Stanmore, 'I agree with Leonard. It looks like the evening will be a success.'

Charles breathed a sigh of relief. The expenses for the event had been manipulated to hide the significant sum he'd embezzled from the partnership's accounts. It was important that there was more investment, otherwise there would be very close scrutiny of the costings and his deception would come to light sooner rather than later. If he was found out in a few months' time, it wouldn't matter. By then he would be living in America with new funds under a new name. No longer would he be troubled by his gambling debts. Losing the large house in Shrewsbury would be a pity, but it was mortgaged to the hilt in any case.

'The food was very good, it was a pity you missed it,' commented Warren.

'Good. I only hired the very best staff from the top restaurants in the county,' replied Charles, which was far from the truth. He had hired some half decent staff, paid them poorly and doubled the actual cost in the account books as part of his plan to cover the embezzlement. The food and wine, purporting to be from the best suppliers had actually come via some very dubious sources.

'It's a pity that bounder Harry Foden was invited for the after-dinner soirée,' said Stanmore. 'He took a considerable sum off one of our guests in a few hands of cards over the port and cigars.'

Warren nodded his agreement. 'I've done business with him privately. He's very influential in parts of Birmingham and is looking to extend his interests. I wouldn't have invited him here though. That's down to Charles.'

'He's a personal acquaintance and I had no option,' grimaced Charles, not wishing to explain further.

'If you aren't too pleased to have *him* here, then I've got more bad news for you. Let's join the others in the drawing room,' suggested Stanmore.

Warren and Charles followed the taller man out of the room, and crossed the entrance hall once more. As they did so, the under-butler hired for the evening exchanged a glance with Charles which he hoped had not been noticed by his companions. Then the servant turned and disappeared downstairs to the servants' quarters.

***

John Kelly had been well paid and promised a glowing reference for future work. Sacked from his previous employment for drunkenness, he was lucky to be under-butler, even on a temporary basis. Tonight though, he was sober and determined to follow his instructions to the letter, however strange they seemed.

Rushing through the servants' quarters, he exited into the rear courtyard which was in darkness. Young, fit and of a wiry physique, Kelly sprinted out of the enclosed courtyard and into the grounds beyond. Turning to the right he ran around the Eastern boundary wall of the mansion, past the stone colonnades, until he was outside the wall of the drawing room. Reaching out, Kelly grabbed the lead drainpipe that ran from the roof and began to climb. He had no fear of falling, as he had taken a practice run the previous evening in preparation. Reaching the first floor he took a couple of steps along a ledge, the most precarious part of the climb, placed a cloth against a specific section of window and gave it a gentle tap. Having used a glass cutter to prepare the window on his practice climb, a small circular section of glass fell into the room, making the slightest of sounds. Kelly paused, waiting to see if someone would enter the room and switch on a light. It was unlikely, for the valets and ladies' maids of the small number of overnight guests were in the servants' kitchen; and would remain there until the party ended.

'Here goes,' he muttered as he put his hand through the opening. Carefully, Kelly undid the catch and pushed the sash window open until it was wide enough to squeeze through. Immediately, he retreated to the drainpipe, scurried down it and went to the nearest bush. Bending down, he picked up an old shoe he'd hidden earlier, and placed it close to the wall where it would easily be found. Taking a deep breath Kelly sprinted back the way he had come, and as he reached the servants' quarters he lit a cigarette.

'Having a crafty smoke are you Mr Kelly?' asked the cook as he entered the kitchen.

'Just had a minute by the back door Mrs Evans,' he replied.

He had been absent about ten minutes, though it had felt like an eternity. Just one more thing to do later in the night; a quick visit to the generator located in the laundry room, and then his assignment would be complete.

***

Warren smiled as the three partners entered the drawing room. 'Everyone seems to be having a good time,' he observed, dabbing his sweating forehead with a handkerchief once more.

Everything was indeed in full swing, with two dozen of Shropshire's elite in ebullient mood. The room's magnificent crystal chandelier sparkled above the revellers, and the enormous mirrors at each end of the room made the gathering seem even larger.

A fire had been lit whilst the guests had been dining, and now heat radiated from the marble fireplace, causing some of the male guests to adjust their collars.

'That's Dunstan the property magnate, and he has agreed to double his initial investment,' said Stanmore. He pointed to a grey-haired worthy who must have been at least in his seventies. The magnate had settled at a piano and was merrily playing a polka tune, to the delight of several ladies who clapped in time.

'And there, gentlemen, is our prize main attraction,' added Stanmore, drawing his companions' attention to an elderly, aristocratic figure in the far corner. Charles Landell followed Stanmore's gaze towards his great aunt, Lady Deansmoor, who was holding court before several enraptured guests. Not that they were fascinated by what the haughty dame had to say; it was what she wore that drew their attention. Around her neck, Lady Deansmoor wore a necklace on which was suspended a large teardrop sapphire. It sparkled with such brilliance that Charles was temporarily speechless.

'I assume you've seen it before Charles,' stated Warren, lighting a cigarette.

'No, never. It is usually kept in a safe. It took a lot of coaxing before I finally managed to persuade her to bring it along.'

'It was certainly worth it. Lord Berwick is also playing his part. They've set up the card table and he seems fairly affable.'

'Perhaps for now, but your guest, Foden, is joining the game. Charles, I don't like him. Can't you get him to leave?' asked Stanmore.

Landell grunted. 'I only wish I could,' he admitted. 'But....'

Suddenly he froze, 'Christ! What is he doing here? Why didn't you warn me?' he exclaimed.

Stanmore rested his hand on the startled man's shoulder and gave a sarcastic grin. 'I did mention earlier that I had more bad news for you.'

The object of Charles's displeasure was a well-built, dark-haired man in his early thirties with large side whiskers who stood partially obscured by the men near the fireplace. He held a large glass of brandy and was talking to, or rather being talked to, by an attractive dark-haired woman of a similar age.

'Inspector Chard has been sent here by the Shrewsbury Borough Police Force to keep an eye on the famous 'Sabrina's Teardrop'. God knows why. If anything, it should have been the Shropshire Constabulary's responsibility to send a man. Not that I think it's necessary anyway.' Stanmore tapped the side of his nose. 'I detect Mrs Ferguson must have had a word in the ear of the Chief Constable. She certainly has been monopolising the inspector at every possible opportunity.'

'What do I do now?' demanded Charles.

'Just keep on the fringes and get into conversation with the guests. He'll be occupied with Mrs Ferguson and at the rate he's drinking I doubt he'll trouble you.'

'Yes,' added Warren, 'just enjoy the party. In a while you'll be as relaxed as everyone else. Just you see.'

Charles nodded, but was concerned what the night ahead would bring.

***

By one o'clock in the morning, the guests were still in ebullient mood, some regretting they'd called for carriages to be ready at 2 a.m.

Inspector Thomas Chard poured himself yet another brandy and cursed inwardly. 'Load of pretentious bastards!'

He had never been the worse for drink on duty before, but tonight things were different. Five years ago, he had returned to his home county of Shropshire, having made a name for himself as a detective sergeant in Manchester. He'd been appointed as an inspector in the Shrewsbury Borough Police Force and life couldn't have been brighter. Yet now, everything in his personal life was in turmoil and he didn't know how to deal with it. To make matters worse, he had been ordered to attend this function on the pretext of ensuring no-one stole Lady Deansmoor's sapphire. He'd been puzzled at first, as Atcham was outside his jurisdiction, but then all became clear as soon as Della Ferguson pounced on him.

The inspector gave a wry smile as, through an alcoholic haze, he noticed her approach once more.

'Thomas dear, put that glass of brandy down. You've nearly drank a whole bottle of the wretched stuff. Come and dance with me.'

'I am sorry Mrs Ferguson, but I am on duty,' came the slightly slurred reply as the inspector straightened his posture.

'Stop calling me Mrs Ferguson, Thomas. You were happy to call me Della once upon a time, and many other things besides,' giggled his admirer. 'If you don't want to dance, then just take my arm and let me lead you somewhere more private.'

Chard had to admit that Della was a very beautiful woman, He still found her smile captivating. Warm, welcoming, it drew him in, and without thinking he allowed himself to be led through a door into the adjoining chamber.

The Sultana Room was a quiet retreat from the boisterous drawing room and only two ladies were present, taking a discreet inhalation of cocaine at a far table.

'Let's go into the alcove,' suggested Della, leading them to a long low Ottoman settee upholstered in red silk.

The inspector let himself be guided to the alcove and he did not resist when Della sat alongside him and held his hand.

'Where is Major Ferguson?' he felt obliged to ask.

'Reginald doesn't like these sorts of things. He can be a real bore sometimes,' complained Della. 'Anyway, he is away on business, so couldn't have come. I'm glad you know; because I've had rather a lot of champagne and he would not have approved,' she added, wagging a finger.

Chard gave an involuntary grin at the admonishing expression on Della's face. She always was able to make him smile; something he hadn't done in weeks.

'I'll tell you a secret, Thomas. You're only here because I persuaded nice Superintendent Edge to let you come. No-one really wanted a policeman to guard Lady Deansmoor's sapphire.'

'I'd guessed you had something to do with it,' grimaced Chard. 'There are other things I should be doing.'

'Your superintendent agreed because he is concerned about you. It's a break from your troubles, just for one night.'

Chard smiled. 'Perhaps you are right,' he conceded.

'Then come with me.'

Taking his hand, Della led Chard from the alcove, grabbing a half-finished bottle of champagne which had been discarded on a table. Exiting by a different door, Della led Chard to the foot of the grand staircase.

'If a man can't hit his own wife then who can he hit? The country's gone to the dogs!' ranted Lord Berwick, out of sight in the adjoining picture gallery.

'Quick, before we are seen!' urged Della.

Befuddled by the brandy, Chard followed her obediently up the staircase, steadying himself by holding the gilded rails. At the top there appeared to be a dead end, just a scarlet blank wall.

'I can't find the knob,' giggled Della. 'Ah there it is.'

A concealed door opened and Chard now found himself in a narrow corridor.

'Where are we going?' asked the inspector, feeling strangely vulnerable.

'We'll have some privacy in one of the rooms, just for a few minutes.'

All of a sudden, everything went black and Chard was unable to see a thing. 'What's going on?' he demanded, a hint of panic in his voice.

Della gave a wicked laugh. 'The generator must have failed. It'll take them ages to fix it. Now's our time. I can feel a door handle. Come here!'

Chard was pulled into a darkened room and immediately, Della's lips were on his.

'You shouldn't have left me, Thomas,' she murmured.

'Things just didn't work out. It was a long time ago.'

'Five years isn't very long.'

'Much has happened since then,' countered Chard as Della nibbled his ear whilst simultaneously starting to undress him.

'I shouldn't have married Reginald, but you gave me no option.'

'At least he's rich, which I guess is why you're here tonight,' suggested the inspector, making no attempt to resist her advances.

'He has investments which is how I managed an invitation, but my reason for being here is you.'

'You know we can't be doing this…' argued Chard without any real conviction.

'I would kill to have you back Thomas. Just remember that.'

Della bit Chard's neck playfully and the inspector succumbed to the inevitable, helping his former lover out of her dress.

Ten minutes later, their coupling was interrupted by a woman's scream from somewhere in the building.

'What was that?' asked Chard, listening intently.

'Don't stop! Don't you dare stop!' scolded Della.

The inspector obeyed, ignoring the raised voices somewhere in the distance.

Minutes later, Della's moans were interrupted by the sound of footsteps in the corridor outside, followed by the door being flung open.

Chard looked across, dismayed to see Lord Berwick holding an oil lamp, an expression of utter shock on his face.

***

The following evening, John Kelly finished his meal and got up from the table.

'Where are you off to Johnny boy?' asked his elder brother. 'I thought your job was only for last night.'

'It was Sean. Indeed it was, and well worth my time.'

'So where are you going? I hope you're not up to no good. I've got a respectable job and if you get into trouble then it'll be me who suffers.'

'Don't worry yourself, Sean. I just want to collect what I'm owed.'

'I thought you said you'd been paid in advance.'

'Cash yes, and handsomely. But I've also been promised a fine reference, and that's what I need to go on the straight and narrow. My benefactor said he would send it on to me, but I want to make sure. I thought it would be worth calling on him, around the back at the tradesman's entrance of course,' answered John.

Sean grunted. 'I don't know whether to believe you this time, but if you're telling the truth, good luck to yer.'

Kelly went into the cold winter's night and headed into Shrewsbury town. He passed the cattle market and considered calling into The Globe to take a whisky against the chill night air.

'Best stay respectable,' he lectured himself. Choosing to avoid the centre of town, he crossed the River Severn over the Welsh Bridge then walked on until he finally reached Kingsland. He knew Charles Landell's address, having made his own discreet enquiries after receiving his original instructions. Even so, it took some time to find the large house, set in its own grounds.

'Here it is,' he said with satisfaction.

Kelly looked around to see if anyone was watching his movements, then quickly threw himself against a hedge as he noticed an old man walking his dog on the other side of the road. The dog walker seemed to be moving erratically as if drunk, then stopped for a moment. Kelly watched as the man pulled out a hip flask and took a swig before continuing on his way.

Waiting until the man had gone out of sight, Kelly moved away from the hedge and approached Landell's property.

'Strange, I would have thought it would be closed,' he muttered as the large wrought iron gate swung open at the merest push.

By instinct, Kelly crept stealthily towards the property, noticing that only one window seemed to be lit. Abruptly he froze, as voices could be heard. There was someone at the door. It was Landell and he was talking to a visitor.

'Well! Well! I wonder what you're doing here?' exclaimed Kelly under his breath.

TWO

Eighteen months later
September 1896 Pontypridd, South Wales

Inspector Thomas Chard sat alone at a table in the Ivor Arms, sipping his first beer of the evening. It had been a long hot summer and a busy one for a policeman. Whether the heat had caused more people to turn to crime or not he couldn't tell. One of his constables had been severely injured that very week by an ironworker called Pullman, a man formerly of good character. It made the inspector feel melancholy, and nostalgic for his former life in Shrewsbury.

He remembered the night when everything went wrong. At least his drunkenness had lessened the immediate feeling of shame. It was somehow worse looking back on it. Della in just a chemise and himself in only his shirttails, coupling against a chest of drawers; whilst Lord Berwick's shocked face gradually developed into a lascivious grin.

By the time the generator had been repaired, they had dressed, sobered by the realisation that their reputations would be ruined. Lord Berwick was not known to be discreet. Shamefaced, they had walked downstairs to find the place in pandemonium. The servants had all been called up from below stairs, guests were checking their belongings; and Lady Deansmoor was being comforted by someone he hadn't noticed earlier in the evening, Charles Landell. Before he could say a word, one of the hosts, Leonard Warren, had rounded on him.

'You're the policeman here! Lady Deansmoor's jewel has been stolen. Where were you?'

That was the same question levelled at him by Superintendent Edge the following morning.

'Damn it all Chard! What a mess! Where were you? No, don't

answer. It's a rhetorical question. I know where you were and probably so does half of Shrewsbury by now. If you had just disgraced yourself, then that would be one thing, but you've made our force look incompetent. One of the most valuable jewels in the country stolen from right under your nose. Can you imagine how I'm going to explain to the Shropshire County Constabulary why I had one of my men on duty on their patch? I bloody can't.'

Chard had understood his superintendent's foul mood and would have been just as angry if he had been in Edge's position. The Shropshire County Constabulary had been called in, everyone had been interviewed and the servants searched. A broken window had been found in a first-floor bedroom and beneath it a discarded shoe. A search of the surrounding area had been ordered, with the guests finally allowed to leave at 6 a.m. When Chard had been ordered to report to the police station, he had managed only an hour's sleep and still felt hungover.

'I only sent you because you're my best detective and you've had a hard time of things. We were all worried about you; and when Mrs Ferguson had a word with me, I thought it was a good idea to give you a break. More fool me,' the superintendent complained.

The admonishment had continued for some time before the superintendent finally announced his decision.

'You are suspended with immediate effect. There will of course have to be a disciplinary hearing which will probably see you dismissed. I suggest you resign before that happens. In the meantime, I will try and find you a position with another force. Hopefully in a couple of years this unfortunate incident will have blown over and we can consider your return.'

Chard gave a rueful smile as he recalled the accusing stares from his colleagues as he left the station in disgrace.

The superintendent had been generous in finding him another position. He had served in the army with a fellow officer who had become a superintendent in the Glamorgan County Constabulary. In a matter of weeks Chard had arrived in the busy South Wales town of Pontypridd as their new inspector.

Pontypridd, or Ponty as it was often known, was both an industrial and a market town; with iron and steel works, textile mills and numerous coal mines. It sat astride the road, rail and canal networks which connected the ports of South Wales to the coal-producing valleys. Chard had found it difficult settling in to a place that had initially felt so different to anywhere he had previously experienced. Yet now, eighteen months later, things had changed.

He had discovered a genuine warmth in the local people, who he'd come to know and trust. With the odd exception, he respected his colleagues, who were forever struggling due to a lack of resources. And he felt comfortable in his house situated close to the police station, especially since appointing a 'maid of all works', on a full-time basis. Chard took another sip of his beer and went to scratch his sideburns, before stopping himself. It was an old habit from times gone past before he had trimmed them short. Instead he stroked his neat moustache in thought.

'Perhaps I'll never go back,' he murmured to himself.

The inspector's reverie was interrupted by a bang, as the pub door, which was always stiff to open, was flung back with force.

Everyone turned to stare, as in rushed a sturdily built police constable with mutton chop whiskers.

Chard looked up in astonishment. One rule was sacrosanct amongst his constables. The Ivor Arms was where he liked to relax, and none of them were to enter unless in cases of dire emergency.

'Where's the inspector?' demanded the constable, looking in the direction of the bar.

'I'm here Constable Morgan. There had better be a good explanation for your interruption,' responded Chard, from his table in the corner.

'Sorry sir, but it's urgent. Please could you come outside? It's a matter of life and death.'

Chard groaned, but dutifully picked up his hat and followed his constable out of the pub, into the night.

***

'There's Mr Pennel is waiting for us,' said Constable Morgan pointing to a young, frail-looking man who stood by the front door of his small terraced cottage next to the river.

On the way to the cottage, Morgan had explained that

Mr Pennel's baby son had died in his mother's arms earlier in the evening. The sad event appeared to have unhinged Mrs Pennel and she was threatening to kill herself.

'Oh, thank God you've come, Inspector. The constable said you would be the best person to call. When my Maria saw his uniform, she broke a glass and held it to her own throat. He said you might be close by and in plain clothes.'

'Why didn't you send for a vicar or minister?' asked Chard.

'That's the first thing I suggested to her,' answered the husband, wringing his hands in despair. 'She said that she was damned in the eyes of God and if I fetched the minister from the chapel, she would do herself in. I went outside in desperation and saw the constable.'

'I did try my best sir, but it just seemed to make matters worse, so I thought of you,' added Morgan.

'Do you have any other family?' asked the inspector.

'None in the town.' Replied Pennel.

'No other children?'

'None. We have not been blessed. Maria twice gave birth to still-born daughters. This was our first boy.' Pennel wept as he spoke.

Chard nodded and patted the husband's shoulder. 'I'll try my best,' he promised, removing his hat and passing it to Constable Morgan.

'She's downstairs, in the back of the house,' informed Pennel.

With considerable trepidation, the inspector walked to the front door and gently pushed it open.

'Maria...?' he called in a soft, gentle voice.

There was no reply, so he walked through the tiny hallway to a door leading into the back room. Giving a very light knock, he called out once more.

'Maria...? Can I talk with you?'

There was no reply.

'I am going to come in. There's no need to be afraid,' assured the inspector.

Again, there was no response.

'All I am going to do is talk and then I'll leave if you want me to.'

Very slowly, Chard pushed open the door and entered the room. It was dark, except for a small oil lamp which threw a little light on one corner of the room. Mrs Pennel, a shawl around her shoulders, sat there cradling a small bundle in her arms.

The inspector took a step forward, but was halted by a scream from the bereaved mother.

'Come no closer! You're not taking him!' she yelled, using her free hand to pick up a sharp shard of glass from her lap.

Chard took a step backwards and raised his hands in supplication. 'I won't take him if you don't want me to,' he answered softly.

There was silence for a few moments, then, seeing that the inspector was going to come no further, the woman put down the piece of glass

'Who are you?' she asked.

'Just someone who means you no harm. You can call me Thomas if you like.'

Again, there was silence.

'Do you want to tell me what happened?'

Once more there was silence. Chard stood and waited without a sound for what seemed an eternity. Then suddenly Mrs Pennel gave a long low moan.

'I killed my poor lovely boy. I killed my Adam. I am damned.'

'I can see that you wouldn't have wanted to harm Adam,' said Chard quietly.

'I didn't mean it. Honestly, I didn't mean it.' The woman leaned closer to the light and Chard could make out her red-rimmed, moist eyes.

'Tell me what happened. I won't judge you,' promised the inspector.

Mrs Pennel paused, as if unsure whether to say any more, then she spoke. 'You see, we don't have much money. My Arthur is not in good health. He does his best, but I have to take in work to keep us fed. It's sewing for a shop in town – piecework you understand. I only get paid for what I do.' Her words sounded apologetic, as if being poor was an admission of failure. 'I have to get up early to cook and clean, then I start my sewing. With all my housework on top and looking after Arthur I get very little sleep and it's so hard to cope.'

'I understand,' answered Chard in a comforting voice.

'I used to manage but since Adam came along it's been such a struggle,' pleaded the poor woman. 'He would cry and cry until I rocked him to sleep. He would wake me in the middle of the night stopping my sleep. Then again in the daytime, stopping me from working. I was at my wits' end.'

'Then what happened?' asked the inspector, inching forward.

Mrs Pennel was by now in full flow, releasing her anguish. 'A friend gave me that!' she snapped, pointing at a broken bottle which had evidently been thrown against the wall. 'It's an "infants' calmative tonic" said to be recommended by "all good parents". I gave my Adam a few drops and it seemed to settle him down on the first night. By the end of the week though, he would cry all the more until I gave him some. Then he stopped eating, he just didn't want anything. I tried stopping the tonic but it made matters worse. I didn't know what to do. We can't afford a doctor and I was afraid that if I went to the workhouse infirmary, they would take him away from me.' Mrs Pennel suddenly noticed that Chard had come nearer. 'Stop!' she yelled, taking up the piece of broken glass. Blood ran from her hand where she had grabbed a sharp edge but she paid it no intention, and raised the shard to her throat.

'Wait! I'll stay here. Just put the glass down. Tell me what happened next,' urged the inspector.

'I gave Adam some tonic during the night, perhaps a little too much, I was so tired. Then this morning he wouldn't eat again, or drink for that matter. He just slept, so I let him be. He just lay there all day.' She sobbed and her hand lowered the glass away from her throat. 'Arthur had found some work but it was a twelve-hour shift, so he didn't get back until this evening. Just before he was due home, I went to wake Adam to give him some food but he wasn't breathing. I shook him, hugged him, even hit him, but nothing could make my Adam wake up. Not even a mother's kiss.' Her tears fell in earnest and the bereaved mother began to rock back and for in abject misery.

'You poor, poor thing,' empathised Chard, deeply moved by the distraught woman's situation. 'It is a tragedy, but you did not intend to hurt your child.'

'It's my fault. I am damned.'

'Things can be made right. You must think of your husband now, your Arthur.'

'I have murdered his child. Our only child,' Mrs Pennel answered, full of grief.

'From what little I have seen of your husband he appears concerned for your safety. That wouldn't be the case if he didn't love you very deeply,' reasoned Chard.

There was silence as the inspector let his words sink in.

'Will he ever forgive me?' she asked pitifully.

'I believe he would. Don't forget, this is a tragedy for both of you. You need each other desperately now,' said Chard gently.

There was a slow, almost imperceptible nod from Mrs Pennel and Chard moved to within an arm's length.

'We have your Adam to think about. He needs to be at rest,' continued the inspector.

'I can't let him go,' came the pitiful reply. 'Please don't take him from me?' she begged.

Chard saw that Mrs Pennel had let go of the shard of glass and was making no attempt to pick it up.

'I won't take him from you, but perhaps you could give him to me. He needs to be looked after now. You know his time here is over. It is a sad parting but it must be done.'

Mrs Pennel looked up and Chard could see the realisation in her eyes.

'Come now and do what you know you must, then let your husband comfort you,' persuaded the inspector, holding out his arms.

The mother sighed and wiped a blood-stained hand across her tear-streaked face. Then she kissed her child's cold brow and placed the small bundle into Chard's arms.

'Thank you,' said Chard softly as he turned and left the room, holding the dead body as if it was the most precious, delicate object in the whole world.

Outside the house, Constable Morgan and Arthur Pennel stood waiting.

'Is she alright?' asked Arthur anxiously.

'Yes, but she needs to be comforted as I am sure you do,'

answered Chard. 'We'll have to come and take statements tomorrow, but not until the afternoon. Make sure a friend or neighbour can stay with your wife for a couple of days until she is more settled.'

Arthur nodded his agreement, but before going inside he looked at the face of his dead son, stroked his head and turned away as his tears began to flow.

'I'll take the child to the infirmary sir,' offered Constable Morgan, making to take the small burden from his superior.

Chard made to reply but found he couldn't speak the words. Instead, he just shrugged away his constable and started out on the long walk to the infirmary at the other end of town.

THREE

Chard felt drained. His breakfast of bacon and eggs, prepared by his maid Lucy, had barely been touched. Pushing his plate away, he made to go upstairs and get himself ready for duty.

'Are you alright Mr Chard?' enquired Lucy, worried that he was dissatisfied with her cooking.

'Just a bit out of sorts. Nothing to worry about,' he assured her

A few minutes later, having put on his uniform jacket and cap that marked him as an inspector of the Glamorgan County Constabulary, Chard re-appeared and managed to give his servant a smile.

'I am very content with how you've been doing Lucy. For someone who has never been in service before, your work is very satisfactory. There's no need to be concerned.'

Lucy curtsied, pleased at the compliment, then went to the hallway in order to open the front door for her master.

Chard stepped out onto the pavement and took a breath of fresh air. The cold chills of autumn had yet to appear, bringing the inevitable smoke from numerous coal fires that would be lit, even in the early mornings. The walk to the police station was less than a hundred yards away, though it did mean having to cross a road busy with horse-drawn omnibuses, carts and carriages. Fortunately, Chard's uniform did mark him as someone of importance, and accordingly a cab driver slowed his vehicle and gestured for the inspector to cross. Chard waved an arm in acknowledgement and had to admit to himself that he was finally getting used to his formal dress. When he had arrived at Pontypridd the previous year (courtesy of Superintendent Edge having served in the army with his new superior), Chard had assumed he would be continuing as a detective in plain clothes. Superintendent Jones however, had other ideas. His view was that the duty of an inspector was to inspect the work done by the sergeants and constables, mainly by administration. Other than that, he was to uphold the reputation of the constabulary through presenting an impeccable, distinguished appearance; which necessitated always wearing full uniform on duty.

As soon as the inspector entered the busy police station, he noticed Constable Morgan trying to attract his attention.

'What is it constable? We can talk about last night later, after I've had a chance to get my feet under my desk,' snapped Chard.

'It's not that sir. The superintendent has been looking for you. I'm not sure what it's about, but he had a frown on his face.'

The inspector raised a quizzical eyebrow. Usually, on the rare occasions that the superintendent wanted to see him first thing, it was because there was bad news.

'I'd better find out what it's about then,' he commented, heading immediately towards his superior's office.

He found Superintendent Constantine Jones in his office seated behind his large, highly-polished, oak desk. His uniform, more heavily braided than Chard's, was as usual, immaculate.

'Take a seat, Inspector. I have received a telegram and its contents puzzle me,' he stated whilst stroking his large bushy moustache.

'How can I help sir?' offered Chard.

'I know very little about your time at Shrewsbury. Superintendent Edge asked me if I had a post for you as a favour to him, but never said why. I never asked and you've never told me.'

Chard's face flushed. 'It's a private matter, sir. What relevance has it got to the telegram?'

'I'm not sure it has any relevance, it's just a feeling,' replied the superintendent thoughtfully. 'Do you a recall an Inspector Warboys from your time at Shrewsbury?'

'No sir. The name is unfamiliar. Might I ask why?'

'The telegram says that he is coming here later today with another officer. It asks me to ensure you are present when they arrive. Do you know what this could be about?'

'Not a clue, sir. I am as mystified as yourself,' replied Chard.

'I have a bad feeling about this Inspector, I really do.' Superintendent Jones paused as if to say something else but then gave a dismissive wave. 'Carry on Inspector, just don't leave the station.'

Chard couldn't help but feel perturbed by the discussion as he headed back to his own office. His thoughts on the matter were however, interrupted by Constable Morgan.

'Regarding last night sir…'

'Come into my room, we can discuss it there.'

They went inside the inspector's office and Chard closed the door firmly behind them.

'I put the dead child into the care of Nurse Harris who was on duty at the infirmary last night.'

'Will there have to be a post mortem?' asked the constable.

'Yes, and a coroner's inquest.'

'You don't think she did away with the child deliberately though, do you sir?'

'No, of course not, Constable. It's a tragedy, but not the first of its kind. I should have picked up the broken bottle of tonic to check the contents, but you can guarantee it'll include a dose of morphine in it. If it's given too often an infant can become addicted. Then it will lose its appetite. The child will constantly demand more and the mother, often driven to distraction will eventually give in. If they are unlucky, the dosage will stop the infant breathing.'

'Do you think Mrs Pennel will be prosecuted?' asked Morgan.

'It depends on the post mortem and the view of the coroner at the inquest. The worst case would be a prosecution for wilful murder, though I think that's unlikely. Wilful neglect is another possible charge,' answered the inspector, looking troubled. 'I believe she was guilty of neither.'

'What's to be done sir?'

'Unfortunately, I've been ordered to remain in the station until some visitors arrive later in the day. You will have to act on my behalf.'

'Only too willing sir,' replied Morgan. 'The sergeant wanted me to do some paperwork, but having done an extra evening shift last night, I doubt I could concentrate on it.'

'With our shortage of men, we've all got to work extra hours Constable, and the money will no doubt be useful if Miss Roper accepts your proposal. Talking of which, I assume you'll be happy that I'm sending you up to the infirmary?'

Morgan failed to suppress a grin. 'May has promised to give me a definite answer by the end of the year.'

'Your hopes are high then?' asked Chard, aware that Morgan had proposed to the young medical clerk earlier in the year.

Nodding in reply, Morgan, despite his mutton chop whiskers, looked like the bashful young man that he really was. 'We seem to be getting closer, if you get my drift, sir. What do you want me to do at the infirmary?' he asked, keen to change the subject.

'Have a word with Doctor Henderson. He'll be doing the post mortem and signing the death certificate. Let him know that in my opinion the cause of death appears to be accidental and the child died in its sleep. A tonic was administered by the mother which may have had some effect, and we'll get the bottle to him later on so he can look at the ingredients. Understood?'

'Yes sir. When are we going to interview Mrs Pennel?'

'I propose leaving it until later this afternoon to give the woman time to compose herself, but it will have to be done today. Unfortunately, I have no idea how long I'm going to be tied up with these mysterious visitors. If I am still in with the superintendent at five o'clock, then you'll have to go and take a formal statement. If that's the case don't forget to pick up the broken tonic bottle while you're there.'

'I won't forget, sir. I'll let the sergeant know you've given me some duties and I'll make a start by going to see May... I mean Doctor Henderson,' replied Morgan.

Chard grinned as his constable left the office before realising the wider implication of being ordered to stay at the station. Grimacing he looked at the pile of paperwork on his desk that he could no longer find an excuse to ignore.

***

It was two o'clock in the afternoon when Chard's labours were interrupted by a knock on his office door.

'Sorry to interrupt, sir. I thought you should know that the visitors are at the front desk.'

'Thank you, Sergeant Morris. I'll go ahead into the superintendent's office whilst you fetch them through,' replied Chard.

By the time the sergeant escorted the visitors into the superintendent's office, both Jones and Chard were stood in their immaculate uniforms, ready to greet their guests formally.

'Good afternoon, I am Inspector Warboys and this is Constable Fugg,' said the larger of the two men in an accent from the north of England.

Chard frowned. He didn't know the big, heavy-jowled, man who spoke, but there was something about his demeanour which was distinctly unfriendly. His colleague, a shorter individual with hair so blond that it was almost white, Chard did know. Fugg was a detective constable who had served under him at Shrewsbury, and he wasn't a man to be trusted.

'Could I trouble you for some identification, gentlemen; as you appear to be out of uniform?' asked Superintendent Jones politely, but with a degree of annoyance.

Warboys produced his police warrant, which he handed to the superintendent. 'I am afraid we do not wear uniforms. The constable and I are detectives.'

Chard could not help but look at his superior's expression. Although on several occasions the inspector had come close to getting the superintendent to agree they needed a detective department, it was still something which Superintendent Jones resisted. It was the informality that irked him.

'If some forces feel the need to let their officers swan around in their private clothes when on duty, I suppose it is up to them,' responded Jones, his expression one of disapproval. 'I am Superintendent Jones and this is Inspector Chard, formerly of Shrewsbury. I assume you are acquainted?'

Warboys looked directly at Chard for the first time, though Fugg averted his eyes. 'I haven't had the pleasure until now,' answered Warboys with an insincere smile. 'I only took up my position after Inspector Chard left.' He slowly looked Chard up and down before continuing. 'Constable Fugg told me all about you, but you still aren't quite what I was expecting.'

'How can we be of help, Inspector Warboys? We are very busy at this station, so if you wouldn't mind coming to the point?'

interrupted Superintendent Jones, who had clearly taken a dislike to his visitors.

Warboys turned and looked at Chard, ignoring the superintendent. He reached into the inside pocket of his jacket and pulled out a folded document. 'This is an arrest warrant.'

Stepping forward he put his hand on Chard's shoulder.

'Thomas Chard. I am arresting you for the murder of your wife, Mrs Sofia Chard and of Mr Charles Landell.'

FOUR

'What are you talking about man? You cannot be serious!' erupted Superintendent Jones.

'The cuffs, Fugg,' ordered Warboys, still ignoring the superintendent.

Chard felt stunned and made no effort whatsoever to resist as a pair of handcuffs were snapped around his wrists.

'Desist at once damn you!' insisted the superintendent, stepping forward.

'The paperwork is all in order,' responded Warboys, holding out the warrant for the superintendent to take, whilst still staring at Chard.

Face red with fury, Jones inspected the document, then thrust it into Warboys's chest.

'This is a mistake. The inspector isn't married.'

'Is that what he told you?' answered Warboys.

'We've not discussed it, but this is nonsense isn't it, Inspector Chard? You aren't married?'

Jones looked at Chard who had turned a deathly white.

'Well he certainly isn't married now!' interjected Fugg.

'That's quite enough, Constable,' snapped Warboys before speaking once more to the superintendent. 'I don't suppose he told you why he had to leave Shrewsbury?'

'I understand it was a personal matter. He was recommended by an old comrade in arms whose opinion I trust. I will contact Superintendent Edge immediately,' growled Jones.

'You can try,' replied Warboys, 'but you will have no success. He's gone to the continent on extended leave. I am temporarily in charge of the station. The warrant is legal and must be executed.'

The dispute was interrupted by a knock on the office door which was opened tentatively by Sergeant Morris.

'Is everything alright, Superintendent?' he enquired, having been alerted by the raised voices emanating from the office.

'I am not so sure it is, Sergeant. Just wait outside for the time being,' ordered Jones. Sergeant Morris gave the visitors a glare before leaving, though the shadow of his huge frame could subsequently be seen through the glass of the office door.

There was an uncomfortable silence once the sergeant left the room.

Chard felt sick inside. His legs felt unsteady beneath him and his mouth was dry. He tried to come to terms with what he had been told, but it didn't make sense. Shaking his head to try and recover his senses, Chard realised everyone was looking at him.

'How? Where...?' was all he could manage to say.

'Don't come that nonsense with me,' responded Warboys. 'You know exactly what you did.'

'Inspector, tell me this is all a mistake,' demanded Jones, addressing Chard.

'My wife is in America,' he replied weakly.

The superintendent's eyebrows rose in astonishment.

'You mean it's true, you are married? Earlier this year you were courting Mrs Murray...'

Chard gave an embarrassed shrug.

Warboys laughed sarcastically. 'He can't keep his dick in his trousers. That's why he was sent down here in the first place.'

'Chard I cannot believe this...' gasped Superintendent Jones.

'I think we'll be on our way now, Superintendent,' said Warboys triumphantly. 'Fugg, get the door. We'll be on the next train out of here.'

Constable Fugg opened the office door only to find the way blocked by Sergeant Morris, who looked over the visitors' heads to catch the eye of the superintendent.

'Let them pass, Sergeant. Then come inside. We need to talk,' ordered Jones.

Sergeant Morris obeyed reluctantly, and the two officers from Shrewsbury left, with their handcuffed prisoner walking between them.

The superintendent pulled an edge of his moustache in thought as he watched them go, before ushering Sergeant Morris into the office.

'They believe Inspector Chard murdered his wife,' he informed the sergeant.

'I didn't know he was married, sir. Besides, he's not the sort to murder anyone.'

'I can't believe it myself. It must be a mistake, but on the other hand there clearly is some truth attached to it. I don't know quite what to think,' admitted the superintendent.

'Is there anything we can do, sir?' asked Morris.

'Practicalities to begin with. I understand he has a servant?'

'I have heard it mentioned. A maid I believe. Constable Morgan should know. He's about to go and do an interview for the inspector, regarding an accidental death last night.'

The superintendent drummed his fingers on the desk as he deliberated. 'If it's an accidental death then he can leave it until tomorrow. Do you think he would have met Chard's maid?'

'I understand he has had reason to call at the inspector's house before, so the chances are that they've spoken.'

'Good. No doubt the men will be commenting on why Inspector Chard has been led away in handcuffs. Advise Morgan in strictest confidence of the reason. Tell him to see the maid, explaining that the inspector has had to leave on urgent business. She needs to pack a suitcase with a change of clothing for a night or two away, together with anything else she feels would be useful. Morgan is to pick it up then go home, change into civilian clothes and set off for Shrewsbury police station. The train service from Cardiff to Shropshire is hourly. If he gets a move on, he could get there by nine o'clock tonight,' stated the superintendent.

'If you don't mind me saying so sir, Morgan did an evening shift yesterday and is due a break. He wouldn't get back from Shrewsbury until the early hours.'

'He's a young man, so he can sleep on the train. I'll authorise the price of an hotel room out of station funds. Make sure he knows I want him back here by midday tomorrow, with all the information he can glean.'

***

Chard put his head in his hands as he sat on the hard wooden bench of the cell, contemplating his predicament. The walk through Pontypridd police station in cuffs had been humiliating. At least on the train he had managed to sit in such a way as to hide the manacles from the view of most passengers. In a way, it had helped that Warboys would not discuss anything about the charges. It meant Chard had time to compose himself and attempt to comprehend what was happening. Clearly Sofia, who he had once loved, had been killed. Yet, he did not know the circumstances. Where had it happened? How had it happened? Why was he the suspected murderer? As far as Chard was aware, Sofia was living somewhere in America. It just didn't make sense.

The train to Cardiff had been on time and the connecting service took them to Shrewsbury in only two hours. It was a very familiar sight that greeted Chard on their arrival. Cabs waited outside the ornate frontage of the county town's station in the shadow of Shrewsbury Castle, with traffic queuing up the hill leading to the town centre. Trying to keep his bonds hidden, yet also conscious that he was in full inspector's uniform, minus his cap, he went obediently with his captors. They walked up Castle Foregate into the town, continued past the grand Raven Hotel, before going down Pride Hill and turning off into the town square. The police station was situated on the far side, on the bottom floor of a hotel adjacent to the town's music hall.

Having been made to empty his pockets at the front desk, Chard had been pushed none-too-gently into a dimly lit cell.

'Now will you tell me exactly what I am accused of?' he had demanded.

'I've told you. Murdering your wife. We'll take a statement in the morning, it's been a long day,' Warboys had grunted before Fugg had locked the cell door.

That had been two hours ago. Despite having recovered some degree of composure, he was still unsettled.

Chard looked up expectantly in response to a noise in the corridor. A police constable appeared moments later, keys in hand.

'A visitor for you.'

'Frazer, isn't it? You joined the force just before I left the town.'

'That's right. Most of the lads had nothing but good to say about you,' Frazer paused, 'until the jewel robbery,' he added. 'The grasshoppers took the piss out of us for months afterwards.'

The constable turned away and called back down the corridor. 'Come on through.'

To Chard's delight it was Constable Morgan, soberly dressed in a tweed jacket and flat cap who appeared at the cell door. He carried a suitcase in one hand and a small hold-all in the other.

'Leave the bag outside. You can take the case in,' Frazer ordered.

Morgan dropped his own bag and stepped forward, looking concerned at Chard's plight.

'I've had to take some items out of the case, your razor and so forth. They're in your visitor's bag,' Frazer informed Chard, before locking the door and disappearing back to the night desk.

'I'm sorry to find you like this sir. I'm sure it's all a mistake,' sympathised Morgan.

'Constable Morgan, how...?'

'The superintendent ordered me to come. Lucy packed the case whilst I ran home to change and I got the next train to Cardiff for the Shrewsbury connection. There's a change of clothes in the case.'

'Good. It somehow feels worse being locked up whilst in uniform. Did you have any difficulty finding me?' asked Chard, opening the case to examine the contents.

'I asked a railway porter where the police station was and he said to go up the bank and ask there, which I thought was odd, as it would be closed at this time of night. Anyway, I asked where the bank was and he pointed up the hill to the left.'

Chard laughed, despite his predicament. 'They call a hill or incline a bank up here.'

'That explains it then. I eventually asked someone on the street and they directed me to the town square. Another person sent me to the town hall and where I found a policeman who sent me away in no uncertain terms.'

'He'll have been a grasshopper,' said Chard, stripping off his uniform.

'A what?'

'County police as opposed to the borough police. They used to wear green uniforms some years back. They have their administration office and a holding cell across the square in the town hall,' explained Chard, putting his uniform into the case and hastily putting on his change of clothes.

'We'll have to be quick, sir,' said Morgan. 'The constable said I could only have ten minutes, and I have orders to return first thing tomorrow. What have you been charged with exactly, and is there anyone else I need to inform?'

'All I know is that they claim I murdered my wife, which isn't true. I don't know the circumstances of where, why or how. No doubt all of that will be thrown at me tomorrow.'

'We didn't know you were married, sir.'

'Let's not get into that now. It must be late. What time is it?'

'After nine,' answered Morgan. 'Is there anything you want me to do?'

Chard's mind was racing, but at least he was now thinking more clearly than he had all day. 'Go out of the station and go left to the end of the street. Book yourself in at The George Hotel, then come back to the square.'

'I doubt the constable will let me back in to see you,' said Morgan doubtfully.

'That's not important. Go past the Magistrate's Court, that's the building with the undercroft in the centre of the square. A bit further along, on the left, you'll find a pub called The Plough. There used to be a local reporter called Banner who often drank in there. He might know something pertinent to my case.'

'How will I know him?' asked Morgan.

'Just ask if "Old Nosey" is about,' answered Chard. 'If you find out anything useful then leave some sort of message for me before you return to Pontypridd in the morning.'

'I'll do my best. Even if I get nowhere, I'll come back and see you as soon as I can.'

***

Chard was woken early the following morning, grateful to have had his nightmares interrupted.

'Hands out whilst I cuff you,' ordered Constable Fugg. 'We heard about your visitor last night. Inspector Warboys is none too pleased.'

Chard declined to comment whilst the handcuffs were applied, waiting until he had been taken into the interview room before speaking.

'Good morning, Inspector Warboys. It is going to be very embarrassing for you when this ridiculous mess is sorted out.'

Warboys, stood by a table with two chairs, the only furniture in the grey-painted room, glowered. 'A bit cocky today, are we? A change from the sullen, quiet fellow you were yesterday.'

'You had told me my wife was dead, for God's sake. How did you expect me to react? I was in shock,' snapped Chard.

'I see you've had a change of clothes. I heard that you had a visitor last night, but he'll be the last for a while. The men are under orders not to let anybody through and, in case you are expecting any form of assistance from former colleagues, only myself and Fugg will be interviewing you. Sit down in the chair!'

Fugg pushed Chard towards the chair facing Warboys, and took out a notebook.

'Just tell me what all this is about,' demanded Chard.

Warboys grunted. 'Very well, if you want to play the innocent, I'll start at the beginning. A month ago, bailiffs went to take possession of a property in Kingsland because the owner had defaulted on payments and ignored written demands. The house was furnished and they needed to take an inventory. They had been in there for two days before they got around to examining the cellar, the entrance to which had been barred. Eventually, they got it open and inside they found two dead bodies. One was that of Charles Landell, the other was that of your wife.'

'What had happened to them?'

'As if you didn't know, you animal!' shouted Warboys. 'It would have been a mercy if the cellar had been airtight. They would have suffocated inside a day. Instead, they died of hunger and thirst, it would have taken a long time.'

Chard felt a cold sensation run through his body and he gave an involuntary shiver. He felt physically sick and wanted to gag.

Warboys stopped talking and watched Chard's discomfort with disdain, convinced it was just an act.

Eventually, Chard felt composed enough to ask a question.

'You said the bodies were discovered a month ago. If such was the case, why wasn't I informed immediately?'

'Because she had been identified by documents in her possession as Sofia Verdi,' replied Warboys.

'Her maiden name,' explained Chard.

'We subsequently found that out after the inquest. One of the mortuary assistants thought, even with the decomposition of the body, that he recognised her. Further enquiries were made and lo and behold, we found it was none other than Mrs Sofia Chard.'

'I believed she had left for America.'

Warboys scoffed. 'That's what you told Superintendent Edge in confidence. He confirmed it. But you told no-one else.'

'It was no-one else's business,' responded Chard defensively.

'Yet everyone in the station new that your wife had left you for someone else. It was common knowledge, though who the other man was remained a mystery.'

'I repeat, it was a private matter,' said Chard.

'You obviously hated your wife,' accused Warboys.

'I did not.'

'We made enquiries with your former neighbours. There had been violent arguments between you for many months.'

'Loud, angry arguments, but not violent,' denied Chard.

'Still, it must mean you did not love your wife.'

'We had grown apart. What is the saying? Marry in haste and repent at leisure. That's what happened. It was an ill-advised marriage and we were never meant for each other. She met Landell and wanted to leave.'

'So that's why you killed her,' accused Warboys.

'No. Sofia told me she wanted a divorce, but it would obviously be easier for me to initiate it. I was reluctant because of the embarrassment involved.'

'Far easier to murder her though. That would save your reputation, if you got away with it that is.'

Chard ignored the comment. 'As it happened, Landell wanted to take her to America to start a new life with him. We agreed she should establish an address over there. I would then accuse her of adultery and the court proceedings would take place in America, thereby avoiding public embarrassment for myself.'

'We've only got your word that they were going to America. Landell never mentioned it to anyone, not even his business partners,' countered Warboys.

'That would have been his decision. How could I know what was in his mind?'

'Let's just pretend you're telling the truth, which I very much doubt. Why hadn't you commenced divorce proceedings? Surely your wife would have been settled in an address after this length of time?'

Chard sighed, realising his explanation would not sound convincing. 'Sofia should have written to me as promised, but didn't. To be honest I didn't really care. She had gone and I was happy to be living a new life in South Wales as a single man. Without a divorce Sofia would have been unable to marry Landell, so eventually she would have needed to get in touch. As for me, I had no intention of ever getting married again, until....'

'Until what?' asked Warboys, picking up on the hesitation.

'I did enter a relationship earlier this year, which might have led to something, so I sent a letter to an agency in New York. I just enquired if they would be able to trace Sofia and what their fees might be.'

'A clever ruse to provide some defence should your wife's body ever be found,' snorted Warboys. 'What did this agency say?'

'They said that given the approximate dates of departure and the likely ports of disembarkation, they should be able to trace her for a moderate fee.'

'Then, you can produce that reply when you go to trial, though it won't help unless the judge is extremely gullible.'

'Unfortunately, I can't. Nothing came of my romance and I threw the agency's reply on the fire,' answered Chard.

Warboys smiled. 'You used to have a reputation of being a smart officer. To me you seem rather stupid.'

'Call me whatever you like, but I'm not a killer.'

'Oh, but I think you are. I think you let those two poor people starve to death.'

'Tell me this,' insisted Chard, 'when were they locked in the cellar?'

'I'm the one asking the questions,' responded Warboys aggressively.

'It's a reasonable request,' argued Chard.

Warboys paused a while before finally shrugging his shoulders and agreeing to answer. 'We can't tell exactly. The temperature in the cellar may have delayed decomposition, but we know Landell was last seen on the day after Sabrina's Teardrop was stolen at Attingham. An event during which I understand you played a very dishonourable part.'

Chard ignored the slight. 'Where was he seen?'

'He came into town to give a further statement to the County Police that afternoon. Sometime later, a member of the public thought they saw him talking to someone in the Quarry Park. Unfortunately, that was all the detail we could get.' Warboys put his elbows on the table, and leaned forward until his face was just inches from his prisoner. 'Let's get back to the night of the jewel theft. I understand it was a rare old party.'

Chard said nothing.

'I suspect you saw Charles Landell at the party and were overcome with fury at seeing the man who'd taken your wife. As a result, you formed the intention of killing him, and did so the following evening.'

'You will have heard the scandal from gossip-mongers and so you should be aware that I wasn't in a fit state to form an intention of anything,' answered Chard. 'I didn't even know he was there until after the theft took place. He certainly wasn't there at the start of the evening.'

Warboys scoffed. 'I believe that soon after the event, having failed at your marriage and your job, your hatred grew. You were a social disgrace, with no future and an embittered heart; so you sought out a target for your fury. That target was your wife and Charles Landell.

You will appear before a magistrate as a matter of urgency and subsequently be sent for trial for your capital offence,' Warboys leaned closer once more, to whisper malevolently. 'Then you will hang.'

FIVE

It was mid-morning before Morgan arrived back in Pontypridd. He went home and hastily changed into his uniform, before reporting to the police station where he found Superintendent Jones in a very anxious mood.

'There you are, Constable. I would have thought you would have caught the first available train,' he admonished.

'I did, sir,' replied Morgan defensively, 'after making one more attempt to see the inspector. I saw him last night, but this morning my request was refused. I couldn't even leave a message. They said I wouldn't be able to see him until after he's been before a magistrate.'

Aware that a number of other officers had stopped working and were trying to listen to the conversation, Superintendent Jones gestured with his hand. 'Come into my office.'

Once inside, and with the door firmly closed, the superintendent sat at his desk and sat back with a worried expression.

'Now then, Constable Morgan, what did you find out? Is there any truth behind the accusations?'

'Yes and no, sir. When I spoke to Inspector Chard last night, he didn't deny that he'd been married. As to the charge of murdering his wife, he said they hadn't told him any of the details.'

'Is that all he said?' asked the superintendent, drumming his fingers on the desk.

'We had very little time together, but he did ask me to try and find a local newspaper reporter. He was desperate to know more facts about the case and wanted me to leave a message if I found anything out.'

Jones stopped drumming his fingers and stared at Morgan. 'Do you believe him?' he asked earnestly.

'How do you mean, sir?'

'I mean do you think he was really unaware of the facts, or was he pretending not to know about the murder?'

Morgan looked shocked. 'You can't be serious, sir. The inspector wouldn't lie.'

The superintendent absent-mindedly pulled at the edge of his moustache as he gathered his thoughts. 'I would like to think so. This whole thing seems to be out of character for Inspector Chard, but he didn't inform us he was married.'

'He didn't tell us he wasn't either though,' said Morgan.

'A fair point I suppose,' conceded the superintendent. 'Returning to your conversation with him, did you find the reporter he mentioned?'

'I did try, sir. The inspector asked me to go to a pub in the town square. It was easy enough to find and no-one seemed to object to my asking about the reporter.'

'You were in luck then?'

'Unfortunately, no. They said he was out of town and wouldn't be back until the end of next week.'

'So, your efforts were wasted,' commented the superintendent.

'Not entirely, I did get into conversation with a couple of men at the bar. I asked them about any news of a murder in the town that came to light recently.'

'And…?' asked Jones expectantly.

'Two bodies had been found in the cellar of a house on the outskirts of the town. They'd been locked in and had starved to death.'

'Good God! And that is the crime of which Inspector Chard has been accused?'

'I assume so, sir. The men I spoke to couldn't remember the victims' names.'

'I can't believe he could do such a thing. I really can't,' said Jones emphatically.

'Neither can I sir. May I make a suggestion?' asked Morgan.

'Yes, by all means.'

'I've got some leave owing. I would like to use it to go back to Shrewsbury and find out more about the case.'

The superintendent looked pensive. 'Perhaps it would be a good idea, though it is your choice to use your leave for that purpose. My immediate concern is how to manage with one less constable and without an inspector. I will raise the matter with the Chief Constable. It might be possible to get someone in on secondment from another division.'

'How soon could that be done?' asked Morgan.

'At least a week, maybe two. I don't think such a delay will be detrimental. If the Shrewsbury police said you can't speak to Inspector Chard until after he's been before a magistrate, then there's no point in rushing back. Hopefully the charge will be dismissed at the initial hearing and the inspector will be freed regardless. Have faith in British justice, and all will be well.'

Constable Morgan nodded, feeling far from convinced.

***

It was early evening and Morgan stood patiently outside the main gate of the workhouse. Dressed in his best suit, he pulled an old pocket watch from his waistcoat pocket to check the time. Eventually, there was a creak as the wicket-gate started to open, causing Morgan to quickly put away the watch and straighten his posture.

'Goodnight Miss Roper,' came the watchman's voice from within.

'Goodnight Bert,' came the reply in a gentle, soft tone.

May Roper stepped through onto the pavement and at first didn't notice her admirer.

She wore a plain black skirt, high-necked white blouse and a short black jacket. Her auburn hair was neatly pinned up and topped by a small, black flat-crowned hat.

Morgan gave his most disarming smile as soon as May's eyes met his.

'Don't you smile at me, Idris Morgan,' came the expected response from the infirmary clerk, whose face was flushed with annoyance. 'Where were you last night? I was dressed up to the nines waiting to be taken to the theatre.'

'I'm sorry, but I had to go to Shrewsbury in a rush. There was no time to send you a message. I only got back this morning, then this afternoon I had to interview the parents of the child who died the other night.' Morgan put his hand into his jacket pocket and pulled out a crumpled piece of paper. 'Whilst I remember, here's the label off the broken bottle of tonic they gave him. The broken glass and any contents had been thrown away. I had to retrieve the label from their bin. Can you give it to Doctor Henderson in the morning?'

May took the paper and absent-mindedly put it in her jacket pocket whilst trying to take in what had just been said.

'Shrewsbury? What on earth are you talking about?' asked May in puzzlement.

'Something really serious has happened. Come, take my arm and I'll tell you as I walk you home.'

Her anger dissipating, May took the constable's arm and they set off on the walk down the grey stone terraced streets towards the Ropers' home where May lived with her parents.

'Doesn't the inspector come from Shrewsbury?' she asked.

'Exactly the point,' answered Morgan, 'and what I'm going to say is going to come as a shock to you.'

'No! I don't believe it!' proclaimed May angrily, after hearing the accusation laid against Inspector Chard. 'He's a kind man and if it wasn't for him, I would have been killed not so long ago.'

'I was there as well you know,' said Morgan defensively, recalling the inspector's first case in Pontypridd.

'That's not the point. You aren't the one wrongly accused of murder.'

'To be honest, we don't absolutely know he's innocent,' argued Morgan.

May snatched her arm away angrily. 'You what, Idris Morgan? Are you saying you believe these awful lies?'

'Now calm down May. All I'm saying is that we need to find out more about the case. To which end, I'm going to use up my overdue leave in order to find out the truth.'

'How do you mean?' asked May.

'I'm going back to Shrewsbury in a week or two and I'm going to find out everything. If there's a way to prove the inspector innocent, then I'm the man to do it,' said the constable emphatically.

May looked at her beau with sympathy, and stroked his mutton-chop whiskers, before giving him a gentle kiss. 'Oh, you daft thing, Idris,' she said, shaking her head sadly.

***

In a richly decorated office in the City of London, a man sat behind his desk whilst another stood before him.

'You understand what is required?' asked the seated figure, contemplating his visitor.

Elijah Cole was an unusual man, or so everyone thought. Clearly a man of means (though no-one knew the source of his wealth), he chose to take occasional employment rather than live a life of idle pleasure. Although pleasant in appearance for a man in his early forties, with a dark complexion and neatly-trimmed van Dyck beard, he wasn't very tall or muscular in stature, nor was he strikingly handsome. Yet it was his stare that people remembered. There was something about the eyes which could disarm the most abrasive of women and strike fear into the most vicious of men.

'I understand perfectly,' Cole replied.

'You were unsuccessful the last time we called on your services.'

'That was unfortunate, but rather out of my control. There will be no mistakes this time. I assume my terms are agreeable to you?' asked Cole, raising an eyebrow.

'They are. Here is the contract duly signed,' said the seated man begrudgingly as he held forth a folded document.

Cole took the piece of paper and put it inside his jacket pocket without looking at it. 'Then consider the matter resolved. I know my objective and I won't fail,' he assured.

The seated man watched his visitor leave, pleased the meeting was over, and hoped that Cole would indeed keep to his word.

SIX

It had been over a week since Constable Morgan had visited him in his cell, and Chard wondered if his friends and colleagues in South Wales had deserted him. He sat alone, locked in a room at the magistrate's court, staring blankly at the bare, cream-coloured walls. Mr Tayleur, a local solicitor had defended him to the best of his considerable ability.

'There is no way the magistrate will allow the case; the evidence is entirely circumstantial. Motive is there certainly, and having told your former superintendent that your wife had gone to America, when she clearly hadn't, does look rather bad,' he had admitted to Chard before the hearing. 'Nevertheless,' he had continued, 'there is no actual evidence that you had been near Landell's house prior to your move to South Wales. No, I believe we will get this thrown out of court.'

So, it was with a degree of optimism that Chard had entered the courtroom; but it did not last.

Much to Mr Tayleur's annoyance, the prosecution asked permission for a witness to be heard, and the defending solicitor had stood in puzzlement as an old man was brought in. He wore a dark suit which had seen better days and walked a little unsteadily to stand before the magistrate. Despite being several feet away, Chard was able to catch the slight whiff of whisky that clung to the man's clothes.

'I understand from Inspector Warboys, that on or around the dates concerning this case you saw a man lurking by the house of Mr Landell.'

'Yes, sir I did as sure as my name is Enoch Rudd,' said the witness, holding his hand over his heart. 'It was on the very date they reckon Mr Landell was last seen.'

'How can you be sure?' asked the magistrate dubiously.

'I remember everything about that night, it was the best of my life,' Rudd had answered with a grin.

'Explain!' demanded the magistrate.

'It was the night my mother-in-law passed away. Ninety-five she was. I thought she'd never go,' replied Rudd, to the amusement of the court, but not the magistrate.

'How did you come to notice this suspicious person?'

'I was taking me dog for a walk. Always do, every night. I was walking past Mr Landell's house, I used to work there you know sir, until he paid me off. Bastard he was sir, if you don't mind my French.'

'Mind your language,' the magistrate had barked.

'Yes, get on with it. We are not here to comment on Mr Landell's personality,' urged the prosecutor.

The witness gave a little cough, then continued his tale. 'I was walking me dog as I said, when I noticed someone across the way. I was going to say good evening, as you do; but he went and dodged as if to try and hide by a hedge. So, I paused to take a snifter from my flask. Not that I drink much mind, it's medicinal for me war wound. The Crimea you see sir, I met Florence Nightingale once sir....'

'Yes, get on with it,' snapped the prosecutor once more.

'As I was saying. I looked across and he thought I couldn't see him, but I could. Eyes like a hawk I have, sir.'

'Do you see that man in the room now?'

Chard had watched as the witness had looked around the room, actually making eye contact with him without any hint of recognition. Then Rudd looked in the direction of Inspector Warboys, who was sat on the prosecution bench. The inspector gave an almost imperceptible nod and the witness turned towards Chard, raising his arm and pointing.

'It was him, sir as God is my judge,'

The case had gone downhill from there. Despite Mr Tayleur's spirited defence, calling into question the reliability of the witness, and a fearful cross-examination, it just led to Rudd becoming very indignant and feigning illness. By the time all the evidence had been heard, the magistrate had been convinced that the case warranted a hearing at the assizes. In the meantime, Chard would be held on remand at the Dana, Shrewsbury's prison.

'Don't worry, Mr Chard,' Mr Tayleur had said. 'The witness they produced will not convince a jury. He clearly has been influenced to give evidence by the prosecution. They know it and I know it. All it has done, is to buy them time to try and find more evidence against you.'

Chard had nodded without saying a word. He knew there would not, could not, be more evidence. Yet here he was for now, a figure in disgrace, humiliated and deserted by his friends.

His miserable reverie was interrupted by the sound of a key turning in a lock.

'Come on, time to go,' announced the constable on opening the door.

Chard stood and walked out into the corridor as instructed, and down the stairs into the town square where the police van waited. He considered trying to run for it, but what would be the point? It wouldn't help to clear his name. Surely, that would happen at the eventual trial when the case would be thrown out of court. For now, Chard realised he would just have to grin and bear it. Once freed, there would be time enough to find the real killer of his wife. He kept that thought at the forefront of his mind as the horse-drawn van set off on the spine-jarring journey, through the town, to the top of Pride Hill then down towards the railway station. Chard was familiar with the route and could visualise the streets outside as the clamour of vehicles and shoppers penetrated the stuffy, windowless van. There was the rumble of a train overhead as they passed beneath the railway bridge, before making a sharp, slow turn up a hill and coming to a stop.

Moments later the back door of the van was unlocked and Chard stepped out, to stand before the gates of the Dana. Two massive semi-circular towers with barred windows stood either side of the main gate and suddenly he felt a sense of panic. The accompanying constable undid Chard's manacles as two prison guards came forward and took his arms.

'All yours, lads,' said the departing constable, eager to get away from what had been a difficult situation. Most of the Shrewsbury officers had been supportive of their former inspector, but Warboys insisted that they would face his considerable wrath if they attempted to communicate with the prisoner in any way.

'This way,' ordered one of the guards, a burly fellow with a red beard. 'We've been told you're a peeler, so you should know what to expect.

Indeed, Chard did. Once through the main gate, he was led off to the left into a long, low building. As soon as he was inside, he was searched and made to strip. The floor felt ice cold beneath his bare feet as Chard walked naked towards the area where he would be 'cleansed'.

'Bastard!' he swore as the first bucket of ice-cold water was thrown over him. Chard was aware that having been renovated, there was a perfectly good shower system in place, but clearly the guards wanted their fun.

The guards laughed at his discomfort. 'No more of that language, or it'll be punishments for you,' they taunted.

After three more buckets had been thrown, the prisoner was given an old towel to dry himself. Then Chard was taken to a holding cell and given an ill-fitting prison uniform.

'Get yourself dressed. Someone will be along for you later, to take you to your new home,' said the guard with the red beard.

Once more, Chard was left alone to reflect. As he stared up at the vaulted ceiling of the cell, he tried to count his blessings. At least the prison was relatively new in parts. It had been built by Thomas Telford and had been a real hell-hole. However, in the last decade it had been substantially rebuilt, making it a lot more humane. The other thing to be glad about was that, being on remand, he would be kept separate from the other prisoners. At least that was the system when he had previously worked in the town. Sometimes they had found prisoners on remand had been (as was he) innocent. So, in order to avoid them becoming 'corrupted' by sentenced felons, it had been agreed with the governor that they would be kept in separate cells on the ground floor. Provided he kept his head down, Chard realised he could endure the temporary incarceration. Then once free, he would get his revenge.

Over an hour passed, and mentally exhausted by the day's events, Chard fell asleep, sitting upright with his head resting back against the hard stone wall.

***

'Wake up!'

Chard shook his head, startled.

'Stand up when a guard enters your cell!

The prisoner blinked then slowly stood up whilst focussing on the man standing before him.

He was very tall, long-limbed, with dark mutton-chop whiskers similar to those favoured by Constable Morgan.

'That's better. I know who you are, Thomas Chard, and I know what you've done. Any nonsense from you and we'll have words. In fact, you'll do some talking to me in any case, but that can wait for now.'

Chard noticed a distinct malevolence in the guard's manner, and it wasn't the sort of contrived malevolence one would use to intimidate a new prisoner. It seemed personal, as if Chard had offended the man at some time in the past.

'Out of the cell and off to the left. You lead the way,' commanded the guard.

As they passed through B Wing, Chard could smell the steam coming from the prison's laundry and there was a hint of carbolic soap in the air. Then came the entrance into A Wing, which would be Chard's home for several weeks until his trial. The building was high, three floors of cells, with windows set into the walls at the height of another floor above. Skylights in the roof gave even more daylight; yet the building was narrow, and cluttered with cast iron stairs, gantries and supports. The effect was stifling, claustrophobic, and Chard shuddered.

'Let's get you settled into your new residence,' gibed the guard, pushing Chard towards the centre of the block.

A cell door on the left was already open, awaiting the arrival of its new occupant.

As the guard shoved his prisoner inside, he muttered, 'I'll come and see you later, and we'll have a nice little chat,' and then slammed shut the heavy metal door.

***

As the day passed Chard lost track of time. The lukewarm, tasteless food pushed through his door earlier in the evening had been sufficient to push away any pangs of hunger; after which he had slept fitfully on the hard wooden bed for a short while. On waking, he sat gazing at the night sky, visible from the barred window set high in the cell wall; wondering how fate had managed to deal him such misfortune. Eventually, Chard closed his eyes and started to drift off once again, only to be woken rudely by the clang of the iron cell door as it swung open.

'Get to your feet!'

Chard groaned as he saw it was the malevolent guard from earlier. Slowly he got to his feet.

'Time for our chat,' snarled the guard, throwing a powerful punch into Chard's midriff.

The prisoner grunted and doubled over in pain.

'Stand up straight when I'm talking to you!' ordered the guard.

Chard's anger started to rise, tempted to punch the guard back, but to do so would probably result in his assailant calling for other guards, and it wouldn't end well. Slowly, he straightened up and, deliberately avoiding eye contact, spoke as calmly as he could. 'You seem to have taken a dislike to me. May I ask why?'

The guard raised his fist, but held it there. 'You will address me as Mr Kelly.'

Chard gave a reluctant nod of acceptance before repeating the question. 'May I ask why you have taken a dislike to me, Mr Kelly?'

'I want to know what you've done with my brother.'

Chard looked puzzled. 'I'm sorry but I can't say I'm familiar with someone called Kelly. Would I know him by any other name.?'

The punch came swiftly at Chard's head, but it was not accurate, and just clipped his ear. 'Don't try to be clever,' warned Kelly.

'I'm not trying to be clever,' replied Chard raising his hands in supplication. 'I'll tell you whatever you like, but I don't know your brother. Why do you think I would know him?'

'Because he came to see you.'

'When?' asked Chard.

'As soon as he found out about the bodies being discovered. It was in the paper. You murdered them at the house of Mr Landell, and it said the owner had last been seen in public at Lord Berwick's mansion, when a robbery took place.'

'So why would he want to see me?' asked Chard.

'Don't try and be clever with me!' snarled Kelly, hitting his prisoner hard in the ribs.

Chard doubled over in pain as the guard continued, his face full of anger.

'John told me it was Landell who had given him a job at the mansion. He was working there when the robbery happened. The following night he went to try and pick up a reference by calling at Landell's property, but there was someone already there, so he came away. He went back later to find the house was in darkness and nobody at home. There was a rumour Landell had gone away, so my brother left it at that. When he saw the newspaper report of the corpses, John reasoned the person he saw on his first visit must have been the killer. He said he knew who it was and intended going to see them.'

'Who did he say it was?'

Kelly kicked Chard in the shin, making him fall to the ground. 'It was obviously you. That's why you're here isn't it?'

'I didn't do it!' shouted Chard, holding his painful leg with both hands. 'If he's gone missing it's nothing to do with me. Why didn't you report it to the police?'

'I did, but they weren't interested. My brother has had a few run-ins with them and they didn't believe my story. They said he's probably got himself arrested somewhere using a false name.'

'If your brother thought it was me, then how would he have been able to find me in South Wales? It's where I've been ever since I left Shrewsbury.'

'I don't know, but I reckon he did find you somehow. If you've killed him then you won't get as far as your trial,' threatened Kelly.

'I want to see the prison governor,' demanded Chard. 'If you don't let me see him, I'll complain to my solicitor,' replied Chard, getting to his feet.

Kelly grinned. 'He's away until the day after tomorrow, but when he gets back, I'll make sure you see him. That's a promise. I'll leave you for now, but perhaps we'll chat again tomorrow.'

SEVEN

A loud bang on the cell door caused Chard to wake with a start. He glanced up at the small barred window to see that it was barely past dawn. He rubbed his face. It felt odd to be completely clean-shaven. His solicitor had insisted Chard should be allowed to make himself presentable to appear in front of the magistrate.

He could hear swearing and general commotion outside, then the sound of footsteps on the cast iron gantries above. The noise went on for nearly an hour, yet no-one came to open his cell door. Chard pulled back the single woollen blanket that covered him, stood and urinated into the metal pail in the corner of the cell.

Eventually, the clamour outside subsided and it was only then that a guard came for him. Chard gave a sigh of relief to see it wasn't Kelly.

'Right, come on, you. Slopping out time.'

Chard picked up the pail and went through the door under the watchful eye of the guard.

'Over there! Just to the right, down the passage to the drains,' ordered the guard.

The floor of the block was clear of other prisoners, their slopping out having finished.

'The others are all safely back in the cells,' the guard informed him. 'Not exactly safe for you being a copper in here. We had a constable in here once, many years ago. It was just after they changed over from the solitary system, when everyone was kept separate. Anyway, the poor bastard didn't last five minutes. Strangled him they did. Very nasty.'

The guard walked behind Chard as they entered the passageway to the slopping out area.

'I don't like to see prisoners "topped" on my watch, so when I'm on duty I'll see you're kept separate.'

'I'm very grateful,' said Chard with sincerity, as he emptied his pail to the drains.

'You will be kept in your separate cell, shower separately once a week, and enter the exercise yard on your own, twice a day. Because you are on remand, you will be excused sewing mailbags and such like.'

Chard felt it was worth saying something about his treatment by Kelly, though only tentatively. 'I think I've got on the wrong side of one of your colleagues Mr...?'

'Burnes,' answered the guard.

'I am afraid Mr Burnes, that Mr Kelly has taken a dislike to me.'

'I'll not hear tittle-tattle about my colleagues,' responded the guard firmly. 'Just be glad you're being kept away from the other prisoners. Only the governor himself can override that.'

With that admonishment the conversation ceased and Chard was returned to his cell. As the guard had promised he was not given any work, but was taken alone to the exercise yard later in the morning and best of all there was no sign of Kelly. All in all, things could be worse. At least it was bearable and, confident that he would eventually be freed at his trial, Chard looked forward to clearing his name.

***

Late in the afternoon, Chard's cell door opened and in stepped an unexpected visitor, dressed in civilian clothes.

'Morgan!' exclaimed the prisoner, standing up to shake his constable's hand.

'Five minutes! No more!' ordered Burnes who stood at the entrance. Morgan nodded his acknowledgement and the guard exited, locking the door behind him.

'I showed him my warrant card and he let me in as a favour,' explained the constable.

'I'm so glad to see you,' said Chard. 'I thought all of you might have given up on me.'

'Never, sir. We knew we would be refused access to you until after the trial; and assumed you would have been freed anyway. Superintendent Jones sent a telegram to the court yesterday; and when we got the reply that you'd been sent here on remand, we had a meeting. I volunteered to come up here today and find out if there is anything I can do to help. I've taken leave of absence so just let me know if there's anything I can do. We still only know the very basics of the case.'

'I'll be as succinct as I can. Do you have a pencil and paper?'

'No sir, they made me empty my pockets before I came in. They're with my coat and suitcase at the main gate,' answered Morgan.

'Try and remember it then. And drop the 'sir'. I don't think it applies at the moment.' Chard took a deep breath before continuing. 'I was married, but we weren't happy. My wife left me for a man called Landell. However, we had come to an agreement. She and Landell were going to America and then I would get a divorce through the American courts on the basis of adultery. By doing it in America, it would avoid unnecessary publicity and intrusion into my affairs over here. Landell is, or rather was, a businessman. For whatever reason, he told nobody about the plans to go to America and so there's nobody to back up my story.'

'That was ages ago though,' said Morgan. 'What about your plans for divorce?'

'That's exactly what the police said. The truth is, when Sofia didn't write to me from America, I felt ambivalent about it. I just didn't care. It was only when I became embroiled with Mrs Murray a few months ago that I tried tracing her. Then, after that relationship fell apart, I just left it again,' explained Chard.

'What else have they got against you?'

'Landell was last seen alive in public at a party. I was present at the time and there was an incident which I haven't got time to go into. The following night a witness claims to have seen me lurking outside Landell's house. I wasn't there, but I don't have an alibi. Landell's body was subsequently found with that of my wife. They'd been locked in a cellar and starved to death. The police have the motive of my wife's desertion, the assumed deliberately fake story of her being in America, and a witness placing me at the scene.'

Morgan gave a low whistle. 'It's pretty damning. Not that I think you're guilty,' he added quickly.

Chard smiled. 'I'm not worried about my forthcoming trial. The witness is plainly unreliable and my solicitor will have had plenty of time to destroy his reputation. I also think I now know who the witness saw.'

'You do?' asked Morgan, raising an eyebrow.

'There's a guard here called Kelly. Apparently, his brother had been hired by Landell to work at the party I mentioned. When the bodies were discovered, the brother said he'd gone to Landell's house the night after the party to pick up a reference.'

'It seems unusual to do such a thing at night,' commented Morgan.

'It is strange, I agree. Anyway, he must have been the man seen by the witness.'

'In which case, we just need to get hold of him and prove it.'

Chard grimaced. 'I haven't finished. When he was there, he saw someone else visiting Landell.'

'Even better then. I'll go and speak to him and make him tell me who he saw,' said Morgan firmly.

'Unfortunately, he apparently went to confront whoever it was, believing it to be the murderer; I assume to blackmail him. The guard's brother hasn't been seen since. Kelly thinks he went to South Wales to find me and that I've done him in.'

'What can I do then?' asked Morgan.

'I think I'll be okay. I doubt Kelly will do me real harm and once the witness is shown to be unreliable, I'll be set free. Then I will want to discover the real killer and track him down. If you want to help in the meantime...?'

'Just tell me what you need doing,' volunteered Morgan enthusiastically.

Chard gave a grateful smile. 'Perhaps you can go back to finding the reporter who I mentioned to you the last time you were here. He might have some information which could be useful.'

'I'll do that tonight and see you tomorrow.'

'Where are you planning on staying?' asked Chard.

'No idea. I can't afford to stay in the same hotel as last time. My pockets aren't that deep. I just want some cheap lodgings,' answered the constable.

Morgan's explanation was interrupted abruptly as the cell door was flung open, 'Time's up!' ordered the guard.

'Ask for directions to the Welsh Bridge. On the far side of it is the Bridge pub. They'll point you in the direction of a decent lodging house,' Chard said quickly to Morgan as the latter was hurried out of the cell by the guard.

The door was slammed shut, leaving Chard feeling uplifted, knowing there were friends still willing to support him.

***

Morgan wandered into the town square. After leaving the prison that afternoon, he'd asked a passer-by for directions, and found the pub recommended by Chard. Over a pint of ale, the landlord had suggested he try a lodging house on Frankwell Quay, known to have clean rooms at a reasonable price. Having inspected the rooms and settled in, he'd slept for a while before taking a meal and returning to the town centre.

It was early evening, yet the square was still busy with cabs for hire in front of the magistrate's court building. The doors of the music hall were open, but it was too early for customers. Young men and chaperoned young women promenaded around the square, hoping to catch each other's eye. Workmen, tired from a day's toil, and businessmen out for an evening meal, walked purposefully to their intended destinations. It seemed a town at peace with itself and Morgan felt he could enjoy his stay in other circumstances, but not tonight – there was a job to be done.

'Good evening, landlord. I'm looking for a gentleman called Banner. Apparently, he's known as Old Nosey,' enquired Idris on entering the Plough.

'You're in luck. That's him, over there, in the corner,' came the reply. 'He drinks whisky if it helps. Will it be two you'll be wanting? That'll be sixpence,' said the landlord pointedly, holding out his hand.

Morgan handed over the money, and once served with the drinks, took them across to Banner. He was an elderly man with thinning hair and a red nose, who sat at a table, scribbling notes into a small book. His patched tweed jacket had seen better days and the stem of a pipe stuck out of its top pocket.

'Mr Banner?'

'Who's asking?' came the reply, without looking up.

'The name's Morgan, Idris Morgan. I thought you might like a drink.'

Banner stopped scribbling and looked up. 'Take a seat. I should take a break anyway,' he decided, taking the proffered glass of whisky. 'I assume you want something. What is it? Have you got a story to sell?'

'No. I'm new to the town and need some information,' said Morgan, taking a seat opposite the reporter.

'Shrewsbury sits inside a wide loop of the River Severn,' replied Banner, deciding to toy with the stranger. 'The railway station and the castle are at the open end of the loop. The main crossing points to the East and West are the English Bridge and the Welsh Bridge respectively; and we've got a big park called The Quarry. What else do you need to know?'

'Not information about the town, information about a murder,' clarified Morgan.

Banner looked interested. 'What murder?' he asked.

'A man by the name of Landell and a woman called Sofia Chard.'

'The former Inspector Chard's wife,' nodded Banner. 'He was put on remand yesterday. Were you in the courtroom? I was there standing at the back, but I didn't see you.'

'No, I only arrived today,' answered Morgan. 'Mr Chard is a friend of mine and I want to find out if there is anything the magistrate missed.'

'In what way?'

'I don't know. Let's start with the discovery of the bodies. Who found them?'

'Bailiffs entering the house. The man in charge was Scratch Harper. It shook him up,' answered Banner.

'Were there any marks on the bodies?'

'I spoke to him as soon as the news broke and asked him that very question. He said the bodies were too far gone to tell. He did say one thing though…'

'What was it?' interrupted Morgan eagerly.

'He said their hunger must have been terrible because Landell had tried to eat…'

'No!' interjected Morgan, 'I don't want to know!' The constable took a sip of his drink before asking another question.

'How compelling was the evidence in the courtroom, from your point of view?'

'All circumstantial really, but I can see why the magistrate felt compelled to put Chard on remand. The motive was glaringly obvious, and there was a witness placing him at the scene of the crime on the probable night the deed was done. Not that the witness was a reliable one. Enoch Rudd is a drunk with bad eyesight and will say anything for the price of a pint. He won't fool a judge. I dare say your friend will go free at the assizes.'

Idris felt a degree of comfort in the reporter's opinion. 'Did Landell have any enemies?' he asked.

'He clearly was in debt, which was why the house had been mortgaged. I obviously can't see the bank having him killed, but he might have owed money to others. I did speak to his business partners, a Mr Jeremy Stanmore and a Mr Leonard Warren. Neither seemed that sorry about Landell's death.' Banner paused. 'I'll admit there's something about the case which doesn't sit right. Chard had a good name in the town, for a policeman that is. Until he disgraced himself at Lord Berwick's.'

'What did he do?' asked Morgan, puzzled.

'You mean he hasn't told you?' Banner gave a sarcastic laugh. 'Are you sure he's a friend of yours?'

'Quite sure,' answered Morgan, slightly offended.

'Then you'd best ask him?' answered Banner, finishing his drink. 'You'll have to excuse me, but I have a prior appointment at Newman's Vaults. A reporter's work is never done.'

Morgan watched the reporter leave, then gave a sigh.

I'm no further forward now than I was before, he thought. At least the inspector's hopes that they'll clear him at his trial seem realistic. I'll visit him tomorrow, then I might as well go home.

EIGHT

Unlike the previous morning, Chard wasn't alarmed by the banging on the cell door which woke him up. His life would be one of routine for the next few weeks. Something to be endured with fortitude. At least he would have a few minutes to clear his head before having his solitary turn at slopping out. His thoughts wandered, not for the first time, to the identity of the real murderer of his wife. She had made no real enemies since they had married, nor friends for that matter. His sweet Italian bride had become sullen and argumentative soon after he took her home to the small town of Wem, a few miles north of Shrewsbury. It was too rural, '*troppo noioso*', too boring, for her. Yet, although her haughty attitude to the people in the town was noticeable, no-one could have wanted to actually kill her. No. The killer must have been known to Landell. But what was the motive?

Unexpectedly, the cell door swung open, catching Chard by surprise. The other prisoners could still be heard on the gantries, making their way back to their cells, not yet locked up after slopping out.

'On your feet, prisoner!'

Chard looked towards the door where the guard Kelly stood, looking mightily pleased with himself.

'Come on! Get up! I've arranged what you wanted. You should be pleased I've done you a favour,' said Kelly, in a way that left Chard feeling uneasy.

'What might that be, Mr Kelly?' replied the prisoner, feeling tempted to swear at the guard, but determined to try to keep on the good side of his tormentor for the time being.

'You wanted to see the governor didn't you. To complain about how I welcomed you the other night? Well, you can. He's a very jovial fellow, only appointed to the post a month ago. You should get on like a house on fire. Come on, follow me. I won't even cuff you,' Kelly added pleasantly.

Very puzzled by this turn of events, Chard followed Kelly out of the door and into the main floor of 'A' Block. Most of the other prisoners were by now back in their cells, but a couple of prisoners on the gantry above pointed angrily at him, and another turned and spat; a gobbet of phlegm landing inches away.

'Someone seems to have told them who you are,' smirked Kelly without turning around.

'They were bound to find out eventually. I've put enough of them inside,' shrugged Chard, as they walked out of the prison block and into the gatehouse which also housed the governor's office.

'I expect the governor will be unhappy that you haven't been able to keep my identity secret for more than a couple of days though,' suggested Chard.

Kelly gave no response and continued to lead the way until they reached the door of the governor's office, which he rapped hard with his knuckles.

'Come in!' came the terse response. There was a slight accent to the command and Chard frowned, as it seemed somehow familiar.

Kelly pushed his prisoner inside, then stood to attention behind Chard as the governor finished signing some papers and looked up from his desk.

Chard felt the colour drain from his face, and swallowed hard as he recognised the middle-aged man who sat before him. Chisel-faced, with a neatly trimmed grey moustache, the new governor was none other than Major Ferguson; the husband he had publicly cuckolded at Lord Berwick's party.

'How are you settling in?' asked the governor, with a glint of cruel satisfaction in his eye.

Chard realised immediately there would be no point whatsoever in complaining about his treatment. It would only give Ferguson satisfaction. Instead, he avoided the governor's gaze and stared at a point on the wall about two feet above the man's head.

'Splendidly,' he replied.

Kelly punched Chard hard in the kidneys, causing him to fall to his knees.

'You will address the governor as "sir". Now get to your feet!' commanded the guard.

Chard struggled back up, catching sight of Ferguson's smile as he did so.

'Splendidly, *sir*,' he emphasised.

Ferguson tapped a pencil against his desk absent-mindedly, as if his thoughts were elsewhere, considering a serious issue. It didn't fool Chard. The governor clearly had something already in mind, but was theatrically drawing it out to keep his prisoner on edge. Finally, he spoke, a harsh Scottish accent giving an edge to his words.

'I am worried about your safety. Are you aware of the Separate System?'

Chard knew it was a rhetorical question. Every police officer was aware of the Separate System of prison confinement. Convicted prisoners were kept entirely apart from each other. They weren't allowed to converse, and even when allowed out for exercise they were made to have a peaked cap over their heads covering their eyes. Then they would place a hand on a fellow prisoner's shoulder and walk around in a large circle whilst remaining silent. They would be allowed to see each other and sing hymns in the prison chapel, but not to converse. The idea was that they could not be corrupted by each other, leaving them to reflect internally on their own sinful ways.

'My predecessor was impressed with Gladstone's report on prison reform which came out last year, and decided to trial a more relaxed approach. Something that I have, for the time being, allowed to continue.' The governor paused for effect, clearly enjoying Chard's discomfort.

'They say that under the Separate System many prisoners became insane. Driven mad by an inability to come to terms with their sinful souls. Unable to gain a perspective of their foul deeds through communication with their fellow inmates. Many a time a prisoner would be found hanging in their cell when the guards came around in the morning. Am I not correct, Kelly?'

'Yes sir. So I believe,' obliged the guard.

'I think questions might be asked if that were to be my fate… sir,' said Chard, aware Ferguson could not possibly do something so blatant as to fake his suicide.

'Oh, don't misunderstand me,' replied the governor, his voice reflecting an attitude of mock concern. 'I am concerned for your health. It is incumbent on me to keep you fit and healthy for your appointment with the hangman. Not just physically you understand, but mentally. We have been keeping you alone in your cell and then separate from everyone else. I feel there is a real danger that if we keep you so secluded, you might go the way of those poor fellows under the Separate System who went insane.'

'I have to be kept segregated for my safety, as you know sir,' responded Chard.

'Yes, of course. However, we need to strike a balance. Perhaps someone to share your cell. Then you would have someone to watch over you when you go out into the exercise yard with your fellow prisoners. Do you know of someone suitable Kelly?' asked Ferguson, looking at the guard.

'Oh yes sir. I have the very man. You just leave it to me sir.'

It was then Chard realised that one way or another, Ferguson would ensure he would never get as far as a trial. His life was already in danger.

***

There had been tears, it had been inevitable; and lies. There had to have been lies, May reasoned. Her father had raged that she would not be allowed back in the house. 'You cannot go unaccompanied. It's unseemly. If that lad has anything to do with this, I'll horsewhip him!' he had threatened. Mrs Roper had wept as she tried to calm her husband. 'I'm sure May knows what she is doing, dear. She has come so far with curing herself of her "affliction". If she feels there is a clinic that can help her further then I'm sure a short stay away will be beneficial,' Mrs Roper had reasoned.

May patted the small pocket in her jacket where she kept her bottle of laudanum. Her "affliction" was an addiction to the drug which she was being slowly weaned off, under the watchful eye of her employer, Doctor Henderson. The fact she had lied to him, about having to visit a sick aunt, was regrettable. It might, in due course, result in her dismissal. It was a terrible gamble, but she had to risk it. Inspector Chard had, in the past, saved her life and also kept her addiction secret. He clearly was in trouble, yet the best Superintendent Jones could do was to send one of his constables to help. Poor Idris. She loved him... probably. He was brave, and handsome beneath his muttonchop whiskers; but she doubted his ability to help the inspector. Not that he was stupid. Far from it; but by the sounds of it, this was something beyond the ordinary, and he would need help. That was why, unknown to him, she had set off early that morning for Shrewsbury. It was an adventure, not ever having travelled outside Wales, but so far everyone had been ever so kind.

'There's a Young Women's Christian Association opened up in Princess Street only a few weeks ago, Miss. They might be able to advise you,' a helpful railway porter had said on her arrival.

She had found plenty of cabs outside the station; and for a cheap fare one of them had taken her to Princess Street which ran just off the town square. Luckily there were a small number of rooms for the discerning Christian lady of respectable appearance, and May had paid for her accommodation before settling in and resting until midday.

Now she stood in the square, close to the police station, wondering how on earth she could possibly find Idris in this busy town. Surely, she couldn't go on her own to the prison? But then, why not? The purpose of coming was to help Inspector Chard, and he would know Idris's whereabouts. Purposefully, May walked into the police station and smiled politely at the desk sergeant.

'Excuse me Sergeant, but I'm a visitor to your town. Could you give me directions?'

'Certainly Miss,' replied the sergeant, only too willing to be distracted by the attractive young lady standing before him. 'Where do you want to go?'

'The prison, please,' replied May.

The sergeant furrowed his brow. 'And why would you be wanting to go there, Miss?'

'I have a friend in there.'

'You've got a friend in prison? You don't look the sort.'

'What sort, Sergeant?' asked May innocently.

'Never you mind. Go ahead onto High Street, turn right up Pride Hill, down the other side until you reach the railway station, under the railway bridge, then first on the right. You can't miss it,' said the sergeant. 'Now on your way,' he added tersely.

May reddened at the sergeant's rude tone, but at least she had been able to take in his directions. Turning on her heel, she marched out of the station into the fresh air.

Finding Pride Hill was easy enough, she had come along it earlier in the morning, and remembered noticing a café as the cab passed by. The black and white timbered building was next to a shop called Randles selling corsets for the *most discerning* lady. Having glanced at the price in the window of the 'New Flexible Hips' corset, May gave a sigh and went into the café next door, taking a window seat, and ordering a light luncheon.

She had just finished her meal and put her cutlery together for the waitress to remove her plate, when a familiar figure walked past the window. May took out her purse and paid her bill before hurrying out into the busy street.

Eyes turned to stare at the smartly dressed young woman, rushing in a most inelegant way up the hill, calling out as she went.

'Idris! Idris! Wait a moment!' called May.

Finally registering that someone was calling his name, he turned and looked in astonishment to see May coming towards him.

'What the hell are you doing here?' he blurted out, without thinking.

'Don't you use that language, Idris Morgan!' scolded May.

'Sorry, but I mean…what…?'

May read the expression in her sweetheart's face. He didn't look angry, nor pleased, just confused. 'I've come to help,' she explained.

'But who's with you?'

'I've come on my own.'

'On your own? You mean your parents let you?'

'I don't need my parents to give permission. I am twenty-one after all,' snapped May. 'They don't know why I'm here, but at least they do know I'm in Shrewsbury.'

'Does your father know I'm also in Shrewsbury?' asked Idris, with a worried expression.

'Not as far as I know. I dare say he'll find out at some point,' shrugged May. 'Don't worry about it. We can cross that bridge when we come to it.'

Idris didn't look the least bit reassured. 'I'm just off to the prison to see the inspector,' he said.

'Good, then we can go together,' responded May, taking his arm.

***

Despite the intimation of the governor that there would be unpleasant changes to his imprisonment, Chard had been returned to his own cell and left undisturbed. Finding it unbearable to contemplate being found hanged in his cell, or murdered in the exercise yard, his mind had turned to the almost impossible task of escape. There has to be a way, he mused. A few possibilities had come to mind, but they all needed outside help or the complicity of a guard.

Chard's thoughts were interrupted by the door of the cell opening. He tensed ready for another unpleasant confrontation with Kelly, but to his relief, it was Idris Morgan who entered.

'I had to bribe my way in this time,' he said. 'We've got just a few minutes.'

'Did you find anything out last night?' asked Chard eagerly.

'Nothing much. I've got the name of the bailiff who found the bodies but that's it. Other than the fact Landell was obviously in debt.'

'Who did he owe money to?'

'The mortgage hadn't been paid, but he was in business and had an income, so he must have been in debt to someone else.'

'Try and find out who that someone else is. Perhaps ask his former business partners, Jeremy Stanmore and Leonard Warren. My solicitor, Mr Tayleur who has an office in Dogpole will give you their details.'

'Where?' asked Morgan

'Dogpole. It's a street. Just ask anyone in town,' answered Chard irritably.

'Is there anything else I can do?'

'Yes, but I am afraid it might get you into trouble,' said Chard solemnly.

'What is it?'

'I need you to go out of town via the English Bridge, turn right and after about two hundred yards you'll find Trinity Street on the left. There's another narrow side street just off it, leading to Brougham Square. Ask for George Lamb's house. He's someone who owes me a debt.'

Morgan repeated the directions to confirm he understood, then nodded. 'What do you want me to do when I find him?'

'Tell him to arrange for a rowing boat to be hidden by the bank where we used to fish together. Also say that I want him to wait on the river bend at Uffington at midnight, for the next five nights.'

Morgan's eyes opened wide with shock. 'What? Are you going to try and break out? Are you serious?' he exclaimed, trying to keep his voice down. Realising he had questioned Chard's judgement, Morgan blushed and adopted a calmer manner. 'Sorry sir, I mean Mr Chard. I mean why would you want to escape? You've said yourself you will be acquitted. It's just a matter of time.'

'I am afraid it's time I don't think I'll have,' answered Chard grimly. 'There are people here who mean me great harm and my instinct tells me that if I don't get out, it'll be the end of me.'

'You must be exaggerating, surely,' said Morgan dubiously.

'No. I'm deadly serious. Other than contacting George Lamb, I don't want you involved. If I need to send you a message though, how can I get hold of you?'

'I'm staying in the lodging house next to the river in Frankwell.'

'Good. I'll only send you a message if I really need to.'

'What if I find out anything useful about Landell?'

'Leave anything like that with George Lamb. I just hope he won't let me down. He does owe me a great favour, but helping me escape might be too much to ask.'

'I'll do my best to persuade him, and we'll see what we can get out of Landell's business partners.'

'We?' asked Chard. 'You needn't involve George Lamb in finding out more on Landell.'

'I didn't mean him. I've got May with me.'

'You've got May…?' exclaimed Chard, as shocked as Morgan had been when he'd mentioned the escape.

'She's outside the gatehouse. They wouldn't let her in. Not even with a bribe.'

'But how…?'

'She's staying in Shrewsbury for a few days,' explained Morgan.

'So, you and her are…?' started Chard with raised eyebrows.

'Oh no sir! Nothing like that!' denied Morgan hurriedly. 'She's staying at the YWCA. I didn't know she was coming until she found me on my way here. She seems to be behaving very headstrong,' he said, shaking his head.

'I wouldn't disagree for one minute,' said Chard. 'May used to be like that when I first met her. Perhaps she's getting back to her old self. Just keep her out of all this,' he added.

Morgan frowned. 'It's a side to her that I haven't seen…'

Suddenly, the cell door was kicked open.

'What's going on in here?' shouted an enraged Kelly. 'No visitors! Get out!' he yelled at Morgan, who immediately bristled and started to advance on the guard.

'Morgan! No! Or you'll end up in here with me,' advised Chard urgently.

The constable took a deep breath, then nodded to his inspector, before leaving the cell with reluctance.

Kelly turned to Chard briefly before closing the door. 'I've got something special planned for you later,' he threatened.

NINE

Nice – The South of France

Lady Deansmoor was pleased to have finished her afternoon constitutional along the Promenade des Anglais. Yes, the view of the sun's rays shining on the Bay of Angels was truly magnificent, but it really was just too hot. Still, it was better than being at home, and the offer from an old friend of free use of the apartment for the whole summer was an opportunity which could not be refused.

'Oh, this is so much better, Finnick,' she proclaimed to her lady's maid as they entered the cool interior. 'Bring me some tea. Damn French cafés can't make tea, not even in Nice.'

Lady Deansmoor walked to the window blinds and opened them a fraction, letting a blinding shard of sunlight light up the chaise longue on which she would recline.

She scowled in response to an unexpected knock on the door of the apartment, followed by Finnick's footsteps as she hurried to answer it. Lady Deansmoor heard the door being opened, then some sort of verbal exchange.

'What is it Finnick?' she called.

The maid entered the room carrying something in her hand. 'It's a telegram, from England, your Ladyship.'

Lady Deansmoor snatched at the telegram and read the contents. Finnick watched as the grand dame scowled, then picked up a small china vase, which she hurled against the wall, shattering it.

'Get out! And don't come back for an hour, I need to think!'

A terrified Finnick, used to her mistress's tantrums, immediately headed for the door.

'When you get back, make arrangements for a journey. We're going back to England,' shouted Lady Deansmoor at her fleeing servant.

After the maid had left, Lady Deansmoor read the telegram once again. She knew who it was from and what the cryptic message meant. 'Annual charge be damned! I shouldn't have paid before,' she admonished herself. 'If this continues, I'll be in penury. No, something needs to be done.'

***

May waited impatiently for Idris to re-appear through the prison gate. She was still indignant at having been summarily refused entry by the guard. Finally, with some relief she saw her suitor exit the Dana and, with a worried expression on his face, approach and take her arm.

'What happened? What did the inspector say?' May demanded.

'It's complicated,' replied Morgan, leading her away from the prison, back towards the town.

'You look worried. Why? What's going on?' she asked.

'I can't tell you. It's best you don't know.'

'Idris, what exactly can't you tell me?' came the indignant response.

'Like I said. I can't tell you. What I can say is that the inspector needs our help. We need to find a way of speaking to the business partners of the man who was murdered. The inspector suggested we speak to Mr Tayleur, his solicitor, who may provide some details.'

'What does he want us to do when we find these business partners?' asked May.

'The inspector reasoned that the victim might have been killed by whoever he owed money to. The partners might know the answer, though how we get them to tell us is beyond me.'

'I'm sure we'll find a way,' replied May, confidently. 'Let's go and see the inspector's solicitor straight away. Where is his office?'

'You won't believe this,' replied Morgan as the couple walked under the railway bridge leading past Shrewsbury station, 'but it's in a street called Dogpole.'

'Dogpole? These English people have ever such funny names for places sometimes,' reflected May.

Morgan was by now getting familiar with the uphill walk from the railway station into the town's main streets, and after a brief word with a messenger boy outside Newton's milliners, the pair soon found themselves at their destination in Dogpole. Entering the premises, they stated their business to a prim, bespectacled receptionist who invited them to wait in an adjoining room. It was half an hour later before the solicitor became available.

'Do come in,' welcomed Tayleur as he came into the waiting room to greet them. 'I hope I haven't kept you too long.'

'Not at all. We are only too pleased you could make yourself available to see us,' replied May graciously.

The solicitor gestured with his arm that they should follow him as he led the way to his private office, and soon they were sat comfortably in fine leather backed chairs facing Tayleur's polished oak desk.

'I understand from my receptionist that you are friends of my client, Mr Chard,' said Tayleur.

'That's correct. My name is Idris Morgan, and I am a constable in the Glamorganshire County Constabulary. This is Miss Roper.'

'We've just come from the prison. Or to be more precise, Idris actually went inside whilst I waited at the gate,' explained May.

Tayleur looked at her attentively. 'I trust Mr Chard is in good health? He is currently in a most unfortunate position but I am confident it is only a temporary situation. I believe the prosecution will drop their case before it comes to trial, unless of course they find any more evidence.'

'Do you think Mr Chard is safe in there?' asked Morgan.

Tayleur gave a somewhat condescending smile. 'Oh yes, he's perfectly safe. The governor will be aware of his situation and he'll be kept away from any of the other inmates.'

May noticed the worried expression on Morgan's face, and resolved to press him on the matter afterwards.

'Now how can I be of assistance?' asked the solicitor.

'Mr Chard asked if we might have a word with the murdered man's former partners. Do you know where we might find them?' responded Morgan.

Tayleur pondered for a moment before replying. 'I believe they've kept their former partner's name in the business. The offices of Warren, Stanmore and Landell can be found on Claremont Bank.'

Morgan noted the puzzlement in May's face. 'It means Claremont Hill. They call hills banks for some reason,' he explained.

Mr Tayleur looked Morgan up and down and had an uncomfortable expression on his face. 'I don't quite know how to put this,' he said slowly, 'but they might not choose to see you. They are very busy men dealing with some very influential investors.'

'I don't ...' replied Morgan.

'We quite understand,' interrupted May. 'Thank you, Mr Tayleur. You've been very helpful. We won't keep you any longer.'

With that, May stood up and tugged on Morgan's sleeve, indicating he should do the same.

It was only after they had left that she took him to one side to explain.

'Idris, don't be offended, but what Mr Tayleur was inferring related to how you are dressed.'

'What's wrong with how I'm dressed? This is my best suit!'

'And very handsome you look too,' mollified May. 'You look very respectable, but these men we need to talk to will be used to dealing with people with money. Lots of money. If you had a frock coat instead of your suit jacket and a top hat instead of your cap, and you wore a waistcoat with a gold chain, then they might let you in.'

'Bloody nobs!'

'Shame on you Idris Morgan!' scolded May. 'Then there's your accent.'

'What's wrong with my accent?'

'It's the same as mine,' explained May. 'A beautiful accent from the valleys of South Wales, but not one you'd hear in the tea rooms of high society.'

'Oh, so you would prefer it if I was a "plumgob" then would you?'

'No *cariad*, I wouldn't, but it is something I could carry off if I needed to. I was once in a play at our church hall and took the part of a countess. I'll give it some thought and we can meet up tomorrow morning to discuss our plans.'

'When and where?'

'Ten o'clock in the town square,' answered May, 'but before I forget, what haven't you told me?'

Morgan shrugged innocently. 'Nothing,'

'You had the same worried expression in the solicitors, when you asked if Mr Chard will be safe, as you had when you came back through the prison gates earlier,' accused May.

'You're imagining things,' replied Morgan, giving May a peck on the cheek before walking away. 'I'll see you in the morning.'

***

Kelly was taking a break and enjoying a piping hot mug of tea, thinking of what he had in store for Thomas Chard, when to his annoyance, he was interrupted by one of the other guards.

'Sean, you're not going to believe this, but there's someone else wanting to visit a prisoner. What do they think this is, a hospital or something? He looks like a foreigner as well.'

Kelly swore an oath and went to the main gate where another guard was standing by the inspection grille and evidently arguing with someone outside.

'What's the problem?' demanded Kelly.

'This gentleman is insisting he should be let in to see a prisoner called Chard,' replied his colleague.

'I'll talk to him. Move out of the way.'

Kelly put his face to the grille, looked at the visitor and sneered. He was finely dressed, so obviously a man of means, but his face betrayed him. 'Some kind of foreign johnny, certainly not from these shores,' thought Kelly.

'I just want to have ten minutes on my own with a prisoner.' The visitor spoke calmly, with no trace of impatience.

'The prisoner being Chard, I understand,' replied Kelly deciding to humour the stranger for the moment.

'Correct,' he confirmed reaching into his pocket to take out a wallet.

'And who shall I say is calling?'

'The name is Cole. Elijah Cole,' came the reply, as a gold sovereign was produced.

'What do you want with him?' asked Kelly.

'Just some time alone with him. It's a private matter,' replied Cole pleasantly.

'He's already had a visitor today and there'll be no more. You can see him being hanged in due course.'

'I understand he is only here on remand. As such, there should be no reason to be quite so strict,' argued Cole, remaining calm. Reaching into his wallet once again, he pulled out two more sovereigns which he held in the open palm of his hand so Kelly could see.

'He's caused us some trouble, so he's in the punishment cell,' lied the guard. 'No more visitors, not even his solicitor.'

Cole smiled and stared hard at Kelly, this time producing a bank note. 'Are you sure you can't be persuaded?'

'I'm sure of one thing,' replied the guard.

'And what's that?' asked Cole.

'I'm sure you can stick your money up your arse and piss off!'

Cole glared back silently, before turning around and walking away.

TEN

It was later in the evening, after having eating a filling bowl of mutton stew with dumplings, that Idris Morgan set off on his other errand. He had changed into older, more comfortable jacket and trousers which he'd packed, but still kept his favourite flat cap. Annoyingly, it had started to spot with rain, and Morgan wished he'd brought a coat. He left the town via the English Bridge for the first time, and the hill leading down out of the eastern side of the town was far steeper than he expected. Crossing the bridge over the River Severn, Morgan stopped to look at the sight before him. Beyond a railway bridge, through the drizzle of rain, could be seen the impressive bulk of Shrewsbury Abbey. Instinctively, Morgan started to walk in its direction before remembering he had to turn right. Not entirely sure he'd remembered the directions correctly, the constable asked a couple of street urchins where he might find Trinity Street, then threw them a halfpenny in payment. He was very glad he did, because he felt sure he would have missed it otherwise, for the entrance was quite narrow.

'Get out of the way!' yelled the driver of a cart which could barely fit in the narrow roadway.

Morgan turned sideways on the pavement as the large carthorse clattered by, the side of the cart missing him by less than a foot.

'I'm looking for Brougham Square,' called Morgan to the driver.

'Just there on the left,' he replied, pointing back up the street with his whip, before turning his attention back to the horse.

Morgan made his way into the narrow turning; which then dog-legged into a square which might originally have been a mews. Despite the damp weather and the late hour, a number of children were out, playing barefoot on the beaten earth of the square.

Feeling sorry for the poor infants, Morgan took another halfpenny from his pocket and gave it to the youngest in return for the address of Mr Lamb.

'It's that one mister,' said the child pointing, before running off with the coin.

Curious as to how someone in Inspector Chard's position would know someone who lived in this square, Morgan gave the door a firm knock.

The door was opened sharply and a man Morgan guessed to be in his thirties stood staring at him.

'I thought you were one of those kids, knocking the door and running away. What do you want?' he snapped.

'Would you be George Lamb?' asked Morgan. The man was not quite what he had imagined. Of medium height with a shock of hair the colour of copper wire, and rounded shoulders, the occupant stood arms crossed with a scowl on his face.

'I would. What of it?'

'I understand you know Thomas Chard. May I come in?'

'Why?' asked Lamb.

'He asked me to give you a message, and I'm starting to get wet out here.'

Lamb grunted. 'You'd best get inside then, mon. There's no fire lit though,' he added, turning his back.

Morgan followed him into what was a small room, with a cooking range against one wall, alongside which were two chairs. One was occupied by a generously proportioned, fair-haired woman, who sat knitting a scarf.

'This is my wife, Freda,' explained Lamb, before gesturing to her with his arm that she should put her knitting away and get up. 'Best go out to the scullery, Freda. I think this gentleman and I may have some business to discuss.'

Lamb waited for his wife to disappear through the door at the back of the room before turning back to his visitor.

'So, who are you exactly? You're not from around here.'

'My name's Idris Morgan and I'm a friend of Mr Chard from South Wales.'

'If you're a friend of his then why aren't you calling him by his name? What's with the Mister Chard?'

'Look, I've just come to give you a message. Do you know he's in trouble?' asked Morgan.

'Yes, of course I do. When I heard he'd been arrested I went to the hearing at the magistrate's court and sat at the back. There's no way Tommy killed anyone and the witness had clearly been told what to say. They may have sent him to the Dana but there's no way he'll be hanged. They'll release him soon,' said Lamb emphatically.

'That's what his solicitor says, but...'

'But what?'

'I understand you owe... Tommy, some kind of favour,' said Morgan, changing tack.

Lamb stared silently at the wall, his mind clearly resting on some disturbing memory. It was a while before he spoke.

'Tommy saved my life. We'd been friends as young lads. He was boarding at Shrewsbury School, but preferred to run with the local town lads whenever he could. He left for university and by the time he came back he was a police inspector. I had fallen on hard times and got involved with a bad crowd,' Lamb gave a little cough, and cleared his throat before continuing. 'There was a fight with a rival gang and someone was killed. I was the scapegoat and I would've hanged, but Tommy doesn't forget his friends. He moved heaven and earth to get to the truth, and had me cleared after finding the real murderer.'

'This time he needs your help,' said Morgan firmly. 'He is adamant that if he stays in prison, he won't get to trial. I don't know why.'

'He's not planning to run, is he?' demanded Lamb.

'Yes, and he needs your help. You're to have a boat hidden where you used to go fishing. Then wait by the river bend at Uffington at midnight for the next five nights.'

Lamb looked appalled. 'I can't do that! I can't! If I were to be caught helping him escape... I'm sorry, but no, it's too much of a risk.'

'He's depending on you,' insisted Morgan.

'Things are different. I'm married now. Who would look after Freda?'

'But you just admitted you owe him your life.'

'It's just too much to ask.'

Without thinking, Morgan found himself offering to take an

active part in the escape. 'You just leave the boat and I'll wait for him on the river, if you tell me where Uffington is.'

Lamb paused to consider, before finally looking Morgan straight in the eye. 'To be honest with you, I'm a worried man. We've got a roof over our heads and enough to eat, and I've got a decent job. However, the thing is that Freda's little sister has gone missing. I reported it to the police, but they wouldn't do a thing. I even spoke to Inspector Warboys directly, but he told me to stop wasting his time. My proposition is this. I'll help Tommy on the condition he finds our Cora. There's somewhere I know where he could remain safely hidden, but only if he, and you, find her. If you stop looking for Cora then I'll turn you both in and deny ever having helped you.'

Morgan held Lamb's gaze, cursing himself for getting so involved. 'I don't think there's much option. Just tell me where I'll find Uffington.'

***

Ben Fogarty was glad to get away from the house. His job as manager of the Berwick Estate was busy enough, but his wife had been in a foul mood since he'd got home.

'God knows, I shouldn't have married her,' he muttered to himself as he made his way down to the river.

The light had faded and it was drizzling with rain, but it didn't matter. It would be an hour of peace. The small lamp, held in his left hand, lit the way, but he had used this path so many times over the years that he felt confident of making it blindfolded. He gripped the fishing rod in his other hand tightly, a sense of excitement flooding through his veins. It had been weeks since he had fished for salmon, having injured his arm moving some furniture.

'If the silly cow had been happy with the oak dresser staying where it was, it wouldn't have happened,' he told himself.

Yet now the arm was mended, and the salmon would be starting their swim upstream. The full migration was yet to come but there would be a few early ones, no doubt.

Finding his spot on the bank, Fogarty set down his lamp, unstrapped the fishing net from his back and lay down the rod. The reel and line had been set up with his favourite fishing fly attached before setting off, so there was no real preparation required; other than to gently enter the water until the river came up to mid-calf around his waders, then start to cast.

Fogarty's ears pricked up at the sound of a sudden splash which came from somewhere near the opposite bank.

'Yes!' he uttered excitedly. It was an indication of a salmon taking an insect off the top of the water. Hurriedly, he made his first cast, not clearly able to see where his fly had landed. Almost immediately there was a sharp pull on the line, and never having managed a bite on a first cast before, Fogarty found himself in the fight of his life. The hooked salmon set off downriver with a force that made him feel as if his arms were being wrenched out of their sockets. Gradually he would make some progress in pulling the salmon in, only to have to loosen the grip on the line for fear of it breaking, the fish then launching itself away once more. Eventually though, Fogarty's quarry started to tire, and after a titanic struggle, it was brought to the net. Putting it on the bank, the fisherman dispatched it with two blows of his "priest", the fisherman's small club.

Overcome with joy at what would make a fine meal the following day, Fogarty was tempted to return home straight away, but then decided to try his luck just once more.

Back into the water he went and sent a cast towards the same place, but this time with too much enthusiasm, so that it overshot the mark.

'Bugger! It's snagged!' he cursed.

There were only two options. Either cut the line, lose his favourite fishing fly and try and set up a new line by the light of his lamp; or wade across to the far bank and unsnag the hook from whatever it had latched onto. It was a difficult decision. The river had been quite high a few weeks ago and although the level had dropped considerably, the current could be treacherous. Against his better judgement, Fogarty decided to give it a try. Picking up the rod he used it as a staff to guide his footing, albeit at the expense of getting the reel wet. Halfway across the river the water had risen to just above his knee, and Fogarty was thankful the galoshes he wore were of good quality. When he was a few feet from the other side, the fisherman was shocked to see what had snagged the hook of his fly.

'Oh shit!' he groaned.

There, resting half-submerged, was a man's body.

***

Chard lay in his dismal, soulless cell, desperately trying to think of a way of escaping his confinement. There was no sound to disturb his thoughts, other than the occasional footsteps of a guard on his rounds. Feigning sickness might get me out of the cell to be treated in the infirmary, he thought. Or if I was allowed to mix with the other prisoners then there might be a way out by finding how often the prison received outside deliveries. Maybe I could hide under a cart and make my escape unnoticed? Chard kept thinking of options, but the reality was, he needed help.

Once more footsteps could be heard outside the cell, but this time, instead of them passing by, they stopped. Chard sat up as the door of the cell swung open and the unmistakeable frame of Kelly appeared.

'Prisoner, come with me,' he ordered.

Obediently, for there was no point in refusing, Chard got to his feet, put on his prison issue shoes, and went outside the cell.

'Go ahead until you reach those stairs and go up to the next level. I'll be right behind you,' said Kelly, brandishing a short wooden truncheon.

The prison block was dimly lit, with an occasional gas lamp set into the wall that sent their shadows flickering across the eerily silent space. There was no other guard on the ground floor and for a moment Chard considered turning on Kelly, but then he heard the steps of someone else on the next level. Kelly would no doubt put up one hell of a fight and if not silenced quickly, there would be at least one more guard to deal with. Chard reached the cast iron staircase and walked up to the next level.

'Where now?' he asked.

Kelly gave him a sharp prod with the truncheon. 'Where now, sir!'

'Very well, where now sir?' repeated Chard through gritted teeth.

'Along the gantry and up the next set of stairs to the upper level.' Chard tensed, wondering if the intention was to try and throw him off the top. 'You'll never get away with it,' he warned.

'Get away with what?' asked Kelly. 'Oh, I see. You think I'm going to arrange a nasty fall? Oh no, not at all,' he laughed.

The pair passed the guard whose footsteps Chard had heard earlier and Kelly gave the man a nod.

Chard reached the next open cast-iron staircase and started to ascend to the top floor, looking down occasionally at the dimly-lit ground far below.

'I don't want you dead, yet. I want you to tell me what you did with my brother when he came to find you in South Wales. I've come to terms that you've probably killed him, but I want you to admit it. Then you can be hanged in this prison with me watching.'

'He never came to find me. He had no reason,' argued Chard.

Kelly prodded Chard once more, this time with some degree of force. 'He said he was going to find the man he saw outside the scene of the murder. You've been arrested for it, because a witness saw you there. My brother disappeared some time ago, as soon as the bodies were found; when you were in South Wales. It all fits.'

Getting to the top of the staircase, Chard stopped and turned to face his accuser. 'If I did kill my wife and her lover, then why don't you wait for me to be found guilty and hanged for that? Sir,' he added.

'Because you seem confident that you'll find some way of being cleared, that's why. You'll find some means of getting away with it,' replied Kelly.

'Then why not just kill me, if you are sure I'm guilty?'

'Because if I do, there'll be too many questions asked. I might be charged with murder and you'll go to your grave without having been convicted. I want justice to be seen to be done. You'll be buried in the prison grounds and I can go and piss on your grave every day.'

'So, if you've got to keep me alive, why do you think I'm going to confess to killing your brother?' asked Chard.

'Because life in here can be very uncomfortable. From tomorrow you'll be allowed to mix with the other prisoners, and they don't like you. By the time you've had a few encounters with them, you'll be begging to tell me the truth. There's a risk they'll go too far and kill you, which will disappoint me greatly, but it's one I'm prepared to take. Now move along to the end cell!'

Chard walked to the end of the landing and stood outside the cell door, watching as Kelly took a set of keys from his belt.

'I've worked a double shift today to arrange this. We had to move a bunk bed up these steps and it wasn't easy. You should be grateful,' said Kelly with an evil look in his eye.

He inserted the key in the lock and the cell door swung open.

'Get up! I've got company for you,' he said loudly.

From the bottom bunk a figure moved in the darkness, expanding in shape as it stood up until it nearly filled the space between the bed and the far wall. It stepped forward until the faint glimmer of light from outside the cell barely illuminated the features of an enormous bald-headed man, whose face was devoid of hair, not even eyebrows.

'Make yourself comfortable. This is John Carroll, the Beast of Shawbury,' introduced Kelly.

'Hello Mr Chard. Pleased to meet you,' said Carroll with a smile.

ELEVEN

May glanced at the clock in the hallway of the YWCA before going out into the street. It showed a quarter past ten and Idris would be very annoyed at her lateness. It had been necessary though. Putting her auburn hair into a fashionable style had taken time; and it was fortunate she had brought enough pins and clips for the purpose. Her hat would have to do, though any lady of quality would recognise it was not of the latest fashion. Fortunately, she would be dealing with men, and they weren't the brightest of creatures.

Her pale green skirt with matching short jacket were simply decorated, but smart enough to pass, and the main thing was to project the right attitude.

'Excuse me ma'am,' said a grocer's lad pushing a handcart down Princess Street.

May obliged by moving to one side to give him more room. She smiled as she did so, for normally he would have called her 'Miss'. Clearly she appeared a little more imperious in her looks and the way she was projecting her person.

She turned into the town square and marvelled at how busy it was. In front of the courthouse in the centre of the square, a dozen hansom cabs waited for fares. Crossing in front of them and filling the pavement on either side were people from all walks of life. Well-to-do gentlemen in top hats and frock coats, maids on errands, housewives in shawls, young men in fashionable straw hats for the summer, farmers in from the surrounding countryside; yet no sign of the town's poor. That was probably because the Council offices and the police station faced onto the square, she thought. Vagrants would not be allowed to huddle with begging bowls on the street. Yet they had to be somewhere, for poverty lurked in every town.

May was annoyed with herself for not having been specific as to where to meet in the square, but she assumed Idris would be sensible enough to wait somewhere obvious. Either in front of the courthouse or, ... 'yes there he is,' she muttered to herself. At the open side of the square which formed part of the High Street, stood a statue of Clive of India, and Morgan waited there, tapping his foot impatiently.

May did not hurry. Instead, she walked slowly, as if she had all the time in the world, for it was important to keep in character.

'May, there you are! Where have you been?' asked Morgan, stepping towards her.

May held out a hand dismissively. 'Keep your distance! I am Miss May Fetheringham, cousin of the late Charles Landell; and you are merely my factotum and chaperone.'

Morgan stopped, surprised at the tone and indeed the accent of an upper-class lady, an English one at that.

May smiled and spoke normally. 'There is no way Mr Warren or Mr Stanmore will see you without an appointment, if at all. On the other hand, they may be prepared to see a relative of Mr Landell.'

'Do you think you could get away with it?'

'Why not? Don't you think I can act the perfect society lady?' replied May, switching back to her false accent.

'Of course,' Morgan replied hastily, 'but what if they ask you some awkward questions?'

'We'll cross that bridge when we come to it. I'll just have to make things up.'

'Are you sure you know what to ask?'

'Yes. We just need to find out who Landell owed money to.' May, shook her head, looking angry with herself. 'I should have said to whom Landell owed money. I mustn't make a mistake like that, or they'll spot it.'

'You look wonderful by the way.'

'Thank you. I'd give you a big kiss, but it wouldn't be seemly for a lady of my position,' May answered with mock haughtiness. 'Now, let's find Claremont Bank.'

'I've already made enquiries. We need to head back in the direction of my lodgings, then take a turn this side of the river, before the Welsh Bridge.'

The couple set off out of the square and Morgan enjoyed showing off his newly acquired local knowledge.

'This part is called Mardol Head. The hill going down towards the river is called Mardol and I've been told not to go down there at night, so beware,' he warned. 'Up ahead you've got the town's huge market hall. Not that you could fit our market in Pontypridd inside it…'

May wasn't really listening. She tapped her hidden bottle of laudanum through her clothes, realising she hadn't taken a dose the previous evening. It was just the excitement of everything, it was like a re-birth.

It was no more than a five-minute walk to their destination, and the specific address was easy to find, as the names of Warren and Stanmore were clearly displayed on a small brass plate next to the door of the premises. A blank piece of brass had been placed over what had presumably been Landell's name.

Morgan hesitated and took a deep breath. 'Are you sure about this?'

'Perfectly. Let me do the talking, whilst you stand behind me looking strong but subservient.'

Only moments after pulling the bell cord a smartly dressed clerk appeared at the door.

Without waiting to be asked the nature of their business, May stepped imperiously into the ground floor office, where two other clerks were working busily at their desks.

'I wish to see either Mr Warren or Mr Stanmore. I am a relative of the late Mr Landell and it is important that I address matters of a personal nature.'

The clerk, not entirely sure how to react, tried to step in front of May to prevent her going any further into the room.

'If you could tell me the exact nature of your business, Madam…'

May brushed him aside with her arm. 'I said it is of a personal nature. You may tell them Miss Fetheringham wishes to see one of them immediately, now go!'

The clerk made to argue, but then saw the glint in the eye of the young man with large whiskers who had followed the woman in.

With a nod of acquiescence, he went past the two seated clerks who were staring in astonishment, and rushed up a staircase at the back of the room.

Eventually, the flustered clerk re-appeared at the top of the stairs, followed by a short man in pince-nez spectacles, holding a cigarette. As they reached the bottom step the clerk received a clip across the ear.

'I do not receive visitors without appointments,' scolded his employer, who then looked up ready to lambast whoever had been impertinent enough to interrupt his day.

'Now then, Miss...' he started before coming up short, taking in the attractive young lady standing in the centre of the office.

May watched him look at her from head to toe and back up again, before she held out her hand.

Warren took it gently in his right hand, whilst holding his cigarette behind his back with the other. 'Leonard Warren, at your service,' he said, giving a slight bow of the head.

May was aware he held her hand for longer than necessary, and felt uncomfortable as she felt his thumb rub gently across her skin. Morgan gave a slight cough and she pulled her hand away.

'I am Miss Fetheringham, and this is Mr Morgan, my land agent who is accompanying me to Shropshire on business. I am a distant relative, through marriage, of Charles Landell.'

Warren gave an almost imperceptible grunt at the name. 'And what exactly is your business here?' he asked.

May looked around the room at the clerks who were clearly listening to the conversation, whilst pretending to be busy. She leant closer to Warren and spoke quietly. 'It's rather personal. Could we speak in private?'

Warren's face had lit up at the thought of a private conversation, but soon tutted when he recognised Morgan would probably have to be present.

'Perhaps Mr Stanmore is also available?' added May.

Warren, fingered a strand of his wispy white hair, 'As you wish. Come with me Miss Fetheringham, but we can only spare you a few minutes.'

Putting the cigarette back in his mouth, he turned and led the way up the staircase, a wave of foul-smelling tobacco trailing behind, causing May to hold a hand across her mouth. Morgan followed, muttering under his breath.

At the top of the staircase they turned left and Warren knocked at a door. Without waiting for a response, he entered. 'Jeremy, we have visitors. This is Miss Fetheringham, a relative of Charles and Mr Morgan, her land agent.'

Stanmore rose from behind his desk, with a cold, forbidding expression. 'This is unexpected.'

Warren pulled up two chairs, positioning one opposite Stanmore for May, with the other further behind, indicating it was for Morgan. Then he walked across the room and leant against the window frame, close to Stanmore. 'Apparently, Miss Fetheringham wants to talk to us about a personal matter.'

'I am intrigued,' commented Stanmore, taking his seat. 'But before we start, would you mind putting out that dreadful Turkish cigarette. You know I dislike them.'

Warren shrugged, then stubbed it out on the window sill. 'Go ahead Mis Fetheringham.'

May found her throat go dry, and she gave a little cough. 'My family has been abroad for some time and only just arrived back on our estate.'

Stanmore raised an eyebrow. 'And where exactly is your estate?'

May panicked inwardly. 'In Bedfordshire,' she lied, desperately worried that her accent might fail her.

Stanmore stroked his chin, but seemed satisfied. 'Please do continue.'

'On our return we heard of Charles's death. It was terrible news. I was very fond of him, though we hadn't seen each other for some years. It was upsetting to find out I had missed the funeral.'

'Very understandable my dear,' said Warren, with a consoling smile.

'It wasn't the only thing I found upsetting. You see I've heard rumours.'

'About the manner of his death I suppose. Yes, people will talk,' commented Stanmore, his expression one of indifference.

'Indeed, those details were truly awful, but it isn't what I was ... I mean it isn't that to which I refer,' stumbled May, correcting her grammar. She paused waiting to see if either businessman would make a comment. Thankfully, they just looked as if they wanted her to continue. 'I was also concerned about rumours that he owed money.'

'Damn right he did,' exclaimed Warren. 'Sorry, Miss Fethering-ham. I will mind my language.'

Stanmore leant forward with his elbows on the desk. 'You see neither of us knew about it at the time. He just vanished and we didn't have a clue where he was. Then one day Mr Warren here started to go through the books, and I am afraid to say we discovered Charles had been falsifying our accounts.'

'I can't believe it. Charles would never do such a thing!' exclaimed May in feigned shock.

'We now know that not only had he been taking money from our business, but he had also been borrowing from the bank. Which is why the bailiffs went to repossess his house, and how they came to find the body,' explained Warren.

'Yes, it was a surprise. We assumed he had just absconded with our money,' added Stanmore.

'And probably Sabrina's Teardrop,' agreed his business partner.

May frowned in puzzlement. 'Pardon me?'

Warren smiled benevolently, 'Sabrina's Teardrop is a fabulous sapphire, worth a fortune. It was stolen just before Charles disap-peared.'

'You think he took it?'

'We assumed he had, after we found the anomalies in our accounts.'

'The police think it was a professional gang and they are proba-bly right,' contradicted Stanmore.

Warren shook his head. 'I now think it was the Chard fellow they arrested for the murder.'

'No!' blurted out Morgan, causing May to turn around and glare at him fiercely.

'What Mr Morgan is trying to express, is that we understand he was motivated by the desire to kill his wife and her lover; not to steal a jewel,' she interjected.

'I dare say that's true, but he could have also stolen the jewel, the damn bounder,' exclaimed Warren, this time not apologising for the expletive. 'He was there after all.'

'Where?' asked May.

'At Lord Berwick's mansion. In theory he was meant to be guarding it.'

Stanmore shook his head. 'No Leonard. It can't have been him. He was otherwise occupied at the time, as everyone can remember.'

'I am afraid you are losing me. Could you explain?' questioned May.

Stanmore gave a condescending smile. 'Chard was otherwise engaged, causing offence to one of our valued investors and our personal friend, Major Ferguson.'

'What did he do?'

'It's rather delicate. Major Ferguson was not there at the time.'

'Then how was he causing offence?'

'I think we are getting a little off the point,' interrupted Warren. 'Your question was initially about Charles. I think we have been sufficiently clear that he also owed us money as well as the bank. If you need to know any of his other creditors then I'm afraid you'll have to ask elsewhere.'

'You've both been very kind, but there's just one more thing before I go.'

'What might that be?'

'Presumably your business is profitable? I would expect that if you have invested money on behalf of others then your own personal investments would be benefitting?'

Both Warren and Stanmore seemed to stiffen and they remained silent as May continued.

'So, what puzzles me is why Charles felt he had to embezzle. Can you answer me that?'

Stanmore visibly bristled. 'At the time in question the funds of the business were tied up in ventures which had not yet come into fruition. We take commission on our investors' profits and we had to wait until this year for those benefits to be realised. Both of us have other sources of income, so were able to wait for funds to come through, but Charles did not.'

May nodded, and with a polite smile started to rise from her chair. As she did so, another thought popped into her head. 'If the benefits of the investments only came through this year, then it means the commission, which I assume to be substantial, will now only be shared between the two of you.'

'True,' snapped Warren, 'but I consider that comment to be rather impertinent.'

May heard Morgan get to his feet and she could sense the tension in the room.

'Sorry, no offence intended. We'll leave you to get on with your business. Thank you both for your help.'

Morgan and May left the room and descended the stairway as quickly as they could, without appearing to be rushing. As they got to the front door, it was held open for them by a man of foreign appearance who was on his way in. He had a Van Dyck beard and a smile which, despite her urgency to get outside, May found profoundly attractive. Morgan gave her a gentle nudge and soon they were outside in the fresh air.

'*Duw*, Idris, thank goodness that's over. I don't think I could have kept the accent going much longer.'

'You were wonderful *cariad*,' replied Morgan, pleased they could return to their Welsh accent and dialect. 'I wouldn't have believed you could have pulled it off. You're just like your old self, before you started taking the laudanum.'

'Yes, I hope that soon I'll be able to go without it completely,' she explained, as they walked back towards the centre of town.

'Then you'll keep your promise to give me an answer? I've waited for months now.'

'Of course, but if I am going to agree to marry you, I must be sure I am doing it with a clear mind.' May reached out and took Morgan's arm. 'There is one other condition.'

'What's that?'

'We can't keep secrets from each other.'

'I never would!' swore Morgan enthusiastically.

The pair stopped for a moment to cross the busy road, as they had to wait for an omnibus to pass, before heading towards the market hall.

'Then tell me what the other errand was that you had to carry out for Inspector Chard last night.'

'Look at those old timber-framed houses, aren't they wonderful?' said Morgan hurriedly.

'Stop trying to change the subject,' scolded May.

Morgan stopped and looked into her eyes. 'I can't. It would get you into trouble and the inspector would be furious.'

'I can get furious as well. Do you want to have a chance of marrying me or not?'

TWELVE

'You know you'll need to put on an act Mr Chard, don't you?' 'Yes, Carroll. I'm aware of that,' replied the reluctant cellmate. Chard sat on the top bunk with his legs dangling over the edge, eating a spoonful of greasy stew out of a rusty metal dish.

Carroll lay on the lower bunk, his huge frame barely fitting into it, his own dish laying empty on the floor. 'Why does Kelly have it in for you?'

'Because he thinks I've killed his brother.'

'Did you? I mean we all do things in the heat of the moment.'

'Like you ripping the testicles off the Richardson brothers with your bare hands, I suppose?'

Carroll frowned. 'You know I'm ashamed of what I did, Mr Chard. They had teased me in the village for years, just because I was born ... different. One day I just snapped from their constant bullying, and thought they should find out what it was like.'

Chard sighed. 'Sorry Carroll, I know you regretted it. At least you won't get bullied any more.'

The eunuch gave a high-pitched laugh. 'Everyone is terrified. The Beast of Shawbury, they call me. It's why Kelly put you in my cell.'

'It's a good job he doesn't know you bear me no ill will. I admit I was a bit concerned last night when he put me in here.'

'You looked after my mum. Without me fetching money in she would have starved, but you looked after her and arranged with the church to get her some work, to keep food in her stomach. No other policeman would have done that.'

'She was a nice lady. It was a coincidence I became involved. I remember I was visiting the vicar of St Mary's who I knew socially, when the Richardsons were found. It was the County Constabulary's jurisdiction, but you came to the church to confess your sins and ran into me.'

Carroll nodded. 'Covered in blood I was.'

'Bled all over my suit as well. You were lucky your victims didn't bleed to death, otherwise you would have been for the noose.'

'It would have to be a bloody strong rope to hang me!' giggled Carroll.

Inwardly, Chard felt on tenterhooks. On the one hand he was incredibly lucky his cellmate seemed friendly towards him; but on the other hand, he wasn't sure Carroll was entirely sane.

'We'll have the cell door open soon,' said the eunuch, changing the subject. 'They'll make us take our dishes to the kitchen first and then it'll be out to the exercise yard for half an hour. Just remember to act scared of me.'

'I've told you I'm aware that I need to do that. I'll keep my eyes averted, looking downward and hunching my shoulders as if I'm subdued,' answered Chard.

'Good. There are others in here who bear a grudge and want you dead. I can keep them away from you for a while, but they might still try something.'

'At least Kelly wants to keep me alive for the time being, until I tell him where his brother is. He just wants to make things uncomfortable for me, so I need to convince him I'm scared of you.'

Carroll got to his feet and stretched his huge, fatty limbs. 'I expect it'll be Kelly who takes us over to the exercise yard, just to see how you're getting along.'

As if on cue, there was the sound of boots outside and the cell door clanged open, but it wasn't Kelly who stood there, but another warder.

'Come on, out you come!' he commanded, stepping back quickly as Carroll advanced, holding his dish and spoon.

Outside there was a cacophony of sound, as cell doors swung open and the occupants of the top floor were herded down the staircases at either end of the block. The top floor inmates were evidently being exercised first, as the cells they passed on the lower floors remained locked.

'Get a move on! Dishes and spoons to the kitchen first, then out to the yard!' yelled their escort.

Just outside the entrance to the kitchen stood an inmate wearing an apron standing by two metal buckets; and one by one the prisoners tossed their dirty dishes and spoons into them.

The yelling continued. 'Hurry up! Get outside!'

'It's so good to get outside,' Chard whispered to Carroll, feeling strange to be confiding his thoughts to a convict, and possibly an insane one at that.

Carroll cackled. 'You've hardly been in here five minutes. Wait until you've been in a few weeks, then you'll start to feel like you're going mad.'

'Stop talking! Come on, get moving! Let's see you have a jog around the yard!' yelled one of the guards.

Despite the temptation to look around for a means of escape, Chard kept his head down and his body hunched forward, keeping close to Carroll. After five minutes of jogging, the prisoners were allowed to walk for the next five. Then they were ordered to turn around and repeat the process in the other direction. Finally, they were told to rest, and the men split into small groups, some leaning against the wall, whilst others sat on the ground.

It was whilst Carroll was distracted by another convict and chard was on his own, that three other inmates walked forward.

'What do we have here?' asked the taller of the group.

'Looks like a piece of shit to me,' replied a short, fat convict with beady eyes and a scarred face.

'No, you're wrong. I think it's a dead man, don't you?' disagreed an ugly brute with a broken nose. 'You put me inside, and that means your death sentence.'

Chard was about to raise his head and respond, when he felt an arm the weight of a leg of mutton land on his shoulder.

'Clear off. He's mine,' demanded Carroll, hugging Chard to his sweaty chest.

'You can't keep your eye on him forever,' snarled the tall convict. 'I can see something nasty happening to him.'

'Oi! Keep away there! You three move back, and as for you Carroll, let that man go!' came a yell from somewhere to their left.

To Chard's relief, Carroll released his bear-like grip as the guard who shouted at them approached. With murmured threats, the other three inmates backed off and headed for the other side of the yard.

'That was close. I would have liked to have put my fist in one of their faces,' said Chard, angry and more than a little shaken.

'Sorry if I grabbed you too tight Mr Chard, but I had to make it look right. They have to think I'm committed to protecting you. They're right though, I can't guarantee to be around all the time.'

The remaining few minutes in the exercise yard went without incident and soon the prisoners were back in their cells. Through the metal doors they could just about make out the sound of the floor below being emptied, as its inmates took their turn of outdoor exercise.

'Thanks for the help out there. As much as I hate having to be passive, I know I've just got to survive through this. I'll promise to come and visit you after I get out… if I get out,' vowed Chard sombrely.

'Just bring me a nice big cake!' responded Carroll with another of his high-pitched, slightly insane giggles.

'I wonder why we didn't see Kelly?'

***

It was late in the evening, after the prisoners had what passed as an evening meal, when the cell door opened.

'Get to your feet, Chard.'

Both Carroll and Chard looked towards the doorway, where Kelly stood, waiting for a response. Chard frowned, there was something in Kelly's manner, both in his posture and the way he had spoken. It hadn't been a barked order. Rather, it sounded almost as if it was an unfortunate requirement.

Taking his time, Chard climbed down from the top bunk, giving a shrug of uncertainty to his cell-mate before he turned around to face Kelly.

The guard gestured with his right hand. 'Come with me.'

Chard straightened up, determined after his trying day, particularly the incident in the exercise yard, to put up a show of resistance. 'Tell me why first!' He then waited for the inevitable blow from the short truncheon held in Kelly's left hand; but it never came. Neither was there a reprimand for not calling Kelly "sir".

'I see a night with Carroll hasn't broken your spirit. Perhaps it's for the best. I'm taking you back to your old cell.'

'But you can't Mr Kelly! I liked having company,' objected Carroll.

'I'll find you someone else,' snapped Kelly in response, before turning his attention back to Chard. 'Follow me back to your old cell. We need to talk.'

From feeling despair just a short while ago, Chard now dared to think there might be hope, though why that was eluded him. Feeling intensely curious, he followed Kelly outside and waited whilst the guard locked Carroll in. The pair descended the two staircases to the ground floor in silence.

'You know which cell it is – the door will be open. Get inside and wait for me whilst I check there's no other guard around to see me talking to you,' ordered Kelly.

More puzzled than ever, Chard did as he was told and waited until the guard re-appeared.

'My brother was found last night,' explained Kelly.

Chard's muscles tensed ready to defend himself in case of an attack, but it took only moments to realise it wasn't necessary. Kelly's shoulders were slumped and there was an air of sadness around the man.

'Where?'

'Near Atcham. They say he must have thrown himself in the river and drifted downstream,' answered Kelly.

'He could have gone in anywhere.'

The guard nodded. 'Because they think he must have drifted down from the town and he lived in Shrewsbury, they reported it to the Shrewsbury police. I've been to see Inspector Warboys this afternoon.'

Chard grimaced. 'What did he say?'

'I told him there's no way John would have killed himself. When I last saw him, he was happy enough and eager to go and see whoever it was he saw at Landell's house.'

'Did Warboys believe you?'

'No! He said it was a straightforward suicide and there was nothing more to be said. He made it plain he already had Landell's killer in custody.'

'Me you mean? I've told you, I didn't do it,' argued Chard.

'After I left Warboys I went back to the infirmary and found the doctor who wrote the death certificate. He said the body had been in the water for a long time.'

'You thought he'd come down to South Wales to find me and I'd killed him down there.'

Kelly nodded. 'I know you've been living in South Wales until you were arrested recently. So, either John did commit suicide, or someone else here in Shropshire killed him.'

'Exactly,' agreed Chard. 'If you follow that reasoning, you must understand that whoever killed your brother, must also have murdered Landell and my wife.'

'The governor convinced me you were the man responsible.'

'That's because I cuckolded him,' responded Chard. 'It may take some time, but when I get out, I'll find the real murderer, both of my wife and your brother. I suppose I'll be kept safely in my cell again, away from the other prisoners?'

'It's not that simple. It was the governor who wanted you mixed in with the others, despite him saying he wants to keep you alive to face trial. Having you found hanged in your cell would raise questions, but an assault in the exercise yard by other inmates would be easily explained.'

'If that happened, then nobody would look for the real killer. They would assume I was guilty and got my just desserts.'

'And I would have gone along with it too,' confessed Kelly. 'I persuaded the governor to let me put you in with Carroll for a couple of nights just to shake you up. I hoped an unpleasant time with him would persuade you to confess what I thought you'd done to my brother.'

'He hasn't been too bad, just a little bit strange.'

Kelly grimaced. 'That's one thing you could call it. The last man who shared with him had his little finger bitten off in the night, because Carroll thought it "looked good enough to eat". He is quite insane, but the asylum wouldn't take him off us.'

Chard shuddered. 'Where does that leave us? If the governor wants me mixing with the prisoners, I'm likely to be dead by the end of the week. Then no-one will look for your brother's killer, and I'll be buried with everyone believing I was the murderer, whilst the real one goes free.'

'No doubt you're right,' nodded Kelly. 'The only way to keep someone investigating the truth is for you to escape.'

Chard's hopes suddenly rose. 'I agree, but how?'

Kelly shrugged. 'I don't know yet, but it has to be soon. The governor is away for a couple of days, so I can keep you safe in here until he gets back. When he returns I won't be able to protect you, so we'll have to move quickly.' The guard put his hands to the side of his head and rubbed his temples as if trying to stimulate thought. Chard noticed there was a look of weariness and despair in his eyes

'Everything has happened so quickly today that I can't think clearly,' continued Kelly. 'I'll mull it over tonight and hopefully will come up with something. Just be ready,' he said firmly before leaving the cell.

Chard listened to the key turn in the lock, took a deep breath and let out a grateful sigh, perhaps his luck was changing.

THIRTEEN

Chard had passed a fitful night, his mind fully active as he tried to devise a plan of escape in case Kelly could not. He resolved however, not to tell the guard that he had already made plans to get away once outside the walls. Though it would depend on whether or not George Lamb had agreed to help.

The day had been no better. He was safe in the cell, but all he could do was pace up and down the small space, mind whirring as idea after idea was worked through and then rejected. It came down to only one conclusion.

It was mid-afternoon when Kelly did finally appear, looking fraught with worry. 'There's only one way it can be done,' he said.

'Yes. The problem is the cell door, isn't it? I couldn't possibly pick the lock, so the only way is to get your keys.'

Kelly nodded. 'I had thought of taking some clothes from 'C' block, then putting out a call for the midwife. Sometimes the new female prisoners come in and find they're pregnant. Then with a shawl over your head you could pass the gatehouse pretending you're the midwife on her way back out.'

Chard gave a rueful smile at the suggestion, appreciating the inventiveness. The women prisoners could not be seen or heard from 'A' block, and he had forgotten they existed.

'Surely I would have been properly checked by whoever was on duty at the gate though?' he asked.

Kelly shook his head. 'I would have arranged for it to be me, or like tonight, a guard called Bailey. He only does night shifts because the lazy bastard knows there's not much to do. It also means he can have a secret drink on duty and spend half the shift sleeping.'

'That still wouldn't explain away how I got out of my cell. No, there's only one way to get your keys,' said Chard grimly.

'You need to overpower me and steal them,' confirmed Kelly,

'and it needs to be tonight. I've just started my shift and Bailey takes my place at eleven. When he comes on duty I'll say I want to go to your cell, to rough you up before I go home. All the other guards think I still hold you responsible for my brother's disappearance, so it won't seem unusual.'

'So I hit you and steal your clothes. What happens then?'

Kelly rubbed his chin as he worked through the scenario in his head. 'By then there'll just be a guard on each of the two floors above us, plus one in each of B and C blocks. You should be able to pass unnoticed. The only difficulty will be getting through the main gate. You can open it yourself, but Bailey will be in the gatehouse, so will have to come out and close it behind you. Otherwise, if he hears it open without having been alerted, it'll cause suspicion and he might raise the alarm straight away. I suggest you rap on the gatehouse door, then start to open the gate yourself. You should be halfway through by the time Bailey comes out of the gatehouse. Then if you grunt a 'goodnight' to him as you walk away, he might not recognise it isn't me.'

'Possibly, but I'm not as tall as you,' Chard pointed out.

'He isn't the most observant of men, but if he does get suspicious you might have to overcome him; or be fast on your feet. What you do once you're outside, I don't know,'

'Let me worry about that,' answered Chard, not willing to divulge his plan. 'Even if I do get away cleanly, I expect I won't have long before the alarm does eventually get raised.'

'If Bailey thinks he's just let me out, then he obviously won't come looking for me. I can pretend to have been unconscious, but unless you seriously injure me, that pretence would only be convincing for say ten minutes.'

'I'll tie you up. This prison uniform is shoddy stuff. I can easily tear it into strips.'

'Good,' said Kelly, 'it should give you plenty of time before I'm discovered.'

'Then we're set. When you come tonight, I'll be ready.'

***

In a second-floor office in the centre of Birmingham, a grim-faced man wearing an expensively tailored suit sat at his desk, counting a pile of banknotes.

'It's all there Mr Foden,' assured the burly young man standing before the desk.

'I don't really doubt it, Pitt. On the other hand, it is best to keep good practices when it comes to money.' Foden run a hand over his close-shaven head and stared at his enforcer. Young, sometimes impetuous, but loyal, Pitt could be counted on to carry out orders. His appearance reflected his youth, with a fashionable long fringe of hair nearly to his eyes and the back of the head shaved short. 'We need to expand our interests further west. Do you have that little sporting event in hand? I've made the necessary contacts to ensure some people of importance will attend, but the detail is down to you.'

Pitt adjusted the bright blue silk scarf around his neck, before telling his employer what he wanted to hear. 'All in hand, Mr Foden. I've also made contact with Harbury and he seems willing to make the other wager. It's just a question of the amount.'

'Excellent,' replied Foden enthusiastically. 'Shrewsbury is a wealthy town. I'll make the wager sufficiently large to ensure he's crippled financially, and then we can take over.'

'What if we lose?'

'It is something I could absorb, but I'm counting on you to make sure we don't lose.'

Foden lit a cigarette and took in a lungful of tobacco, before releasing a flow of smoke out through his nostrils. 'What about our cargo in Dale End? Undamaged I take it?'

'A bit unruly, but nothing's been done,' answered Pitt.

'Good. I haven't been able to finalise the export arrangements yet. We have to acquire another item first. It's a line of business we could do without, but it will give us contacts.'

'There's just one other thing, Mr Foden. One of the boys, Jimmy Two-Fingers, was arrested last night. He glassed a lad from Aston.'

Foden rolled his eyes in exasperation. 'Probably a copper new to the area. Don't worry, I'll have him out by this evening. We've got a busy time coming up and we need all the men on the ground we can get.'

***

Chard was filled with adrenalin by the time Kelly arrived. It had seemed like an eternity since nine o'clock, when the light through the bars had started to fade. The prison issue shirt had been easy to tear apart and Chard stood bare-chested as the guard gave him the good news.

'Bailey is settled in at the gatehouse and he's already half cut. I saw him take a swig from a hip flask as soon as he thought my back was turned. He thinks I've come to give you a beating. I said I would give him a knock to close the gate behind me when I leave.'

Chard sighed, relieved his waiting was over. 'I've made some strips for tying you up.'

'Good. These are the keys you will need to take with you. There is also a bar you'll have to move on the main gate, but it isn't difficult, even Bailey can do it on his own.'

Chard took the keys and waited whilst Kelly got out of his uniform.

'If you're caught of course, then I'll deny I had anything to do with you getting out.'

'I understand,' replied Chard, 'I'll end up with some sort of punishment, but that won't matter because Ferguson will have me mixing with the other prisoners and I'll be killed anyway.'

'You're more than likely right. For that matter, it wouldn't do me any good saying the governor set you up deliberately. Nobody would believe me. There would be no proof, and I would lose my job. I'm taking enough risk by helping you to escape.'

'It's the only way. I've got a lot more to lose than you have, so I'll find him, whatever it takes,' vowed Chard.

'Then there's only one thing to be done,' said Kelly, 'if you…'

Before the guard had time to finish his sentence, Chard had unleashed a ferocious punch, powered by all the built-up anger from the four nights he'd spent in his cell, into Kelly's cheekbone. The force sent the guard backward into the cell wall, where he slumped to the ground, unconscious. Chard quickly stripped Kelly, then used the strips of torn shirt to bind his hands and feet, then gag his mouth. Trying on the man's uniform gave Chard some concern as it was far from a perfect fit, with the longer trousers bunching at the ankles. The boots, at least, were the right size.

Cautiously, with heart pounding, Chard edged open the cell door and peered around it. No-one was in sight. The gentle echo of slow-moving footsteps from the guard on the iron gantry of the floor above was the only sound to be heard. Stepping outside the cell, Chard closed the door behind him as carefully as possible, but the turn of the key in the lock seemed unbearably loud. Keeping close to the wall, he made his way as silently as possible to the end of A Block and entered the adjoining complex. Remembering Kelly's words that B Block would have a guard on duty, Chard kept perfectly still once inside, listening. After a few moments, unable to discern the whereabouts of the guard, he considered his options. Either he turned right, past the laundry and out through the entrance through which he had been brought on his first day; or he went left towards the governor's office and out through the visitors' entrance. Both ways led to the yard and then the main gate. Instinct told him to take the former route and Chard moved stealthily towards the laundry and the prisoners' reception buildings. As soon as he got close to the laundry he realised he'd made a mistake. There was the sound of shuffling and grunting coming from just ahead. Peeking his head around the entrance of the laundry, he could just make out the outline of figures writhing in the darkness. He had found the guard, who was clearly fornicating with a prisoner amidst a pile of dirty laundry. Presumably it was a female prisoner fetched over from C Block, but Chard decided not to dwell on the matter. Instead, he retraced his steps towards the governor's office.

Exiting into the yard without difficulty, there was now just the main gate to negotiate, and only the guard Bailey in the way. The gate was relatively easy to open but seemed to make a tremendous racket, which presumably the prison guards were used to hearing, for it didn't draw any particular attention. As soon as the gap was wide enough for Chard to get through, he went to the gatehouse door and gave a rap with his fist to alert Bailey that the gate needed locking behind him. Chard had just gone through and out into the street when he heard the gatehouse door open and he heard Bailey muttering loudly.

'You could have waited until I came out Kelly, you ignorant bugger!'

Relieved to be outside the prison, Chard took a breath, then set off to his left, away from the town, down a long street of terraced houses. It was dark and there were no gaslights, but there was a little moonlight and up ahead he could hear the roaring of the weir. At the end of the street, close to the weir, Chard knew he had to turn left onto a narrow road which was bounded by farmers' fields on one side and the river on the other. Eventually, the moonlight illuminated the outline of a small island in the middle of the river, and from that point, he started to count the number of large trees which lined the avenue. Praying his memory of the old fishing spot had not failed him, and George Lamb had not let him down, Chard lowered himself down the steep river bank at what he believed to be the correct spot. There was no option but to enter the water, and he shivered as the cold water came up to his thighs, the current tugging at his legs. Frantically, he looked around, trying to make out any signs of a boat in the darkness. There was overhanging foliage to either side, but it was just too difficult to see. Fighting the flow of the river, Chard waded to his right, feeling his way as best he could, and receiving cuts and scratches for his efforts. Then, reaching underneath some bushes projecting from the bank of the river, he felt the stern of a small rowing boat. Feeling around it, Chard found it was kept in place through being secured to two iron pegs in the riverbank. They had been driven in so hard that he couldn't extract them, and instead had to pick at the knots of the rope instead. He heaved himself into the tiny vessel, barely large enough to contain him and the current took no time in carrying it away downstream. There was a single oar in the boat and Chard had difficulty in keeping a straight line, but he was free, and hopefully his escape wouldn't be noticed until the morning.

***

Chard knew the river didn't follow a straight course downstream from Shrewsbury, for it headed north east, making a number of loops, then changed direction to the south; before flowing southwest towards Atcham. Working out exactly which river bend was the nearest to Uffington, where he hoped George would be waiting for him, proved to be a challenge. However, a scramble up the riverbank and across a field had allowed him a sight of the church tower's outline. Relieved to have found the right location, he returned to the river's edge and waited; as it was probably not quite midnight. In fact, it was just a few minutes later when he heard a curse close by, as someone had evidently stumbled whilst crossing the field.

'*Ych a fi!*'

'Morgan? Is that you?' whispered Chard, familiar with his constable's cursing in Welsh.

'Sir? Where are you?'

Chard stood up. 'Over here! What are you doing here? Where's George?'

'It's a long story. Let's just get you away from here. I've got a pony and trap on the road and the sooner we're under cover the better. I've got a spare key to the Lambs' house so I'll drop you off nearby.'

'What about you?' asked Chard, confused.

'I've got to stable the pony before returning to my digs to get some sleep. We'd better meet tomorrow evening and decide what we're going to do. Frankly we're all in trouble, and I mean all of us.'

FOURTEEN

'Come on now, wake up!'

Startled, Chard shook himself awake. He was lying on a hard floor, with something under his head, which he suddenly remembered was the uniform jacket taken from Kelly. There seemed to be a blanket on top of him, but he couldn't recall putting it there.

'You've been dead to the world. Rise and shine, I've got a cup of tea for you,' came the unfamiliar voice once again.

Chard shook off the blanket and sat up. A fair-haired, plump lady with a round, smiling face stared at him, holding out a cup. He remembered being dropped off by Morgan in the early hours of the morning, taking the spare key to George Lamb's door, and entering as silently as possible.

'I'm Freda, George's wife. He said to call you Tommy.'

'Pleased to meet you,' replied Chard, taking the cup. 'Where is George?'

'Gone to work. I found you asleep when I got up earlier this morning and when George came down for breakfast you still hadn't stirred, so I just put a blanket over you, to keep warm.'

Chard realised he must have been more mentally and physically exhausted from his problems than he had thought. 'Thank you. I am sorry to put you to trouble. I know I've put you at risk by my being here.'

Freda smiled. 'George explained you're going to find my Cora in exchange. I'm so worried about her.'

'Sorry? I don't understand. Who?'

'You know, Cora. She's twelve years younger than me and more like a daughter than a sister.'

'I'm sorry, but I don't know anything about it,' apologised Chard.

Freda looked puzzled. 'I thought you understood. George told me it was agreed with that nice young friend of yours. We'll keep you safe on the condition that you find my missing sister. Otherwise,

I'm afraid we won't be able to help you. It's a big risk for us to take. George reckons you are the cleverest man he knows though, and if anyone can find Cora, then it's you.'

Chard took a mouthful of tea and slowly swallowed it, whilst he gave himself time to think. If Morgan made the arrangement then he obviously knew what he was doing, he reasoned.

'Of course I'll help,' Chard said eventually.

'Good,' said Freda, nodding affirmatively. 'Now take a couple of these.' She offered a couple of small cylindrical pills.

'What are they?'

'Bile beans. Good for the digestion. Knock them back and then I'll make you some bread and dripping for breakfast, whilst you make yourself comfortable in George's chair.'

'I'll leave the pills if you don't mind. Just tell me about this sister of yours.'

'In a moment, I'll prepare food first.'

It was a few minutes before Mrs Lamb returned from the scullery with a plate of bread spread with beef fat, giving Chard time to consider what he needed to do. Morgan wouldn't have agreed to the condition of finding the missing girl unless there was no other option. Also obtaining a change of clothes, some money and where to begin on clearing his name couldn't be started until George returned from work. Listening to what Freda had to say about her sister would occupy him whilst he waited.

'Would you like to tell me what happened to your sister?'

Freda took the other chair by the fireplace. 'I had to raise her after our mother died. 'She was six years old, and I was only eighteen myself. That was twelve years ago. She was a bonny girl, blessed with good looks, and that's what caused the trouble.'

'How so?'

'Cora went into service at fifteen and the master of the house took a fancy to her. She was no angel mind,' added Freda, shaking her head. 'That said, when she got into trouble, there was no help from the father of the child. Cora was just thrown out and left to fend for herself.'

'I assume you offered her help though?' suggested Chard.

'She was too ashamed to tell us about it. We didn't know until it was too late. With no money to feed her little one, she took to the streets, selling her favours,' explained Freda sadly.

'How did you eventually find out?'

'She came to us after the police had picked her up and sent her in front of the magistrate. One of her neighbours let it be known she had a little one, and it came up in court. The magistrate ordered that the boy should be taken from her, as she was clearly unfit to raise him. He was put in the children's home at Montague Place. Cora was distraught, which was why she finally came to us for help.'

'It's a pity she didn't come to you sooner, by the sound of things.'

'George and I spoke to the authorities and we did manage to get something hopeful out of them. They suggested that if Cora entered the Salop Home, behaved with good conduct, and obtained employment to show she could properly support herself and her child; then they would release the boy back to her care.'

Chard was familiar with the good works of the Salop Home. It was a charitable institution which took in young women who had fallen into bad ways, on a voluntary basis. They usually had to pay a small fee, unless sponsored; though their keep was funded by the work they would undertake there as part of their training. The institution took in laundry as part of teaching the girls how to support themselves, as well as giving them instruction in sewing, cooking and other skills that would help them find a place as a domestic servant. Once considered suitably skilled and of good character, the home's benefactors would endeavour to place the girls with an employer.

'Did the Salop Home accept her?'

'Oh, yes. They could see how eager she was to have her child back. George and I paid her fee, but they made it clear to us that once Cora was accepted, then they would expect her to be cut off from her previous life, until she had left and fully settled into her new employment.'

'I can see it being a good general rule. I know from being a police officer that even when a "bad girl" tries to reform, it only takes a little bit of contact from her past to send her back to her old ways,' said Chard sagely.

'I agree,' nodded Freda, 'but we know for a fact she has left the home, yet there has been no word from her.'

'How do you know she's left?'

'As quite a long time had gone by without any news, George went to the Salop Home to make enquiries. They told him she had left to take up employment, but they were not at liberty to give any details. They insisted that if she wanted to get in touch, Cora would no doubt write to us; but perhaps she wanted to forget her old life and start afresh.'

'Maybe they're right,' proposed Chard. 'It wouldn't be unreasonable to think such might be the case.'

'No!' said Freda firmly. 'She wouldn't forget about her little boy, or me for that matter. I'm convinced something has happened to her.'

'Did George make any further enquiries?'

Freda used a finger to wipe away a tear that had started to form. 'Yes. He asked around and fortunately our Cora is so attractive that someone noticed her. They said they saw her in the company of a man, heading for the railway station.'

'Did they know who the man was?'

'They thought it was a businessman called Warren. George found a man of that name who answered the description, but he denied having anything to do with it.'

Chard pursed his lips as he considered the possible coincidence. 'There might be nothing in it, but one of the people who might throw light on the murder of my wife is also a businessman called Warren. Perhaps our interests might coincide.'

'We are only taking the risk of helping you on the condition that you keep looking for Cora,' reminded Freda.

'Regardless of what I plan to do next, I am going to need a few things. I can hardly go wandering about in a prison guard's uniform. Would you be able to go into town for me?'

Freda nodded. 'What do you need?'

'Any old shirt, trousers and pullover, the older, scruffier and dirtier the better. The same goes for a long coat, and if you can get the type of broad-brimmed hat the cattle drovers wear, it would be ideal.'

'I'll see what I can do. Anything else?'

'A roll of bandage, some overripe fruit like plums or pears, and also some blackberries or wimberries. I know it sounds a bit odd, but they are necessary. An old walking stick would be handy too,' added Chard.

'I'd better write it all down. You don't want much do you?' commented Freda sarcastically. 'It'll take more than one trip to get all this. I hope you're going to pay me back.'

'That's something I'm going to have to speak to George about,' replied Chard with a frown.

***

Inspector Warboys was startled as his office door was flung open and a red-faced Major Ferguson stormed in unannounced.

'Tell me, Inspector, what are you doing to find the escaped convict?' he demanded.

Warboys got to his feet quickly, annoyed at the intrusion. 'How dare you sir! How dare you interrupt me unannounced whilst I am in discussion with one of my officers!'

Ferguson gave a cursory nod of acknowledgement to Constable Fugg, before responding to Warboy's admonishment. 'I am sorry, Inspector but I see policemen outside calmly walking about in the square when there is a dangerous fugitive on the loose.'

'If your men had done their job properly then there wouldn't be a dangerous fugitive on the loose,' accused the inspector.

Ferguson's faced flushed again. 'The man is an animal. My best guard had been instilling some discipline into him when he was viciously attacked,' he responded defensively. 'A message was sent to me early this morning and I returned to the Dana as soon as possible.'

'By which time we had already been there and taken action,' countered Warboys.

'What action, may I ask?'

'He will obviously want to get away from here as far and fast as possible. That means the railway. Given he has been living in South Wales for the last eighteen months, the likelihood is that he will want to head there. On the other hand, I am aware that before taking up his post in Shrewsbury, he had worked in Manchester, so he may go north. It is, after all, the same line.'

'I take it then, you've alerted the Great Western Railway Police Force?'

'Obviously! They will have people looking out for him, especially at Cardiff and Manchester stations. They'll also keep a close look out at Crewe, in case he swaps trains to head for Liverpool where he could get passage abroad.'

Ferguson visibly calmed down and composed himself. 'Are you sure he won't head East, towards the Midlands?'

Warboys shook his head. 'What would be the point? He either has to flee the country, or find somewhere to hide and that's a lot easier if you have friends to help you. No, he has either taken the GWR as I've suggested, or he's still in this area.'

'Why would he remain in Shrewsbury?' asked Ferguson doubtfully.

'Money,' replied the inspector. 'He took the guard's uniform so will need a change of clothes, and then he needs to at least get the train fare. That means either robbing some poor bastard, or relying on old friends. Unfortunately, he appears to have had quite a few of them during his previous time here. We've spoken to his former colleagues in this station and they have by and large not been very forthcoming. Constable Fugg has given me a few names though and we'll follow up on them.'

'Surely even an old friend wouldn't risk imprisonment for helping an escaped felon?'

'It should cut down the possibilities, that's for sure,' agreed Warboys. 'The most likely area for us to consider would be Wem, where he used to live, but it's outside our jurisdiction. I'm meeting with the County Constabulary in the next hour to enlist their help.'

'Why haven't you done that already?' demanded Ferguson.

'Because I'm waiting for Fugg to draw a decent sketch in order to get a wanted poster printed to give to them. A task, I might add, which wouldn't be necessary if you had taken a photograph of him when he entered the Dana.'

Ferguson grunted. 'We only take the photographs once prisoners have been convicted, not when they are only on remand.'

'I suggest you consider changing that in future,' reprimanded Warboys. 'Anyway, if he is still around the town, we will catch him.

Take solace that he has proved his guilt by running away. When we get hold of him, he won't escape again and you can hang him in your prison. After having been before judge and jury of course,' added Warboys.

Ferguson remained silent for a moment before replying. 'Of course,' he acknowledged through gritted teeth.

***

It had been a long, tedious wait whilst Freda had been out of the house. The curtains had been left open, as was the Lambs' custom, so as not to draw suspicion. As a result, Chard kept out of sight in the small scullery, in case a neighbour should glance through the window. When Freda eventually returned, he was pleased to see nearly everything on her list had been obtained. The only thing missing was the walking stick, but it wasn't essential. Pleased with the purchases, Chard went upstairs to the small bedroom to change out of his stolen uniform, and was glad to see the clothes Freda had obtained were a reasonable fit; the exception being the overcoat. It was clearly too big, but that would suit his purpose.

Despite the complication of having to find the missing girl, Chard was feeling better than he had in days. True, he was on the run and if caught would face further charges of assault which, (if he wasn't killed in the prison) would also count against him in the murder case. However, he was free and could at least have some form of control over events; rather than accepting whatever fate decided. At the moment, the only thing to test his nerves was the constant chatter of Freda who, having failed once more to foist bile beans on his system, was keen to extol the virtues of Clarke's Blood Mixture which she had bought whilst in town. Chard had politely declined and then pretended to go to sleep on the floor in the corner of the room, out of sight of the window.

It proved to be early evening before the key turned in the lock of the front door and George Lamb entered.

'George, thank you,' greeted Chard as he got to his feet.

The householder held out his hand. 'Tommy, 'ow ar' yer, mon,' he replied. 'It's been a long time. I told Freda to let you sleep this morning.'

'So she said. Thanks for letting me stay the night. Once we've talked, I'll leave you alone and find somewhere else to hide out.'

George nodded then turned to his wife. 'Freda, get the kettle on and make us a cup of tea, will yer? We can eat later. Tommy and I have things to discuss.'

Obediently, Freda went to the scullery to fill the kettle whilst George drew the curtains and gestured for Chard to sit opposite. The cheap fabric allowed enough light to filter through, and the men to see each other without lighting a lamp. 'It's a bit early to be closing the curtains but I think we need to sit and discuss matters in comfort, without people looking in.'

'Freda's told me about her missing sister,' said Chard, taking his seat.

'I'll be honest with you Tommy. It's the only reason I agreed to help you. The risk we're running is tremendous, so I must insist on our deal. I've exhausted every other means of finding her and was about to give up. When your lad, Morgan, called on me I decided it was our last chance.'

'Freda mentioned Cora was seen with a man called Warren and he might, if it turns out to be the same man, be of interest to me too. However, in the first instance, I need to sort some things out. To begin with, there's the matter of money. I owe you for some bits and pieces Freda fetched from town today.'

'You owe me a damn sight more than that, Tommy. How do you think you got here? I couldn't stay up for several nights just in case you turned up at Uffington because I have to get up for work; but even if I could have, how was I supposed to travel there unnoticed? Morgan volunteered to meet you, but he had no means of transport either. I've had to borrow the pony and trap at short notice from people who don't ask questions. They insisted on a minimum of a week's rental and they'll need to be paid. There'll also be a charge for the stabling and feed.'

Chard shrugged apologetically. 'I'll pay you back, but I can't get at my money for obvious reasons. I was hoping to borrow some.'

'Not from me you won't. I haven't got any. Freda and I have barely enough to live on at the moment. You'll have to ask Morgan when he turns up.'

'What?' exclaimed Chard, appalled. 'He's too involved as it is!'

'We arranged he would come here every evening until you either escaped, or the five nights you specified had passed. He might not feel obliged to come this evening, but I reckon he will.'

Chard frowned and shook his head. As grateful as he was for his constable's help, Morgan's involvement was now a further complication. 'I just don't think…'.

Before Chard could finish his sentence there were three gentle raps on the front door.

'That'll be him,' said George, rising from his chair, whilst his guest headed for the scullery, in case it wasn't.

Chard halted his exit as he picked up the sound of Morgan's unmistakeable Welsh accent.

'Is he safe?'

'Yes, mon. Come on in,' George replied to the constable.

'Morgan, what have you done, getting so involved?' exclaimed Chard.

'There's gratitude for you, isn't it?'

'Sorry Morgan. It's just that I only wanted you to send a message to George here. Helping me any further is just too dangerous. You'll end up in prison yourself.'

'You're going to need all the help you can get. I tore one of these off a lamppost. They're all over the town,' answered Morgan, handing over a poster. It showed a sketch of Chard which thankfully wasn't terribly accurate.

'I can avoid getting caught. It won't be the first time I've disguised my appearance, but what are you going to tell Superintendent Jones?'

'I'm due to return in two days, but I'll ask if I can stay one more week to assist the Shrewsbury police in your capture. The only problem is that I haven't got much money and I doubt the superintendent would be willing to pay for my accommodation.'

'We've just been talking about money,' interjected George. 'It looks like I'll have to borrow more than I have already, but it worries me.'

Chard nodded, sympathetic to his friend's plight. 'I'll write a letter to my solicitor, Mr Tayleur before I leave, instructing him to pay you any expenses up to three hundred pounds from my estate should I be killed. Obviously, if I'm captured alive, I'll deal with it from my prison cell. He can't release money to you immediately because it would show you are helping my escape.'

'I trust you Tommy, but I'll still have to bargain with my lender to wait for payment.'

'Who is your lender?' asked Morgan.

'I've been dealing through a middleman. I'll go out this evening and try and sort something out if I can.'

'Say you are helping an old friend, injured in a mining accident, travelling from Yorkshire who wants to eventually make his way South to claim an inheritance,' said Chard. 'When his money gets through then he will pay you back for the loan.'

George smiled and rubbed a hand through his red, wiry hair. 'You've already decided on your disguise then?'

'Thanks to the things Freda fetched me.'

'Anyone called me?' asked the housewife, coming out from the scullery.

'No, my love, but I think we had better have something to eat now to tide us over, as I'll have to pop out later on. Perhaps we could all share a beer with our food, I've got a couple of bottles under the stairs and…'

Suddenly everyone froze in alarm at the sound of an unexpected knock on the door.

FIFTEEN

'Go and open it, George,' urged Freda, waving Chard and Morgan in the direction of the back door.

The two visitors went as far as the scullery and hid there, aware that if it was indeed the police, then they would have the back door covered in any case.

George went to the door and pulled it slightly ajar whilst the others held their breath, straining to hear what was being said.

'What do you want at this time of the evening?' demanded Lamb, in a manner which suggested the caller was not a policeman.

'Let me in this instant or I will cause a scene. I've come for my Idris and your other visitor,' a female voice remarked pointedly.

'Shit!' uttered Morgan and Chard in unison.

'Best come in I suppose,' shrugged George, as May pushed past and entered the room regardless.

'Miss Roper, what are you doing here?' demanded Chard, who then immediately turned to Morgan. 'What IS she doing here?'

'You've got such lovely hair dear. Just like my George. Would you like a cup of tea?' offered Freda.

'She's not having a cup of tea because she isn't staying,' objected Chard.

'She said "my Idris", is she your wife?' George asked Morgan. 'I don't see a wedding ring.'

'No, I'm not, and with all this trouble he's got into I'm not sure I ever will be,' answered May.

'Everybody stop talking!' demanded Chard. 'Miss Roper leaves right now, as fast as possible!'

May stepped up close to Chard, her expression one of grim determination and anger. 'Don't you dare give orders to us, Inspector. You are an escaped fugitive with no say in the matter. You've dragged Idris into all this at the risk of his career and a jail sentence; and even worse, you haven't told us the entire truth of what is going on.'

There was silence for a moment, until George Lamb spoke. 'I can see you have things to discuss between yourselves, so I'll leave you to it. I've got business to attend to.' As he grabbed a coat and headed for the door, Freda tried to stop him.

'Where are you going George? And what am I going to do with this lot?' she pleaded.

'I'm going to arrange some money so Tommy can begin looking for Cora. It's his main priority,' he added markedly. 'Perhaps he can stay one more night and I'm sure our other visitors will be gone soon. Just make sure I've got a decent supper when I return.'

After Lamb left, May returned to her discussion with Chard. 'As I was saying. You haven't told us the whole truth. To begin with, why did you need to escape from prison?'

'It was as I told Morgan. If I'd stayed, I would have been killed. It was confirmed by one of the guards.'

'Then why didn't you ask to see the governor?'

'Because he was the one who wanted me dead,' answered Chard.

The answer wasn't one May had expected and it temporarily halted her flow of questioning. 'Why would he want that?' she eventually asked, with some hesitation.

'Because I had carnal relations with his wife,' came the blunt reply.

May felt herself blushing. 'Oh, I see. I confess to being rather shocked.' After a short, embarrassed silence she continued. 'How did he find out?'

'The same way everybody found out,' replied Chard, annoyed with himself at the rather direct way he had admitted to his transgression, but now fully committed to the story. 'We were found together by Lord Berwick at a social gathering in his mansion.'

At the confession, Morgan had his mouth open in shock, May's face blushed even redder and Freda found it hard to stifle a giggle.

'How did you come to know the governor's wife in the first place? I assume women don't just jump into bed with you on a whim, Inspector?' asked May, trying to regain her composure.

'I've told Morgan it's inappropriate to keep calling me inspector in my current situation. I doubt I'll ever get my position back whatever happens. As to Della Ferguson, we were lovers some years ago, before either of us married. Eventually, there came a time when I realised she wasn't the person I wanted to spend the rest of my life with. She took it hard but would still flirt with me whenever I bumped into her. Unfortunately, on the night of the party, I was in a weak state of mind because Sofia had left me.'

'When we met Stanmore and Warren, they mentioned a party,' interjected Morgan. 'They said you had offended an investor of theirs, Major Ferguson, but they wouldn't say why. I take it he is the prison governor?'

'So, you did get to see Warren and Stanmore, and yes, Ferguson is now the prison governor, but wasn't at the time of the party,' answered Chard.

'They also said something about a jewel theft and that you were meant to be guarding it. One of them, I can't remember which, suggested you might have stolen it,' said May.

'I would have been a pretty poor jewel thief to have drunk to excess, then bedded the wife of a prominent member of society in the middle of the robbery. As it turned out, I was just a pretty poor policeman,' answered Chard, ashamed of his actions. 'I was nominally there to guard the jewel, but really it was Della who used her influence with my superintendent to get me assigned, so she could flirt with me. It wasn't even in my jurisdiction. Normally they would have asked the Shropshire County Constabulary to have someone in attendance.'

'It sounds very convenient,' commented May thoughtfully.

'How do you mean?'

'Nothing, just thinking.'

'Tell us more about the jewel,' said Morgan.

'They call it Sabrina's Teardrop, a large sapphire of tremendous value. It was found by Lord Deansmoor back in eighteen fifty-nine at an unknown location near Shrewsbury. Rumour has it that he discovered the jewel in the excavations at Wroxeter.'

'Where?' asked May.

'It's the site of a ruined Roman town near here,' explained Chard. 'They say the sapphire must have been buried by some important Roman official before the town was abandoned.'

'Why do you say the jewel is only rumoured to have come from the site?' queried Morgan.

'Because the landowner is the Duke of Cleveland. The sapphire would have been treasure trove and, as it was believed Lord Deansmoor was on the land without permission, he would not have received a penny. It was Deansmoor himself who gave the name Sabrina's Teardrop, because using the name of the goddess of the River Severn suggests it might have been found somewhere near the water's edge. The truth is, nobody knows for sure where it was found. When Lord Deansmoor died he took the secret with him.'

'How mysterious,' commented May.

'Few people outside of their family have ever seen it,' continued Chard. 'Which of course, adds to its mystique. It was one of the things which drew people to the party that night, because they knew Lady Deansmoor would be wearing it.'

'What happened?' asked Morgan.

Chard shrugged, with a look of guilt on his face. 'When I was otherwise engaged, the lights went out and someone stole it.'

'Mr Warren accused you of being the culprit,' interrupted May.

'Impossible! I was with Mrs Ferguson.'

'That's what Mr Stanmore said,' informed Morgan. 'I think it was just a throwaway statement by Warren. They had said earlier on they assumed Landell had stolen the jewel.'

'What else did they say?'

Morgan held May's hand proudly. 'You should have seen her. May pretended to be a society lady and convinced them to answer our questions. It turns out Landell had been stealing from the business, but they didn't discover it until after he had disappeared.'

'If they weren't aware of it before he disappeared, then unfortunately that wouldn't be a motive,' reflected Chard.

'Assuming they were telling the truth,' added May. 'However, they failed to deny that they are both better off financially. The commission on profits generated from their clients' investments only came through after Landell's demise; which means they get shared between two rather than three.'

Chard stroked his chin, the stubble rough against his hand.

'Interesting,' he said thoughtfully. 'Did they say if Landell owed money to anyone else?'

'No, just the bank,' answered May.

'Why did they initially think he stole the sapphire?'

'It came across as if it was just an assumption that if he had been stealing from the business, then he was the sort of man who would also steal a jewel. The police were apparently convinced it was stolen by a professional gang,' answered May.

'You have both performed wonders, and I am very grateful. My main concern now is that neither of you get into trouble on my behalf,' said Chard seriously.

'What will you do next?' asked Morgan.

'As the only people we know would benefit from Landell's death are Warren and Stanmore, then I'll have to make further enquiries about them. However, there are two other things which have to take precedence. I can't do much without some finance, so I am reliant on George Lamb helping me out. Hopefully he can get hold of enough money to keep me in food and lodgings, I'll find out later on.'

'I want to stay for a while longer as I mentioned earlier,' reminded Morgan. 'If you can get some money to spare for another week's lodgings, let me know. I'll offer to help the Shrewsbury police to catch you, as a means of distracting them. You can find me at the lodging house in Frankwell for the next couple of days.'

'What's the other thing you need to do before trying to clear your name?' asked May.

'George is only helping me providing I find Freda's sister who has gone missing. I have to show I'm going to make every effort to do so. She had been in the Salop Home, which helps give a new start to young women who have fallen on hard times. Sometimes the girls who go in there want to cut all links with their past lives, so the home doesn't give any information about them after they have left. It might be a coincidence, but Cora Lamb was last seen in the company of a Mr Warren.'

May raised an eyebrow. 'The same man?'

'Quite possibly,' answered Chard. 'Somehow I need to find out where he might have taken her.'

'That's something I can find out for you,' said May confidently.

Chard started to object. 'You really must keep out of this...'
'You've got little chance of achieving anything at the moment. Certainly not in broad daylight.'

'I can assure you that I am fully capable of disguising my appearance sufficiently to make my way around the town.'

'Really? In that old clothing you are wearing I suppose. It will hardly do if you are going to call on an establishment run by ladies, will it? I've got a far better chance than you, and I can pass any information directly to Idris or Mrs Lamb, without seeing you.'

Freda, who had been listening by the scullery door, piped up in agreement. 'That sounds a good idea, Miss. I've got an old photo of our Cora. She is older now, but the blond hair and her features will be the same.'

Chard grimaced. 'I can see when I'm beaten. Take the photo and good luck Miss Roper. Morgan, you can leave as well, and if I get hold of enough money from George, I'll find you in Frankwell.'

***

Major Ferguson rubbed his hand to ease the soreness. 'Let that be a lesson to you, and don't bother calling for your maid; I've ordered the staff to stay below stairs for the evening.'

With a self-satisfied grunt, he glanced back at his wife who lay face down, naked on the bed, whimpering quietly.

'I'm going out and will not be back until the early hours. I will expect you to be thoroughly obedient at breakfast, or there will be hell to pay,' Ferguson threatened, before striding purposefully out of the bedroom and down the staircase to the hall. The staff had indeed been ordered to make themselves scarce, but he knew his driver would be waiting outside with the shooting brake and its special cargo. 'Damn Chard and those idiots I inherited as prison guards,' he cursed aloud. It just didn't seem possible. There Chard had been, fully in his grasp, and the desire for revenge certain to be satiated. Yet now the impudent cad was free and God alone knows where.

'All in order?' he demanded of his servant as he climbed aboard the brake.

'Yes Major. I take it the location hasn't changed?'

'No. It is as I told you yesterday. Excellent sport has been promised by these Birmingham fellows. There will be blood. Plenty of it by all accounts. So, crack your whip and let's be off,' commanded Ferguson, glancing back towards the bedroom window where the outline of a woman stood, silently watching.

***

It was an hour after Morgan and May had left before George Lamb returned. Chard had been given something substantial to eat by Freda and the items bought for him in the town, together with some sandwiches, had been wrapped up and placed in an old linen bag.

'You can put the bag back down for a start,' said George gravely as he entered the room. 'You're going to have to stay one more night.'

'Why?' asked Chard, looking puzzled.

'Because I didn't know who I'd borrowed the money off. I'd used a middle-man by the name of Nash who arranged the loan. When I said I needed a lot more to help a friend from out of town, he insisted on taking me to the lender. It turned out to be a man called Harbury.'

Chard put his hand to his head. 'Is he still around? What were you doing?'

'You know of him then?'

'Of course, I do! When I worked here, he was the bane of our lives. He's been behind every betting scam and illegal loan racket in Shrewsbury for years. We could never put him behind bars because he always had someone else to take the blame.'

'It was the fact I knew someone from out of town that attracted his interest. He wants to know if you can be trusted. If he thinks you can be, then he's got a task for you. Carry it off and he'll give us what we need.'

'What task exactly?' asked Chard dubiously.

'He wouldn't say, but in order to prove yourself, there's something else you've got to do for him tonight. If you refuse, then you can forget about the loan and I dare say I'll end up with broken legs.'

'But I can't get involved in anything illegal. I'm in a difficult enough situation as it is,' objected Chard.

'It isn't anything illegal. All you have to do is to go to Haughmond Abbey tonight, watch whatever is going on, and report back on everything you see. Harbury will expect to see you under the English Bridge at eight o'clock tomorrow morning.'

'But the abbey is just ruins,' exclaimed Chard, 'and how will I get there?'

'Look, I don't know what all of this is about. All I do know is that there isn't an option. On my way back I rigged up the pony and trap ready for you. It's at the back of the Plough and Harrow. I'll lend you an oil lamp to help you see your way, and a spare front door key for when you return.'

'I'll need half an hour to sort out my disguise.'

George shook his head. 'No time for that. You'll have to make do as you are. Harbury was clear you'll have to set off straight away.'

'It appears I have no choice. I just wonder what I'm getting into,' said Chard grimly.

SIXTEEN

The journey through the outskirts of Shrewsbury had been easy going, with few travellers on the roads and the occasional street-lamp to guide the way. Once he left the town, the road became far more difficult, even though Chard knew the way.

Haughmond Hill was situated about four miles north east of Shrewsbury, on the road to the village of High Ercall. Although not a great height, in daylight the heavily wooded hill provided scenic views of the surrounding, predominantly flat, countryside. At night however, there was nothing other than moonlight to aid visibility and unless carrying a lamp, driving was hazardous. Chard had often visited the hill as a beauty spot in his youth, for it was a favourite venue for courting couples on sunny summer afternoons. Now though, in darkness and with a chill wind, Haughmond Hill seemed sinister and full of menace. As he neared the summit, Chard noticed the outline of a number of carriages, positioned off the road amongst the trees. He carried onwards and observed others, on either side of the road; their horses tied to trees but with no attendants. Chard went past them for another hundred yards, before also taking his pony and trap off the road, extinguishing the lamp, and securing the animal out of sight.

Returning on foot to the suspiciously parked vehicles, Chard moved stealthily into the woods. He guessed he was level with the abbey ruins and could faintly hear raised voices and other, strange, guttural sounds carried on the breeze. Just as he came to the outline of the outer wall of the abbey, he heard a twig snap under a boot.

'Oi! What yer doin'?' came a challenge in a thick Birmingham accent.

Chard turned to face a tall youth who had stepped out from behind the cover of a nearby tree.

'Just wondered what was going on. I saw the vehicles parked up and thought I'd take a look,' he answered innocently.

The youth raised a wooden club and patted it meaningfully into the palm of his hand. 'It's private business, so fuck off before you get a clarting.'

'I'm going,' Chard assured, backing away until he disappeared from sight. After a few minutes he crept back and observed that the young guard had returned to his post, confident that the interloper had been deterred.

'Damn!' Chard muttered under his breath. He hated violence and avoided it whenever possible. Nevertheless, he had to admit it was something for which he had a natural aptitude.

After waiting a few minutes, allowing the lookout to relax, Chard approached silently from a different direction. Aware on this occasion of his presence, he soon made out the sentry's profile and prepared to silence him. The ideal opportunity came when the man gave a silent yawn, raising both arms as he did so. Moving swiftly, Chard ran up and slipped his left arm under that of his opponent, and moved it around to the back of the man's neck. At the same time, he put his right arm across the lookout's throat, with the bone of his wrist pressing into the windpipe. Chard's adversary flailed wildly, but to no avail. It was impossible to shout out with the windpipe being crushed, Chard's body was too close to be caught by a blow from his opponent's right elbow, and it was the lookout's natural reactions which caused his own downfall. It was almost a reflex action to try to free his left arm by pulling it away from Chard's grip, but the very force of doing it increased the pressure applied to the windpipe, without Chard having to put in any more effort. Eventually, the young man's breathing became shallower until eventually he went limp. Chard kept the grip on for five seconds then quickly released the hold, letting the body slump to the ground. After checking for a pulse, he took a scarf from around the unconscious man's neck and used it to tie his hands. Then he removed the man's belt to secure his feet before gagging him with a dirty handkerchief.

'That should hold you,' muttered Chard as he hid the inert form under a bush.

Hoping there were no other sentries placed around the abbey, he pressed forward as silently as possible, towards the outer wall of the abbey ruins. Fortunately, there appeared to be no-one else standing guard and Chard climbed into the abbey grounds without incident. A babble of human voices with the occasional growling of wild beasts could be faintly heard from further within the ruins, but it was impossible to discern what was taking place. Cursing as he stumbled over a piece of long-fallen masonry, Chard approached the high stone wall of the abbot's house, which towered above him. Most of the structure remained, and he listened at the empty doorway before entering.

Try as he might, Chard couldn't recall the layout of the ruins so there was nothing to do, other than try and follow the direction of the voices, which had grown louder. Exiting the other side of the building, he could make out there was an open area beyond, with a high wall to his left. The voices and other animalistic, almost eerie sounds were straight ahead and slightly to the right. Cautiously, Chard moved forward, keeping to the wall. On reaching another high wall, he blindly felt his way to its end, then crossed some open ground to the cover of some more ruined stonework at the edge of what would have marked the abbey's cloister. From his new position he could see the source of the commotion. Outside the former chapter house stood a group of about thirty men, visible by the light of half a dozen oil lamps, hanging from iron posts which had been knocked into the ground. Some of the men had companions, and when Chard saw them, he realised the reason for the secrecy.

'Right then, gentlemen. We've had some good sport so far. But now it's time for some rare entertainment, so if you'll just give us a few moments…'

The voice had the dull monotone of a Birmingham man, but without the broad accent of the look-out Chard had dealt with. He couldn't see who was speaking, but four or five young men wearing bell-bottom trousers and misshapen bowler hats seemed to be marshalling the crowd.

'I've got to get nearer,' Chard told himself. Once in the throng, with his coat collar up and hat brim pulled down, it should be possible to mix in unobserved.

When two of the organisers came from beyond the chapter house carrying a small wooden crate, everybody turned to look, and that was the chance Chard had hoped for. Keeping low, he swiftly crossed the open ground of the cloister, then surreptitiously stood up in the crowd as if he had been tying a shoelace.

'Now then gents. I'm offering three to one for a time of under ten seconds, five to one for ten to thirty seconds, even money up to a minute, and two to one on, for over a minute. These are fair odds or my name's not John Pitt.'

The speaker was a large young man similarly dressed to his fellow 'Brummies'; bell-bottom trousers, sturdy jacket, the brim of his bowler hat re-shaped to a point and tipped over one eye. He also sported a bright blue silk scarf around his neck.

The crate was carried into the chapter house and everyone gathered around it. The single storey building, although small, was largely intact. It had stone flagstones inside and the empty window openings at either end stood only about three feet above floor level. Some of the crowd gathered by the open doorway and the adjacent windows, whilst other onlookers moved around to the openings at the far side of the structure.

'Come gentlemen, do I have any takers? Here's the quarry!' announced Pitt.

Chard readied to steel himself, for he anticipated a pack of rats would emerge from the crate as the end was opened and tipped onto the floor.

Instead, everyone laughed as half a dozen small mongrel puppies scampered out onto the flagstones.

'Y'see in good old Birmingham we train our dogs with these, not rats. It saves chucking unwanted ones into the canals and slowing down the barges.'

'If the beast is going to be anything decent then he'll tear these up in seconds. Those odds are ridiculously good,' commented someone in the crowd.

When Chard looked to see who had spoken, the face seemed familiar. It looked a little like Landell's former partner, Jeremy Stanmore. It had been a long time since they met, so Chard couldn't be absolutely certain of the man's identity; but he definitely recognised the man next to him. It was Major Ferguson.

'I expect you're waiting to see our little pet before you come forward,' said Pitt. 'Here he is. Raised and trained in Small Heath. Barney the Butcher.'

Everybody looked as a short, muscular dog with the powerful jaw of a Staffordshire bull terrier was brought to the doorway of the chapter house. Pitt held him on a leash as a wooden barrier was placed along the bottom half of the doorway.

'As soon as I take the muzzle off and jump the barrier, the time will start. Jimmy Two Fingers has the stopwatch.'

'I'll have ten guineas on ten to thirty seconds,' shouted Stanmore.

'Cautious does it,' warned Ferguson, to no avail.

'Five pounds on under ten!' yelled another man, and soon there was a flurry of notes bring offered by the spectators. One of the Birmingham gang came around with a bucket whilst another wrote names and bets into a book.

'Enough!' said Pitt after a short time, to the groan of those who had been unable to place a wager.

'You should have bet, Major' scoffed Stanmore to Ferguson. 'I'll wager my reputation on winning this bet. Ten seconds is too tight, but he'll chew through the pups in just a few seconds more.'

'Ready!' shouted Pitt as he undid the leash, held the dog's collar with one hand whilst starting to remove the muzzle with the other. In the meanwhile, the tiny puppies wandered around the room, some nervously urinating whilst others wagged their small tails and gave excited yaps. As he watched, Chard felt his stomach churn and he prepared to look away.

'Away!' shouted Pitt as he took off the muzzle and leapt over the barrier, causing the crowd to roar and Chard to avert his eyes.

To his surprise, there followed not the increased roar of the spectators, bestial growls, and the sound of rending flesh; but sudden silence, followed by laughter which carried the tinge of Birmingham accents. Opening his eyes, he was greeted with the sight of the bull terrier licking one of the puppies and wagging its short stumpy tail. The punters looked stupefied, whilst the Birmingham men were in hysterics.

The puzzlement of the crowd was starting to turn to rage when Pitt jumped back into the arena and scooped up Barney.

'I'm sorry gents,' he apologised. 'Just a bit of fun. All of your money will be returned. We wanted to make a point that we could have taken money from you unfairly, but that we would never do so. If you let us run your gaming, of whatever type takes your fancy, then you'll not be cheated. Now, while we return your money, we'll just entertain you by putting in another dog to finish what Barney couldn't. No bets on this event though.'

The man with the bucket and his companion went around repaying the wagers, whilst a larger bull terrier was taken into the chapter house. As the crowd started to shout, Chard walked away, unable to stomach the spectacle.

It was mercifully less than a minute before the shouts settled down and the pitiful remains of the puppies were tossed into the blood-soaked crate.

'That was more like it, Stanmore!' exulted Ferguson after his fellow punter had returned with his wager. The prison governor's eyes were shining with excitement after the bloody destruction of the defenceless animals.

Everyone was alerted by Pitt's Brummie accent calling them to pay attention to the next announcement.

'We've had some bostin' challenges earlier on. Really good scraps. But now we come to the final two bouts. When we arranged this, we asked if anyone wanted to take on a couple of heavyweights from our fair city of Birmingham, one a bullmastiff, the other a rottweiler. Two of you said they were game to bring their dogs. Will you step forward gentlemen?'

Chard was surprised to see the men coming to the front were Stanmore and Ferguson.

'Are you sure you still want to risk your babbies?' mocked Pitt.

'We invested in two pups from the same bitch, brought from overseas. They'll not fight each other, but will happily contest with anything you've got,' scoffed Stanmore.

'Then let's see what the first one will face. Bring in Demon!' ordered Pitt.

The crowd swiftly parted as a handler brought forward a power-fully-muscled rottweiler, a truly impressive beast.

'I am taking bets now if you like. We haven't seen your dog fight, but I'm offering two to one against it.'

Ferguson and Stanmore immediately reached inside their coats, wagers ready. A free for all started with stakes being laid on either side, whilst the Birmingham men frantically altered the betting odds to keep up with the pattern of betting.

'Time to bring forward your dog,' Pitt ordered.

Stanmore smiled at Ferguson. 'Do you mind if I go first?'

'Not at all Stanmore, my boy has taken on a rottweiler before. I want him to feed on the bullmastiff.'

Stanmore signalled to his servant, who was standing some yard back, and the man disappeared beyond the far cloister wall, where presumably the larger dogs were being securely held. The rottweiler was already in the chapter house when Stanmore's servant returned with a muzzled beast, some kind of mastiff, the like of which Chard had never seen. The monstrous creature gave off an air of savagery that made Chard's spine tingle. As disgusted as he was with the thought of two animals being made to fight for the entertainment of men, he could not stop himself from looking into the makeshift arena.

'Hold, Demon, hold!' shouted the Birmingham handler as the rottweiler surged forward while he struggled to remove its muzzle.

It was Stanmore himself who led his own dog into the chapter house and the dog stood obediently as his master undid his restraint. 'This is Razor, a South African boerboel, and trained to my command.'

Whilst the rottweiler, freed of its muzzle, foamed at the mouth and needed a second handler to hang on to its collar, the boerboel remained perfectly still as Stanmore calmly stepped over the barrier.

Pitt stood outside and raised his arm. 'Ready! Go!' he shouted dropping his arm.

'Attack!' yelled Stanmore, as the rottweiler's handlers released their grip and dived for the nearest exit.

The ferocious impact of the two powerful dogs hitting each other in a savage exchange of muscle and powerful, snapping jaws made Chard shudder. Yet even worse was the roar of approval from the onlookers and the bloodlust in their eyes. As he looked away from the contest to study the people watching, Chard noticed someone else was doing the same. It was a man at the back, who from the flickering light of one of the lamps appeared to be a foreigner. He had a neat Van Dyck beard and appeared to be paying special attention to one of the spectators, but it wasn't exactly clear who.

'He's had enough!' yelled Pitt, causing Chard to instinctively look back at the dogfight. The boerboel had a firm grip on the rottweiler's neck and the latter was trying desperately to back away.

'Razor! Here!' commanded Stanmore, causing the boerboel to reluctantly let go, and return to his master's side. The punters who had bet on the rottweiler gave a low groan.

Looking very pleased with himself, Stanmore attached Razor's muzzle, then led him out, passing Ferguson as he did so. 'Your turn next Major. After I've given Razor back to my servant, I'll take a quick piss, then come back in time to see your Blade take on the bullmastiff.'

Chard watched from a distance as Stanmore passed the boerboel to his servant and walked off into the darkness, carrying a walking cane to assist him over the uneven ground.

'Here comes our other heavyweight, Destroyer. A fine bullmastiff from Aston,' announced Pitt, causing all eyes to stare at the new arrival.

Seizing his chance to depart unobserved, Chard set off after Stanmore, to see what he was up to. The businessman had wandered off into the ruins of the abbey church, of which little remained. It was almost pitch black, and although Chard's eyes had become accustomed to the night, he could barely make out his quarry's shape. At the far end of the church ruins was a high grass bank and Stanmore laid his cane down, before preparing to urinate.

'What the hell?' Chard heard Stanmore exclaim. 'Cowering here, are you?'

Chard moved closer and could make out the man picking up his cane and thrashing the ground wildly. Stepping forward silently, he saw that the object of the beating was the docile Staffordshire bull terrier which had made a fool of the punters earlier on. Rather than fight back, it just tried to back away.

Just as Chard decided to intercede, Stanmore seemed to fiddle with the top of the cane and pull it apart. 'Let's give you some cold steel!' he snarled. Pulling back his arm to give a killing thrust with the blade which had been concealed in the cane, Stanmore was shocked to feel pain in his wrist. Someone had grabbed it and locked the joint.

'I don't think you want to use that,' growled Chard, pressing on the elbow with his other hand to lock the whole arm, and leaning against it to force Stanmore to his knees. 'I might have a use for it though,' he added, calmly removing the blade from his opponent's weakened grip.

Letting Stanmore's arm go, Chard deftly swung the weapon around until it was an inch from his captive's throat. 'Don't think of crying out. I'm quite prepared to kill you,' he lied.

'What do you want? There's money in my jacket if that's what you're after, but you won't get away with this.'

'I don't want money; just information,' answered Chard, aware that Stanmore didn't seem to recognise his identity.

'I want to know about Charles Landell.'

'You and everybody else it seems.'

Chard let the comment pass. 'He owed money I understand.'

'He stole from our business and he owed the bank.'

'Who else did he owe? Tell me or I'll run you through.'

Stanmore hesitated, but saw the apparent resolve in his captor's eyes. 'The man who organised this,' he finally replied, gesturing with his arm. 'Though a fat lot of good it'll do you.'

'The fellow with the blue scarf?' queried Chard, his intuition suggesting it was unlikely.

'No, of course not,' he scoffed. 'You want a man called Harry Foden.'

'Thank you. Now get to your feet,' ordered Chard, concerned that his captive's presence might soon be missed.

'I wouldn't thank me. If you go anywhere near him, I'm sure you'll regret it,' warned Stanmore as he stood up. 'Now, who exactly are …?'

Before he could say another word, Chard's fist impacted on his jaw and Stanmore slumped unconscious to the ground.

'I think I've probably chanced my luck enough for one night,' Chard muttered, turning back in the direction of the dogfight. Careful not to stumble in the darkness, he moved as quickly as possible towards the crowd of spectators. Fortunately, they were now engrossed in the spectacle of the second boerboel facing off against the bullmastiff. Major Ferguson was so wrapped up in the intoxicating lust for blood, that he had forgotten about Stanmore's promise to return in time for the fight. The only person seemingly not enthralled by the event, who was looking around trying to spot someone, was the strange, dark-featured man who Chard had observed earlier.

'Ready! Go!' came Pitt's voice, followed by the excited roar of the onlookers mixed with savage growls from the combatants.

Chard moved faster, heading for the outer wall of the abbey ruins and the trees beyond. Having reached the safety of the woods, his heart rate slowed and he felt the sudden desire to laugh out loud. Instead, he went towards the spot where he had hidden the bound look-out, to ensure he hadn't choked on his gag. The man was now clearly awake, but unable to free himself, fury evident in the way he struggled upon seeing his assailant.

Chard gave him a playful kick for good measure then headed for the spot where he had secured the pony and trap.

Hearing a rustling in the bushes behind him he paused, but only for a moment. With his heart starting to race again, Chard ran as quickly as he could, but went sprawling over a tree stump. The sound of the pursuer was getting nearer, so he scrambled to his feet and re-doubled his efforts, finally spotting the pony and trap just a few yards ahead; but whoever was following had got much closer. There was now no option other than to turn and fight it out.

Bunching his fists, Chard turned around to face his opponent – just as Barney, the reluctant fighting dog, waddled into view, his tongue lolling from his huge jaw.

This time Chard did laugh. 'Fugitives in arms then!' he exclaimed, grabbing the heavy, stubby body and placing the exhausted dog on the floor of the trap.

SEVENTEEN

Freda Lamb gave a terrified scream. Having come down the stairs, bleary-eyed and with her thoughts on making her husband's breakfast, she was confronted with a frightening apparition standing next to the fireplace. It was a portly man with a crippled arm in a sling; his face bandaged from forehead to the tip of his nose, leaving a narrow slit for his eyes. Beneath the bandage, on the left-hand side, the skin had a disfiguring stain and seemed to ooze some sort of ulcerous discharge.

'Hush, Freda. It's only me,' came a familiar voice.

Footsteps thundered down the stairs as George came to his wife's aid. 'What's going on?' he demanded, as he reached the bottom step. 'Jesus!' he exclaimed, seeing the same unexpected sight.

'It's me, Tommy,' explained Chard.

There was a sudden knock on the door. 'Quick!' said the clearly shaken Fred. 'Get out of sight! It'll be the neighbours wondering why I screamed.'

Chard obeyed, whilst the housewife answered the door and assured her next-door neighbour that there was no problem, merely that she had seen a mouse.

After, the neighbour had departed, George called Chard back into the room. 'Bloody hell, mon. What do you look like?'

'Clearly my disguise worked,' replied Chard.

'It nearly worked too well. You nearly gave me a heart attack,' complained Freda.

'I've spent the last hour on it. I've borrowed a pin of yours to keep the bandage in place. The discolouration of the skin is from the berries you got me, with patches of the rotten fruit pulp on top. There's also newspaper stuffed inside my shirt to make me look fatter. I wasn't going to bother with the sling for my arm, but there was plenty of bandage left over. I just need to stain it a bit to make it appear an old one. It's also extra insurance. When people see a damaged limb, it's what sticks in the mind. They see the infirmity, not the person.'

'What's that?' shrieked Freda, though not loud enough on this occasion to alert neighbours. Turning around to see what had caused the wet, unpleasant feeling on the back of her leg, she gazed down at the Staffordshire bull terrier that sat with its tongue lolling out.

'He's called Barney,' explained Chard as if there was no more to be said.

The short, muscular dog seemed to almost waddle over to his new master and sat on his foot. 'He does that a lot.'

Freda seemed less than impressed. 'I'm glad you're going then. I hope you're taking that beast with you?'

'He adds to the disguise. The police will be looking for an upright, formerly distinguished member of society, in reasonably good health, speaking as would be expected of a former pupil of Shrewsbury School. They won't be looking for a one-armed, portly man, with facial disfigurement, speaking with a Yorkshire accent, accompanied by a dog.'

'How did it go last night?'

'Let's just say it was interesting. I just hope what I've got to tell Harbury pleases him enough to let me take on the other task; which may, or may not, be illegal.'

'Talking of which, you'd best be on your way to meet him. I'd prefer you to leave over the back fence. People around here tend to mind their own business, but you look so suspicious that people in the square would probably stop you if they saw you coming out of the front door, especially after Freda screamed earlier.'

'Fair enough George, but you'll have to lift Barney over to me. His legs are too short to jump it.'

Chard added the broad-brimmed hat to his disguise, grabbed his small bag of belongings, and having said his farewell to Freda he set off through the back door.

***

Although it was still early, there were plenty of people on the streets. There were also many omnibuses filled with shoppers coming to the market town. Chard walked slowly, with a noticeable limp, Barney padding along at his heels. Occasionally someone stared at him, but on seeing the empty sleeve, looked away in embarrassment. Once over English Bridge, Chard turned down a small set of steps leading to the pathway beneath, which ran alongside the river. On the path, directly under the bridge, a man stood waiting.

'Mr. Harbury I take it. 'Ow do, sir,' greeted Chard in a borrowed accent. 'The name is Smith,' he added.

The heavy-jowled, burly organiser of much of the town's illicit activities, looked askance at the one-armed, scruffy individual who'd addressed him, but said nothing. He took out a cigar, then lit it before scoffing. 'A bloody cripple. Lamb didn't mention that.'

Chard was at least relieved not to have been recognised, for he had interviewed Harbury three times in the distant past, over alleged offences which could not be proved.

Harbury took a large puff of the cigar, then blew the smoke in Chard's direction. 'Take your hat off so I can see you properly.'

Chard obeyed the instruction, removing his headpiece to fully reveal the bandaged upper face and seemingly disfigured skin below.

Harbury grimaced. 'Ugly bastard, aren't you?'

'Haughmond Abbey. I went there,' stated Chard, deciding to speak in a short, terse manner, the better to retain the Yorkshire accent.

'And what did you see?'

'Dogfight, about thirty punters.'

'You're from out of town, I understand. So, you wouldn't have recognised anyone I suppose.'

'Heard a couple of names. There was a Stanmore and a Ferguson.'

Harbury took another puff of his cigar. 'Anyone else?'

'No. But they were mainly gents.'

'Who was running the dogfight?'

Chard noticed that despite the apparent nonchalance of the question, there was an underlying urgency. 'About six men. Young sloggers. Birmingham lads I reckon.'

Harbury spat into the river. 'Fucking peaky blinders! That bastard Foden's trying to take my trade.'

'Foden?' queried Chard, curious that he was known to Harbury. 'An ambitious Brummie shit, he's even got an office in Corporation Street. He pretends to be a gent, but runs a gang of sloggers. They call themselves peaky blinders.'

'George asked for a loan,' Chard reminded his potential unlikely benefactor.

'Last night was just to see if you could be trusted. There was a further task planned for today, but Lamb didn't mention your arm. He said you could handle yourself if there was trouble.'

'Depends on't trouble. There's nowt bothers me. I took down a look-out last night, with no bother,' argued Chard, trying not to overdo the Yorkshire dialect.

Harbury appeared thoughtful. 'I suppose there's not much option. One of my men has been bribed by Foden, but I don't know who. It's why I need someone from out of town. Lamb is too honest to have any connection with Birmingham filth. When he said he wanted a loan to help someone new to the area, it was too good an opportunity to miss.' He paused once more and took a deep draw from his cigar before exhaling another plume of smoke. 'The facts are these. I've got a wager with Foden for a very substantial sum of money. The cash is being held by someone trusted, but I want to make sure it doesn't unexpectedly vanish, so I need to stay around the centre of town. Unfortunately, my main article of investment for the wager is currently locked up in a warehouse and I need someone to take care of it.'

'Doesn't seem too difficult. What's the wager?'

'What do you know about today's football match?' asked Harbury.

'Nowt,' replied Chard in his terse fake accent.

'Shrewsbury Town have turned professional this season and they're playing the mighty Wolverhampton Wanderers. There normally wouldn't be a hope of the Town winning and so Foden offered me the draw. So, providing Town don't lose, I win a fortune.'

'You reckon they won't lose then?'

'Town's midfielder, Morris, is outstanding. He's the key. Providing he plays, Shrewsbury might even win.'

'What's the problem then?' asked Chard.

'He likes a drink before the match and also the peaky blinders will try and nobble him. To ensure his safety, I slipped him a mild drug last night and locked him in a warehouse. I need him guarded and then taken to the ground for the match. If I win my wager, I'll pay you handsomely and clear Lamb's debt.'

Chard glanced down at Barney who was interested by the ducks swimming under the bridge, and smiled. 'Consider it done.'

As he walked away, Chard smiled at his good fortune. From the encounter at the dog fight he knew Landell had been in debt to Harry Foden. And as much as he had cursed inwardly at having been landed with working for Harbury, he now knew where Foden could be found.

***

Morgan finished writing his telegram to Superintendent Jones, then left the post office, heading for the town square. The message had been short and suitably vague, giving the impression he'd been asked to assist the Shrewsbury police in tracking down Chard, without actually saying it.

Being a Saturday, he found the square was even busier than usual, with its hansom cabs coming and going every few seconds, to the peril of any inattentive pedestrian. It wasn't as bustling as a market day back in Pontypridd, but it had the same sense of vibrancy.

Crossing the square, past the courthouse in its centre, Morgan headed for the police station and asked to speak to Inspector Warboys. However, it was a twenty-minute wait before he was ushered into the surly inspector's presence.

'What do you want, Constable Morgan? I'm a very busy man.'

'I've come to assist you in the recapture of Insp... I mean the escaped prisoner.'

Warboys put down the map he'd been studying. 'And how do you think you can help?' he demanded derisively.

'I know him better than you, if you don't mind me saying so, Inspector.'

'You might know him, but you don't know this area. I've got officers stationed around key points of the town, although I'll have to pull a few of them away this afternoon,' he said reluctantly. 'Damn football match!'

'What football match?' asked Morgan, unsure why it should take any precedence over the search for an escaped prisoner.

'Shrewsbury against Wolverhampton. We've heard rumours of potential trouble, so I've got to send a few men, just in case it gets out of control. As soon as the game is over, I'll have them back on the search in town again.'

'Surely you don't think Chard would be still hanging around the town?'

Warboys gave a patronising sigh. 'That's why I'm an inspector and you are just a constable. He'll have no food or money, so he must steal some. He is probably hiding in some disused shed in the daylight and hoping for a chance to break into a house at night. There were no reports of any incidents last night, so the chances are our fugitive will try something tonight.'

'Surely he might have made it on foot outside the town borough?' suggested Morgan.

'Unfortunately, it's possible, so with great reluctance I informed the County Constabulary. They've had no reports either.'

'I still don't think you'll find him in the town,' argued Morgan deceptively.

'Why are you so certain?'

'Because he's resourceful. The inspector always knew how to get out of a tricky situation. I expect he's got hold of some money somehow and has got on a train.'

'Oh yes, and where would he have headed?'

'North, to Manchester,' replied Morgan with a straight face. 'It's where he used to work, and he must have contacts there.'

'Ha!' exclaimed Warboys triumphantly. 'I'm not that easily fooled. You're trying to put me off the scent. I believe you still think he's innocent, and what you really think is that he's headed in the opposite direction, down to South Wales. Perhaps he's made good friends down there and thinks he can hide somewhere in the valleys.'

'I don't think that at all,' answered Morgan honestly, but with a deliberate degree of hesitancy.

'You want me to send men north to Manchester, whilst you follow him to South Wales to help him evade capture. Well, I've got news for you, young man. I'm going to send a couple of men South. In addition, I will write to your superintendent, insisting you remain here with us to help look for Chard around the town. Then I'll have South Wales covered, Shrewsbury covered, and I can also keep an eye on you.'

'I'm not part of your police force,' argued Morgan.

'True, but as soon as I get a reply from your superintendent confirming your assistance, you will be obliged to report here at least once a day. That will limit your opportunity to help our fugitive,' bragged Warboys.

'In which case I'll call here tomorrow, to see if Superintendent Jones has replied,' answered Morgan abruptly.

Without waiting for a response, the constable left the room and headed for the exit, his mind trying to assess the implications of Warboys' comments. Hopefully, the wording of the request to Superintendent Jones would reinforce the contents of his own earlier telegram, giving him an excuse to remain in Shrewsbury. On the other hand, Warboys clearly had his suspicions, and that could prove dangerous.

EIGHTEEN

After having met her beau for breakfast at one of Shrewsbury's many cafes, May had set off for the town's indoor market, leaving Morgan to visit the post office to send his telegram to his superior. She hadn't told him details of what she had planned to do, because he would have raised obvious objections. Nevertheless, desperate needs called for desperate measures, and the inspector's situation needed resolving urgently. Her part in finding out the fate of Freda Lamb's sister would no doubt help him to concentrate on clearing his name.

The building housing the indoor market was a thing of beauty with red, blue and white bricks and a mixture of architectural styles. Once inside, May's senses were assailed by the smell of vegetables, newly baked bread and fresh meat.

'Excuse me, but are there any stalls selling second-hand clothes?' she asked a stallholder selling jars of home-made jam.

'Only fresh produce I'm afraid dear. There's a little shop in Claremont Street which might do you though. Try this blackcurrant jam, I'll knock a bit off if you buy two.'

Feeling obligated, May bought the smallest jar on the stall and left the market. She was feeling the occasional muscle spasm which she knew was an occasional side effect from abstaining from her small dose of laudanum. Having forgotten to take some the previous two nights, she knew another night could not be missed.

Back outside the market hall, May was going to ask for Claremont Street when she noticed a sign indicating it ran alongside the market building. It took her just a few paces along the pavement to find the shop mentioned by the stallholder.

'I'm looking for some second-hand clothes to give to an old aunt who's down on her luck,' explained May.

The shopkeeper, an old lady with a wart on her nose, gave a

practised smile. 'Help yourself to this pile dear. Have a good look through. I'm sure you'll find what you need.'

The old lady assessed the smartly dressed young woman as having a few shillings to spare and rubbed her hands in anticipation.

May took her time, but eventually picked out a number of items and placed them on the counter. She was surprised at the price, which seemed more than was reasonable, but paid nonetheless.

The old lady, for her part, was delighted with the profit made; but scratched her head at the style of garment purchased. 'She's got a strange type of old aunt, that's for sure,' she told herself, before putting the coins in a tin box.

***

'Now clear off and take that mangy dog with you!' growled the red-faced butcher.

Chard took the meat scraps which had been thrust his way as an incentive not to deter other customers with his disreputable appearance, and left the shop. He threw a piece of fatty beef onto the pavement to be immediately gobbled up by Barney, then made his way down the hill known as the Mardol. The street was busy with shoppers and in the hours of daylight it was indeed a quite respectable area, though at night the lower end enjoyed a dubious reputation for drink and debauchery.

Up ahead, Chard spotted a pimply youth in a cheap woollen jacket and a flat cap. Despite the change in headwear, what had given away his identity as a 'peaky blinder' was the brightly coloured scarf and bell-bottom trousers. Like several others Chard had seen around the town, the lad looked to be searching for something; probably the location of the man Morris.

'There's another one Barney. We'd best keep you out of sight, just in case they recognise you,' said Chard to his four-legged companion, pulling him into a doorway.

Once the way was clear, Chard moved back onto the pavement and continued towards Welsh Bridge, crossing over to Frankwell on the other side. Harbury had described exactly where Morris was being detained and given him a key to the storeroom lock. In theory, the drug used on Morris would have worn off and there should be no ill effects. All Chard had to do was to keep him there until just before the match, then escort him safely to the ground. A task probably easier said than done.

***

The storeroom was located at the back of an empty warehouse, close to the river on Frankwell quay. As Chard approached it, he saw a familiar figure headed for a lodging house nearby. Hurrying forward, but incorporating a slight limp, he caught up with Morgan who was returning from his call at the police station.

'Spare the price of a cup of tea for an old soldier?' he asked in a northern accent.

Morgan turned and recoiled as the bandaged face approached his.

'No! Clear off!' he exclaimed, before squinting in puzzlement as the scruffy individual with an accompanying dog, started laughing.

'It's me,' said Chard in his own voice.

After a shocked silence, Morgan spoke. 'What are you doing sir?'

'It's complicated and stop calling me sir. In case anyone's looking, just look angry and pretend you're looking for some spare change to give me.'

Morgan started to fidget in his jacket pocket as Chard continued. 'Whilst sorting out George's money problems, I'm also making progress in my own investigation. How have you got on?'

'Inspector Warboys thinks you are somewhere in the town, but he also thinks you might have gone back to South Wales. He suspects I might want to help you, so he is asking Superintendent Jones if I can be ordered to help him. Not that he wants my help as such, but he does want me to report to him every day, so he knows where I am. In the meantime, I met with May early this morning and she seemed confident about getting information on the disappearance of Mrs Lamb's sister.'

'Good, but I want her kept out of this as much as possible. I'll be going now. I've got to safeguard someone in a storeroom at the back of the warehouse over there,' informed Chard, pointing towards the quay. 'Liaise with George Lamb, but make sure you aren't followed. Now pretend to be very angry and send me on my way.'

Thrusting out his jaw, Morgan shook his fist and Chard backed away, cursing. Then he headed for the warehouse and the storeroom which had been built as an outside annex.

When he got there, he found the lock which secured the door's bolt was rusty and the key was stiff to turn. Abandoning his ruse of an injured limb, Chard slipped his arm out of the sling to help with releasing the heavy padlock. Once undone, the long iron bolt that prevented the door from opening, slid back easily. Chard slipped his left arm back in the sling and pulled back the heavy wooden door, only to be confronted by a very angry man who was clearly ready to launch an attack.

'Stop!' bellowed Chard, who had been blessed with a stentorian voice and a natural authority.

It was enough to make Morris pause, giving Chard time to add a threat.

'My dog here, will attack at my command. He's a ferocious beast with the biting power of a wolf. Once his jaws lock on to your leg there's no escape, and you'll end up a cripple.'

Morris glanced at Barney, who stood staring up at Chard with his jaws open, hoping for another piece of meat.

'He's looking up at me waiting for the word to attack.'

Morris looked from the dog back to the portly one-armed man with the bandaged, disfigured face, and took a step back.

'That's better,' said Chard calmly. 'We're here to protect you. There are people in the town who mean you great harm to stop you playing in the match today. My job is to keep you here until it's safe to leave. Do you understand?'

Morris nodded slowly, his eyes showing anxiety at the sight of Chard's dog, who was tearing apart a piece of meat that his new master had thrown to him.

'Good,' affirmed Chard, realising he had completely forgotten to use his imitated Yorkshire accent and was speaking normally. Accepting it was too late to cover his error, he gave a grunt and took a proper look at the room. It was a fair size, but clearly hadn't been used for some time, as cobwebs hung across a pile of empty boxes in one corner. Against the back wall there were rolls of canvas sheeting and some threadbare sacking. The whole place smelled of damp.

'I woke up on these blankets, with a bag containing my football kit alongside and a basket of food,' said Morris, pointing to a bundle of bedding in the middle of the room. I gave up yelling after half an hour.'

'The warehouse next door seems abandoned; the storeroom walls are thick and the door is sturdy. A passer-by would have to be right outside to hear you,' shrugged Chard. 'If you've still got food in the basket, you may as well share it out,' he added. 'We've got nothing else to do, other than wait.'

***

An hour later, having made himself comfortable leaning against some of the discarded sacking, Chard had unintentionally drifted off to sleep. Barney also seemed comatose, having lain on his side next to his master. The room, which earlier had been lit by sunshine which shone through a small window high in the roof, had darkened.

Morris, with another terrified glance at Barney's closed jaws, edged towards the bag containing his football kit and slowly picked it up. He held his breath and took a couple of steps towards the door.

Without warning there was a tremendous bang which shook the building.

'What the…?' exclaimed Chard, shaking himself awake.

Barney in his turn, got up, with ears held back, looking at his master for an explanation.

Then, with a roar, the rain came. It thumped against the roof like a thousand hammers.

'Sit down, Morris!' ordered Chard.

The footballer looked at Barney, who was looking disconcerted, but alert. 'No point in getting soaked I suppose,' he replied grudgingly.

His captor stood up, determined not to fall asleep, went to the door and opened it a fraction. The rain was so heavy that it bounced off the ground. Chard prayed the match wouldn't be called off, because it would mean Harbury wouldn't hand over the desperately needed payment.

Despite Chard's pleas to the Almighty, the rain continued for a further hour before it eventually settled to a fine drizzle.

'Not too long to wait now Morris. I'll soon be able to escort you to the ground, then you can do what you please after the match. I'm only here to protect you.'

'I should think so too. Anyway, what am I going to do about my pre-match pint? I always like a drink or two before I go on the pitch. Can we call in at the…?'

'Quiet!' interrupted Chard sharply. 'I can hear voices.'

Inadvertently, the door had been left slightly ajar from the last time Chard had checked on the rain, and there was the faint murmur of men talking nearby.

'Hide behind those boxes,' whispered Chard. 'I'll listen in case it's people looking for you.'

'Are you sure?' came a familiar voice. 'I'll bost your head if you've got me soaked for nothing.'

'It took me ages to find you, but I swear it's true. I've been tailing Harbury and I saw him talk to this man with a crippled arm, so I followed him. I'll have to go now, Pitt. Harbury knows someone has been working for you and if he finds out I'm the informer, I'll be dead by the morning.'

'By the end of this afternoon he won't have the money to afford paying someone to kill you. Stay here with me and we'll check this out together.'

'What if I go and get some of your mates?'

'No! I need them looking elsewhere, in case this is a wild goose chase. Now come on.'

Chard stood flat against the wall as the door was opened and the two men stepped in.

The first man was, as Chard had anticipated, the burly young man from the dogfight, John Pitt. He wore the same blue scarf around his neck, but the 'peaky' bowler had been replaced by a flat cap. The other man, a rat-faced, scrawny individual hung back, just inside the doorway.

'Eh?' uttered Pitt, seeing Barney standing in the middle of the room. 'It can't be can it?'

Seeing him momentarily distracted, Chard launched himself forward, aiming his shoulder at the Birmingham man's kidneys. Pitt gave a grunt of pain but didn't go down. Instead he turned and grabbed his attacker and soon the two men were wrestling each other on the ground. Pitt was shaken, having been taken unawares by the bandaged fiend who rubbed his gelatinous weeping sores against his own face as they rolled on the ground. He was also aware that whoever the man was, he was definitely using two arms and not one.

Just when he thought he was getting the upper hand, the peaky blinder yelled in pain as Chard bit his ear, and then managed to get his feet into his midriff. Pushing his legs out with all the force he could muster, Chard sent Pitt flying backwards to land on top of Barney, who gave a yelp. The agitated dog then started to bark and snapped at Pitt's leg. Looking terrified, Pitt's companion pulled out a short-bladed knife., and stepped forward. Chard noticed the movement out of the corner of his eye and grabbed the knife arm, stopping the intended blow. Barney was continuing to bark and snap at Pitt, who got to his feet and kicked out at the animal, catching it a glancing blow. At the same time, there was a yell from behind the crates at the back of the room and Morris stepped out, hurling a football boot at Pitt, causing him to lose his balance and fall over. Morris's second boot soon followed, but this time the missile was aimed at the man with the knife. It glanced the side of the target's head at the same time as Chard gave a twist and broke the man's arm. With a scream, he dropped the weapon. Barney, having recovered from the kick received from Pitt's boot had started snapping at Pitt once more, but not actually biting. It was enough for Pitt though. Faced with two attackers, a snapping dog, and an ally with a broken arm, there was only one thing for it.

'Let's get out,' he yelled.

Chard felt Pitt barrel into him and before he could react, both of the thugs had run out through the door and slammed it shut.

'Quick!' he yelled at Morris, but they were a split second too late.

Both groaned as they heard the sound of the iron retaining bolt sliding into place.

'That's us bolloxed then,' said Morris. 'With the rain outside, there's even less chance of someone passing by.'

'Quiet!' ordered Chard. 'They're saying something.'

Putting his ear against the door, Chard could faintly hear angry words being exchanged. Pitt was telling the man with the broken arm to stop whining. He was to stay outside the storeroom whilst Pitt went to make arrangements to ensure the game wouldn't be called off due to the rain.

'We might be stuck here until after the match,' grimaced Chard. 'And I don't fancy our chances if they come back mob-handed.'

'What's this all about anyway?' asked Morris.

'People with a lot of money betting on the game. Those men need Shrewsbury to lose. I don't suppose they can win without you?'

'It's hardly likely. The eleven names went in yesterday and you can't change them. Even if someone broke a leg, they can't be replaced. Talking of damaged limbs, what's the business with your arm?'

'It's complicated,' answered Chard.

The disguise was rapidly falling apart. He had revealed his fully functioning arm, dropped the Yorkshire accent and the sheen of rotten fruit had largely rubbed off against Pitt's face during their fight. At least the bandage was still in place, as was the padding around the waist, and although the staining from the berries was probably fading, the bristles from his unshaven face added to his unkempt appearance.

'Your dog didn't do much,' complained Morris.

'He only eats footballers,' replied Chard as Barney padded over to sit on his foot.

'That's as may be, but what are we going to do now?'

'Nothing,' answered Chard. 'We've just got to wait and hope.'

NINETEEN

It seemed an age since the bolt of the door had been rammed across, leaving them imprisoned. Chard had lain back on some sacking, his hat pulled down, conserving his energy and listening to the rain hammering on the roof; Morris paced up and down in frustration and anger.

Suddenly Barney, who was lying against his master's legs, gave a low growl.

'What is it boy?' asked Chard, tipping back his hat.

'Someone's opening the door,' said Morris, balling his fists as the sound of the external bolt being drawn back echoed in the room.

Chard stood against the wall, doubtful he could catch the peaky blinders off guard a second time.

A familiar figure stepped inside and just as Morris launched himself towards the door, fists flailing, Chard threw himself forward.

'Wait! He's a friend!'

Morris, his face a mixture of anger, frustration and confusion, stepped back.

'This is Idris Morgan. We used to … work together,' explained Chard.

'I was going into town to track down the bailiff who discovered the bodies…' began Morgan, by way of explanation.

'What bodies?' interrupted Morris.

'…Then I thought to call in and see how you were doing,' continued the constable, ignoring Morris. 'I saw a shifty looking bloke, standing outside in the pouring rain, holding his arm and cursing. I guessed there was something up, and when he told me to piss off somewhere else, I took exception to it. A kick up the arse saw him on his way.'

'It's a good job you turned up. We're probably bolloxed as it is, but at least I've got a chance of getting this chap to the football ground. It kicks off at three o'clock.'

'Then you're cutting it fine. Where's the ground?' asked Morgan.
'It's this side of the river heading away from town, up by the
army barracks.'

'I've got my kit in this bag. Let's get going,' interrupted Morris.

Chard pulled Morgan to one side, out of the football player's
earshot. 'In the unlikely event of things going my way, I hope to get
some funds. We can't keep meeting at George's house, but there's a
pub not far from him in Bynner Street, called the Prince of Wales.
If you're prepared to take the risk, I'll meet you there on Monday
evening at nine o'clock. Just you though, not May.'

'Hopefully May will have found out something about the disappearance of Cora Lamb by then. She told me she has some idea
how best to go about it, and will leave a message at my lodgings if
anything comes to light.'

Chard pursed his lips and shook his head. 'As long as she doesn't
do anything impetuous.'

'I'm sure that won't be the case,' replied Morgan, affronted on
his sweetheart's behalf.

'You've only really known her since her injury. I can assure you
she was quite different before that,' responded Chard.

'Come on! We need to get going!' urged Morris.

'He's right,' agreed Chard. 'Come, Barney.'

Morgan watched Chard, Morris and the faithful dog disappear
into the pouring rain, and started to worry about May. Perhaps he
didn't know her as well as he thought.

***

'Don't go too far ahead,' Chard warned Morris, as they ran up the
road.

'Why? Because your dog can't keep up?'

'No. It's because I can't keep up; there's a danger that when we
get close to the ground someone will nobble you if you're on your
own; and you'll be too exhausted to play.'

Reluctantly, the footballer slowed to a jog.

'That's better,' said Chard gratefully. 'Anyway, there's a chance
the game will be called off due to this weather.'

Morris shook his head. 'Good drainage on our pitch. Our

manager will ask for a delay in case I've been having a drink before the game and lost track of time; which I admit has happened once or twice. I doubt the referee will agree though. You don't think the Wolves team are in league with the men who locked us in do you?'

'No,' answered Chard, panting as they jogged on. 'Wolverhampton lads in a deal with Brummies? Not likely is it? It's to do with a Birmingham gang and a wager that's been made. You don't need to know anything else. It's safer that way. Just make sure you don't lose today.'

As the men, and Barney, who was lagging about thirty yards behind, reached the top of Copthorne bank, they could hear shouting coming from the football ground a short distance ahead.

'Bugger! They must have kicked off,' swore Morris.

Rushing onwards, they came to a pair of closed gates where two elderly men stood, their attention torn between guarding the entrance against non-paying latecomers, and trying to look over the heads of the spectators to get a glimpse of the match.

'Oi! Let us in!' yelled Morris.

One of the gatekeepers turned around, and was taken aback by the sight of a man with a bandaged face in a large-brimmed hat.

'Never mind him. He's with me!' shouted Morris.

The other gatekeeper then turned around and recognised who had spoken. 'Mr Morris! In you come, quickly! We're already a goal down.'

Nudging his colleague, they opened the gate and let both Morris and Chard through.

'Not the dog though!' said the first gatekeeper, but it was too late, for Barney had run through his legs.

There was a good-sized crowd despite the rain, which was finally starting to ease. Some had taken to wearing knitted scarves in the blue and white colours of the home team as they cheered their players on. There were also shouts of encouragement in distinctive Wolverhampton accents, showing the team in old gold and black had its supporters too.

'Out of the way!' shouted Morris as he pushed his way through the spectators towards the half way line and the changing rooms. As the word went round, the crowd began to murmur, which started to build amongst the Shrewsbury supporters until it became a cheer. Not that approval was universal, for there was the odd jeer bellowed at the late arrival.

'About bloody time!'

'You've let us down, you shit! We're already a goal behind!'

Chard watched as Morris reached the side of the team's manager, who gave him a clip across the ear before sending him into the changing room. There was nothing more he could do.

Everything now depended on the men on the pitch, and for the moment the Shrewsbury goal was under siege.

Chard began to be drawn into the excitement of the match and nudged the man next to him. 'I've only just turned up. We're a goal down I understand.'

'Jesus!' exclaimed the man, recoiling at the bandaged face which had suddenly appeared. 'What are you doing scaring people like that mon?' Regaining some composure, he passed Chard a scrumpled piece of paper. There's the team list. They scored in the first five minutes.'

The names, apart from J Morris, were unfamiliar to Chard, but he memorised their shirt numbers and positions, hoping he would be able to enjoy the rest of the match.

When Morris, fully changed into his kit appeared on the pitch, there was an almighty roar. Chard smiled as he scanned the crowd noting the excitement in their faces, until he saw one that was unwelcome. It was Pitt, who was standing with a furious expression on the far side of the pitch, directly opposite. He too was scanning the crowd, and Chard instinctively held the piece of paper with the team list in front of his face. The broad-brimmed hat would no doubt be noticeable amongst the flat caps and bowlers surrounding him, but Chard hoped he would get away with it.

There was a sudden shout from the spectators as Tracey, the Shrewsbury wing forward, raced downfield and shot just over the bar, with the Wolverhampton goalkeeper left stranded. Chard looked back across the pitch and was dismayed to see Pitt had vanished from sight. He tried to spot where the peaky blinder had gone, but his attempts were interrupted by the crowd jumping in excitement as Benbow, the centre forward, shot wide.

'Have a care!' growled Chard to the man behind, who had accidentally pushed him in his enthusiasm, causing him to nearly stumble over Barney. The dog seemed quite happy in the crowd, eating a discarded sandwich whilst resting against Chard's leg.

'Sorry mon! Look! We've got a corner now!'

Shrewsbury, with Morris making his presence felt in midfield, were starting to dominate. Chard watched as the corner kick was taken and in the ensuing scramble, the inside forward named Bliss slammed the ball past the goalkeeper.

'Get in, you bastard!' whooped the spectator next to Chard.

More excitement was to follow as Shrewsbury forced corner after corner, but Wolverhampton looked like holding out until half-time. Then, from another attack, Tracey put Benbow through on goal. This time, he didn't waste the opportunity, and the Wolves goalkeeper lay sprawled in the mud as the ball flew past him. The referee blew his whistle for the end of the half.

Chard was as excited as all the other Shrewsbury supporters, to the extent that he had entirely forgotten about Pitt. With Shrewsbury going in at half-time 2-1 in front, they just had to avoid conceding two goals in the second half.

'It looks like our efforts earlier on were worth it,' Chard whispered to Barney as he bent over to pat him.

The crowd had started to mill about during the interval, and as he squatted down to make more fuss of Barney, Chard noticed a pair of boots passing close by. They were regulation boots. Sure enough, he looked up to see a police constable walking through the ground, ensuring there was no sign of trouble. Holding his breath, Chard waited for the policeman to pass, then gave a sigh of relief.

'I bet you're glad you came,' said the man alongside, tapping Chard on the shoulder.

'I am now,' he replied, standing back up.

'It nearly didn't go ahead you know, what with the weather. I know it's stopped raining now, but earlier on it looked like it would never end.'

'Yes, I was caught in it on the way here. We're both just as wet as each other,' empathised Chard.

'The referee looked like he was going to call it off and send everyone home, but the funny thing is...' The man paused, then shook his head.

'What?' asked Chard.

'That bloke there, with the daft haircut, wearing the bright scarf. He seemed to have a word in his ear and then to everyone's surprise the game was declared to be on. Our manager was furious.'

Chard looked to where the man was pointing. Only about twenty yards away stood Pitt. He was standing close to the touchline and trying to get the referee's attention. Fortunately, the official was in a heated debate with both managers and seemed to be deliberately ignoring the gestures from Pitt.

Having had their half-time orange, and in some cases a cigarette, the teams were ready to return to the pitch. It was soon clear that the Wolves manager had said some harsh words to his players at half-time and had put fire in their bellies. They attacked the second half with a vengeance, and soon it was the young Shrewsbury goalkeeper, Rufus Jones, needing to make a diving save to keep the ball out of the net. However, with Morris putting in some fierce tackles in midfield Shrewsbury gained the ascendancy once more. With the match looking like a comfortable victory for the home team, Chard found he was actually enjoying himself. With luck he would soon have the means to track down one of the suspects for his wife's murder.

'I won't be able to take you to Birmingham when I go to have a word with this Harry Foden fellow,' Chard whispered to Barney as he bent over to give him a reassuring pat.

'No! Stop him!' shouted someone in the crowd.

Alarmed by the outburst, Chard stood up and looked around. The crowd was murmuring and to his immediate relief it became clear their attention was fixed on the pitch.

Wolves had broken clear of the Shrewsbury onslaught and their centre forward was racing towards the goal, with only Rufus Jones to beat. With admirable bravery, the young goalkeeper threw himself at the feet of the opposition forward, to knock the ball away for a corner kick. With a grunt, the Wolves player followed through with his boot and connected with the goalkeeper's head. The referee immediately blew his whistle and ran to the stricken player's side. Jones lay unconscious and the official immediately started to wave towards the sidelines.

'The bastards have killed him!' someone yelled.

'Fucking yam-yams. Let's be 'aving them,' shouted a local slogger, wanting to pick a fight with the visiting supporters.

As if in response, a number of scuffles were starting to break out in the crowd; and the few police constables present waded in with drawn truncheons to stop things developing into a riot.

Meanwhile two doctors had come forward and were hastily examining the injured goalkeeper. Chard, ashamed at his own lack of compassion, wondered how the turn of events would affect his own perilous position. No substitutions were allowed and so it looked like Shrewsbury would have to finish the match with a man down and an outfield player trying his best as goalkeeper.

The time dragged on, with players standing around, hands on hips, wondering when, or perhaps if, they would restart. Gradually the police regained control of the unruly elements in the crowd, with Chard pleased that they would be too busy with their duties to bother about noticing him. Finally, after a full ten minutes, the doctors helped the goalkeeper to his feet and he walked unsteadily towards the goal.

'He's going to continue!' exclaimed the man next to Chard.

Play resumed with the corner kick, which fortunately came to nothing. It was hoofed up the other end of the pitch and from then on Shrewsbury, led by Morris, did everything they could to keep the ball as far away from their goalkeeper as possible. Conscious of the time left in the match, the team in blue and white used every delaying tactic in the book. They queried whether the ball was deflating, took an age to take throw-ins, ensured the person walking forward to take free kicks or corner kicks came from as far away from their original position as possible; but eventually the inevitable happened. Wolves were awarded a free kick in their half and it was sent high towards the Shrewsbury goal. Rufus Jones, still terribly dazed, tried to catch the ball, but missed it and in the ensuing scramble a Wolves player managed to score. With the score at 2-2 and less than five minutes to play, Chard's heart was in his mouth. The draw would be enough, but everything would be down to which team Lady Luck favoured.

Completely captivated by events on the pitch, everything else around Chard had faded into obscurity. Only a lucky glance picked out an unwelcome sight. It was Pitt, with two other peaky blinders; and they were heading straight for him.

'Come on Barney!' he shouted at the dog, giving it a gentle prod with his shoe. Turning around he headed in the direction of the gates, pushing through the crowd as he did so. He had perhaps a thirty yards head start, but it wouldn't be enough.

'Get out of it!'

'Oi!'

'Piss off!'

The spectators, enthralled by the drama of the match, did not take kindly to being barged into by the bandaged stranger. Fortunately, it was also making them less inclined to make way for his pursuers.

Seeing an opportunity for further disruption, Chard snatched a dangling blue and white Shrewsbury scarf from behind a supporter and threw it towards a group of Wolverhampton men standing close by. The local man felt the scarf being taken and turned to see it fallen against the Wolves supporters.

'You cheeky...' he started to say, but rather than complete the sentence, he tapped his friends' shoulders and they rushed the bewildered Wolverhampton men with fists flying.

Chard reached the gates and took a look back. The scuffle had blocked the peaky blinders' route, their Birmingham curses antagonising both sets of supporters. To add to their problems, a couple of police constables were also joining the fray.

Feeling a comforting heavy weight resting against his leg, Chard looked down at his companion.

'I think we just might have got away with it, Barney.'

Familiar with the area, Chard set off at pace, with the dog

scampering behind; but instead of going back toward the town he headed in the opposite direction. It was only a short distance to the army barracks, and turning off the road, behind the cover of its high walls, he slumped down, exhausted.

TWENTY

May checked there was no-one at the reception desk of the YWCA, then hurriedly left the building without being seen. She wore a long, somewhat dingy coat and was bareheaded, despite the teeming rain, her auburn hair tied up in a bun.

'Mind yer back, lady!' called a baker's boy as he rode his bike down the narrow road that led behind the High Street.

May quickly leapt out of the lad's way, reminded that she needed to be more alert. Her plan was daring, and it was important to keep her wits sharp. Even the first part, though not in any way perilous, would be a minor trial. Fortunately, she had noticed a shop that would meet her requirements when she had purchased her second-hand clothing. May crossed the busy road between an omnibus and a carriage. After a quick glance in the shop window, she took a deep breath and entered.

Five minutes later she re-emerged with a small paper bag and clear directions to the Salop Home. The route was easy enough, except for the crowded pavements and the torrential rain. May walked down the Wyle Cop, turning right at the bottom of the hill before reaching the English Bridge, to a part of town known as St Julian's Friars. The Salop Home was easy to find, its name on a brass plaque outside the door. Having found her destination, she headed for the cover of a tree next to the river and discarded her coat, to display a shabby dress with a low neckline. Then she undid her hair, allowing her wet auburn tresses to fall over her shoulders. Finally, she took out the contents of her paper bag and inexpertly applied a gaudy smear of lip stain followed by a rough dab of rouge.

'If they won't even talk to a relative of Cora, then this is the only way I'll get any information,' she muttered to convince herself.

May was not unfamiliar with the ways of 'fallen women'. She had seen several of her home town's less discerning ladies in the infirmary, but trying to mimic their mannerisms would be a challenge. Steeling herself for the charade, she knocked on the door of the home.

'Yes? What do you want?' demanded the dark-haired girl who answered the door. She wore a plain grey dress, with an apron over the top.

May, her dress soaked through, did her best to adopt a plaintive expression and was about to plead her case when another voice snapped sharply from further inside.

'Who is it, Victoria?'

The girl looked sullen and slowly looked May up and down before answering. 'It's a street girl, Mrs Hill. I'll tell her to go away. You're far too busy, what with all that's been going on.'

'You were once a street girl yourself, Victoria. Let her in,' admonished the voice.

'I suppose you had better come in then,' said the girl, giving May a condescending look. 'Follow me and I'll take you through to Mrs Hill's office.'

May was led into a small, but comfortable room that smelled of polish, to stand before a small hatchet-faced woman dressed in black.

'And you are...?' she asked.

'May Fether...,' she faltered as the alias used when May called on Warren and Stanmore slipped her mind.

Mrs Hill looked dubiously at the bedraggled young woman before her, whose dress was dripping onto the polished wooden floor. 'I suppose it must be your "professional" name. Speak up, what's your business here?'

May put on the same innocent expression she used to get around her father when he was in a bad mood. 'I'm sorry ma'am,' she apologised, whilst giving a deliberately unsteady curtsey. 'I've fallen into bad ways these last few months, but I would like to find a path to a new life.'

Mrs Hill sniffed. 'I detect a Welsh accent. What brings you to Shrewsbury?'

'I was taken into service ma'am. My master had me travel with him on business, but he behaved improperly, even though I was just a maiden.'

'A common enough occurrence.'

'I am ashamed to admit I did give in, just the once. Then in my shame I refused him further familiarities, so he abandoned me without any belongings,' lied May with a shaky voice. 'I've had to make my way as best I can, but I am fallen, and cannot return home.'

'Why did you come here?'

'I was told you can take in girls in such sorry circumstances and find them a way to lead a normal, decent life again.'

'You've come at a bad time. Two of our major benefactors have passed away in recent weeks including our financial secretary and we may have to reduce our places.'

'I do know my letters and figures,' offered May. 'I went to school before I was taken into service. I would be happy to help with books and I have a few pennies saved on my person to help with my keep.'

Mrs Hill paused in thought. 'I suppose we do only have eight girls at the moment, and one of those is due to leave.' She stared at May, clearly wondering whether to believe her story. 'Hopefully I will not regret this, but you may stay,' she finally announced. 'I warn you that the rules here are strict. You will wake at dawn and go to bed as soon as night falls. No drink, tobacco or any other vices. You will work in the laundry and will be taught how to sew, cook and act as a maid of all works. If you achieve a good enough standard, and have mended your bad ways, you will be recommended to one of our subscribers as suitable for employment. Do you understand?'

'Yes ma'am,' agreed May, giving another wobbly curtsey.

'Good. Then you had best get out of those clothes and stop dripping on the floor. You can wipe your make-up off as soon as you get to your room.' Mrs Hill went to the door and looked up the stair-well. 'Betty!' she called.

Moments later, a very pretty blonde-haired girl of teenage years entered, dressed in a similar way to the inmate who had opened the front door.

'This is May, who will be joining us. Find her some dry clothes and a bed in your dormitory,' snapped Mrs Hill.

'Oh, thank you, thank you,' exclaimed May gratefully to the matriarch.

Betty had a completely different personality to Victoria, with a beaming smile and laughing eyes. 'Come on then, I'll lead the way.'

May followed Betty up to a clean, brightly painted dormitory with half a dozen beds.

'There's another dorm upstairs, but this is the best one,' informed Betty. 'The other has four beds, but they're all taken. We've got two spare in here, so you can take either one, and mine will be free soon.'

'You're leaving?'

'I should have gone about three weeks ago, but I picked up some illness and was terribly poorly. I'm better now though. Wait there whilst I find you some clothes, then after you've changed, I can show you around.'

May noticed a washstand in the far corner of the room and whilst Betty was gone, she removed her make-up and used a hand towel to dry off her soaking hair.

'These should do you,' said Betty, walking back into the room beaming broadly.

May took the grey dress and white apron, which appeared to be the standard issue clothing for the home, together with a bundle of clean underclothes.

'Strip off and give me your clothes. We'll put them through the laundry, though you'll not be needing them again. No doubt they can be donated to the poor.'

May hesitated, torn between the embarrassment of undressing in front of a stranger and the risk of undermining her story. Gritting her teeth, she forced herself to remove her dress, and hand it to the smiling Betty.

'I'll keep the rest of my things and let them dry overnight by the bed.'

'If that's what you want,' said Betty. 'When you're dressed, come downstairs and I'll show you where everything is.'

Once Betty had left, May put on her new clothes whilst trying to think what to do next. To start asking questions about Cora immediately would look too suspicious, so she resolved to wait until the morning.

***

'This is the laundry, where most of the work is done.'

May returned the smile of her guide, pretending to mirror Betty's enthusiasm. She had already seen the sewing room and the large drawing room where lessons in being a housemaid were given. Two of the other girls had been in the sewing room, the rest were working here, in the laundry.

'That's Sandra, the tall one's Maureen, Jane has the freckles, Bonnie is by the mangle, and of course you've met Victoria,'said Betty. 'She's a bit of a sneak,' she added conspiratorially. 'Work will finish soon. Then we'll have prayers followed by our evening meal. In the meantime, you can help me pack the laundered clothes ready for sending back out.'

May followed Betty into an ante room, where an assortment of clothes had been left neatly folded on three long tables.

'We just need to check where they are going and parcel them up with brown paper and string. These for example are belonging to the vicar of St Chads,' explained Betty.

'You seem very happy in your work here,' commented May.

'Oh, I am. Everyone's quite jolly here really, apart from Victoria. Even Mrs Hill is alright when you get to know her.' Betty paused '… but I miss the men of course.'

'The men?'

'You know what I mean,' she replied with a wink. 'That was always my weakness. I just couldn't say no. The problem is, there's no future in being on the street with everyone wanting to take advantage of you, and running the risk of getting your throat cut. I just hope I'll end up with a young master who's up for a bit of honest fun.'

May gave a polite nod of understanding, whilst feeling appalled at the girl's sheer audacity and lack of morality.

'Come on then, May. Let's get started. You can do the pile over there. They don't need much attention, as they're only being donated to the workhouse for inmates being released.'

***

It was later, in the dormitory, that Betty started to talk once more about her plans for the future. She had volunteered to brush May's hair for her, to get out the tangles caused by the earlier drenching.

Two of the other girls in the dormitory were chatting whilst Victoria lay in her bed, pretending to read.

'Of course, if I hadn't been taken ill, I would already be living in a grand house by now,' she prattled. 'I expect I'll be taken into service by a far more important household than Cora was.'

'Shut up about Cora,' interrupted Victoria. 'I don't know why you still keep gabbing on about her.'

'Who is Cora?' asked May innocently.

'She was my friend and I should have gone at the same time as her. If she'd waited for me to get better, we could have gone together and perhaps ended up in the same place.'

'You still might, so shut up,' snapped Victoria.

Betty bent forward and whispered in May's ear. 'She's just jealous because when one of our benefactors came to consider placing us in service, he only wanted me and Cora.'

'I can see why Victoria is annoyed,' sympathised May. 'It's understandable. Tell me, who is this benefactor?'

'A man called Mr Warren. He's been here before, but I don't like him very much. He smokes those awful Turkish cigarettes and he stinks of tobacco.'

'Why are you so keen to go with him then?'

'Oh, it wouldn't be his household I would be joining, silly,' teased Betty. 'All he does is find us a place in service, and apparently there was somewhere special he had in mind.'

'How long will you have to wait? Mrs Hill said you would be going soon.'

Betty shrugged. 'I just don't know. Cora went at a moment's notice, so I expect it'll be the same for me.'

May grimaced. She had hoped to find out what she could and get out the following day, but it looked like it might take longer. At least she had confirmation that Cora had left with Warren.

After Betty finished brushing her hair, May settled down for the night, removing a small pouch from within the top of her corset and placing it inside the small cupboard next to her bed.

Soon afterwards, Mrs Hill came round to ensure all lamps were extinguished and once she was gone, May reached into her cupboard, carefully removed the small bottle of laudanum, and took a sip. It was hardly a measured dose, but it would be enough to waylay the symptoms of muscle spasms which had started to cause her discomfort.

***

Chard entered Brougham Square concerned whether his recent visits were being noted by any malevolent neighbours. He had waited until darkness fell and hoped his arrival in the dimly-lit square would not draw undue attention. The afternoon's rain had not returned, but there was a chill wind and many homes had lit their fires, leaving the smell of coal heavy in the air. He approached the Lambs' door and gave it a rap.

'Get in! Quick!' demanded George, almost dragging his visitor inside. Barney squeezed through the door before it closed and made for the small mat in front of the fire.

'What's the matter?' asked Chard alarmed at his friend's urgency.

'The coppers have been around today, asking if anyone has seen anything or anyone suspicious.'

'Why call on you? Has anyone seen me?'

'No. They were asking at every house as a matter of course, but it's getting risky, mon. You can't come here again.'

Chard nodded. 'Understood. Has Harbury been in touch?'

George relaxed a little and gave a slight smile. 'He sent someone around. A draw, 2-2 with Wolves doing everything but score in the last five minutes. It must have been quite a game.'

'Unfortunately, I had to leave before the end, but I heard the result earlier this evening. I take it Harbury is pleased?'

George laughed. 'Damn pleased, I'd say. It must have been one hell of a wager. He cancelled my debt, sorted out two weeks lodgings for you at the Plough and Harrow, where the pony and trap is stabled, and handed over a bag of coins.'

'I'm afraid I'm going to need all the money he gave you, George. I've got a lead on the likely murderer of my wife and I'll need money to follow it up.'

George frowned. 'What about our Cora? Remember our deal!'

'I haven't forgotten,' promised Chard, placing s hand on his friend's shoulder. 'Miss Roper believes she can find something out. I hope to have some information on Monday evening.'

'Good, I'll wait to hear from you, but don't come to the house. I'll call in at the Plough and Harrow every so often and ask after you. The landlady's no friend of the police and won't ask awkward questions.'

'Can you look after the dog for me? For a couple of days at least?'

George gave a reluctant nod, then went upstairs and for the money sent by Harbury. 'Take it, Tommy, and for God's sake be careful!'

***

As he approached the Plough and Harrow, Chard remembered that the owner would have been told by Harbury to expect a man with a bandaged face and injured arm. Hopefully a Yorkshire accent would not have been mentioned, it was a lot more difficult to maintain than at first thought.

Pretending he had a useless left arm would not be entirely without risk, because there was always a chance he would bump into someone who'd seen him at the football match; but there was no option. Crossing the fingers of his left hand for luck, Chard pulled open the front door and went inside.

Being a Saturday night, the bar was crowded and on seeing the newcomer enter, with his curiously covered face, they turned and stared.

'Don't gawp at the poor man! I've been expecting him. Lost the use of his arm and half his face in an accident. Shame on you!' scolded a woman's voice.

Through the thick tobacco smoke pervading the room a tall woman with wild grey hair came forward and took his free arm.

'I'm Liz Donnelly, the landlady. Arrangements have been made for you to have a room for the next two weeks if you need it. There's no-one else staying here other than my lodger, Mr Edmonds.'

'I'd like to be able to rest a while,' said Chard, waiting to see if his lack of a northern accent would be queried.

'Then come with me. Your room overlooks the stables and I'll give you a key to the back door, so you can come and go as you please.'

Chard was led upstairs to a small bedroom, and he waited whilst the landlady lit a small oil lamp on a side table.

'You should be quite comfortable. I'll bring you some food later,' she promised before leaving him alone in the room. Chard assumed her keenness to please him was due to fear of Harbury.

He sat down on the bed, which creaked, and looked at his surroundings. The room seemed clean and tidy but there was a pervasive smell of tobacco. All of a sudden, he felt tired, and the enormity of his mission seemed to overwhelm him.

The only motive he had for his wife's murder was that someone hated Landell enough to kill him, and she was unfortunate enough to be with him at the wrong time. Landell had stolen from his two partners and owed money to a villain from Birmingham, so they had to be the most likely suspects. But what if there was someone else?

Chard shook his head. No, it has to be Foden, he told himself.

Without warning, he began to shake inside. He knew it was down to the shock of his recent experiences and the latent grief of hearing Sofia had died so horribly, but could do nothing about it. When the landlady returned with some supper, he asked for a bottle of whiskey.

The food was good and Chard ate it quickly, not having realised just how hungry he'd been, then started to drink. Removing his head bandage, he lay back on the bed fully clothed.

'I'll get you, you bastard,' he muttered before drifting off to sleep, clutching the half-empty bottle.

TWENTY-ONE

May was woken at six o'clock in the morning, with the rest of the dormitory. After their ablutions, the girls had dressed and assembled downstairs for inspection by Mrs Hill. After prayers and a sustaining though not appetising breakfast, the morning chores were allocated and the girls began to work. Much to her frustration, May was sent to the laundry, whilst Betty was taken aside for extra domestic instruction.

It was three hours of hard physical work before the other girls, familiar with the routine, took a short break. May's arms, the sleeves of her dress having been rolled up, were red from being immersed in hot water and she felt sweat dripping from her brow. The possibility of having to stay in the Salop Home for another day or two was worrying. The one week's absence from her job in Pontypridd was up the following day, and her parents would be terribly concerned if she didn't return. Yet things could not be left as they were. Inspector Chard had to be helped, but that wasn't the only reason. For the first time, May felt the grip laudanum had over her was broken. There were still some side effects of not taking it, such as the occasional muscle spasms; but she no longer felt she needed it. Last night's dose was hopefully the last, or perhaps almost the last.

Abruptly, the chattering of the other girls on their break was interrupted by a sharp clap of hands; and all became silent. Heads turned towards Mrs Hill who stood in the doorway.

'May, follow me if you please!'

Puzzled, May followed the matriarch out of the laundry and into the drawing room.

'Close the door behind you,' ordered Mrs Hill sternly.

May did as she was told then stood silently, hands clasped in front of her, with head bowed.

'It has come to my attention that you have broken the rules of this institution.'

May raised her head. 'In what way ma'am?'

Mrs Hill held out her hand. 'Can you explain this? I assume you know what it is?'

May looked at her small bottle of laudanum. 'Yes ma'am. It's laudanum, prescribed for me by a doctor,' she answered truthfully.

'I am shocked! How would you afford a doctor? For that matter why would he prescribe it, when it can be bought openly?'

'But…'

'I'll hear no more! There was also a door key in your cupboard, so you are hardly homeless. I don't know what your game is young lady, but frankly I was dubious about your story yesterday, and this confirms my doubts. Clearly you still have some vices and are untruthful. Pack your things and go!'

May was annoyed with herself for not having hidden her laudanum and the key to her room at the YWCA, rather than just leaving them in the bedside cupboard. Leaving immediately would normally be ideal, but not without knowing when Betty would be taken by Warren.

'I assume the clothes you arrived in are still in the laundry, so pick them up and leave what you are wearing on your bed,' added Mrs Hill. 'Take your bottle with you. The door key and the money you brought is still in your cupboard.'

'Could I have a word with Betty before I go?' asked May hopefully.

'No, you cannot. She is leaving here for a new life this very afternoon and I don't want her thinking about anything else.'

May's hopes rose and she found it hard to suppress a smile as an idea began to form. 'Yesterday, I packed up a parcel of old clothes to be given to the poor. I haven't anything of my own other than what I was wearing when I came here. I don't suppose I could take the parcel for myself, could I?'

'Old clothes?' sniffed Mrs Hill. 'I suppose so. As long as it gets you out of here. Be gone in the next half hour!'

Finding it hard to conceal her joy, May left the room and headed back to the laundry, noticing a smirking Victoria in the corridor.

When she reached the laundry May saw the others were trying not to stare. They clearly sensed something important had transpired, but said nothing as she swept past.

May found her clothes from the previous day without much difficulty. They hadn't been laundered but at least they were dry. Putting them under her arm, she went to look for the parcel. It might not be needed, but it seemed a good idea and May smiled broadly when she found it. Hurrying back up to the dormitory, she changed, took the key and her few coins from the bedside cupboard and left clutching the parcel.

***

Harry Foden picked up the small china vase off the mantlepiece and hurled it angrily at the far wall, where it disintegrated with a loud crash.

'I gave you a simple fucking thing to do, Pitt!' he yelled. 'Just find their best player and keep him away from the match.'

'I *did* find him and I locked him up after a fight with the man protecting him. Blame Carson, our spy in Harbury's camp. I left him guarding the door and he ran off.'

Foden grunted. 'What have you done with him?'

'Nothing for now, Mr Foden. He's come to us because he knows that whoever chased him off is liable to tell Harbury and then he'll be dead. I've sent him to the infirmary to fix his arm. It was broken in the fight.'

'Let him think he can join us, then drop him in the canal after dark,' ordered Foden. Taking a cigarette from a silver case, he lit it and inhaled deeply. 'It was a miracle Shrewsbury managed to hold out for the draw. Luck was against us. The losses can be covered, but in future I'll need to be more selective. Expanding into Shropshire will have to wait.'

'I don't understand why Shropshire was of interest, if you don't mind me saying so, Mr Foden,' said Pitt deferentially. 'It's mostly cattle, sheep and grass.'

Foden sighed. 'It's also rich landowners, men of influence and somewhere out of our usual area where we could hide the profits from other activities. The biggest gamblers in any county are the rich, so control the illegal betting and you also control them. Anyway, there are other things to concentrate on. I've had word that our second piece of merchandise is coming this afternoon. Once she's settled in, I can make the arrangements for our trip across to France.'

'Our trip? You mean I'm coming as well Mr Foden?'

'I'll need you and one other. The girls are a goodwill offering to my contact in Paris. He has a particular liking for blonde-haired girls with blue eyes in his establishments, so I promised him a pair. If all goes according to plan, our activities will reach beyond these shores and we'll be moving into the import and export business.'

'Who's bringing the girl?'

'A man called Warren. I found out he's a pervert with some particular preferences, and he's greedy. He procured the first one for a reasonable payment and a free go on our girls at the Orchid. This second one is a late delivery so he'll get paid less, but when he gets to the Orchid let him have his pick of our regulars.' Foden then gave a hearty laugh and corrected himself. 'No, on second thoughts make sure you offer him Mary. She's looks like a goddess, but I hear she's poxed up.'

Pitt grinned, but then straightened his expression when he noticed Foden staring at him. 'Just remember something Pitt. No-one is indispensable. Fail me again like you did over the football match and it'll be you in the canal!'

*****

May had held her parcel close to her body, hiding her low-cut dress, as she sneaked back into the YWCA. Wearing something more suitable for a respectable young woman's Sunday attire, she stood outside her boyfriend's lodging house, waiting for him to appear.

'May! I am so glad you are alright. I was afraid you might have done something rash,' said Morgan, giving her a hug.

'There's no time for a *cwtch*, Idris,' she scolded. 'Time is of the essence.'

'Why? What have you found out?'

'I've confirmed Cora did leave with Mr Warren. What's more, he's taking another girl this afternoon. If we follow them, they may lead us to Cora.'

'What time this afternoon?' asked Morgan.

'No idea. That's why we'll need to hurry.'

'I'll get my cap and jacket.'

As Morgan turned to go back inside the lodging house, May tugged his sleeve.

'Is there someone who can deliver this parcel to George Lamb's house?' she asked, holding out the large bundle.

'Why? What's inside it?'

'You don't need to know. Is there anyone?'

'There's the owner's son. He seems a reliable sort,' answered Morgan, stroking his whiskers.

'Then give the parcel to him and ask if he can deliver it straight away. I've written the address and a message on this piece of paper,' explained May.

Morgan looked at the message which read "for our injured friend" and shrugged. 'I'll be back in a couple of minutes.'

As soon as he returned, the couple set off across town and found a spot close to the river where they could observe the approach to the Salop Home.

'I saw the inspector yesterday afternoon,' said Morgan as they waited for Warren to turn up.

'How was he?' asked May, her voice full of concern.

'First, he fooled me, wearing a hideous disguise. Then later on I found him locked up in a storeroom and had to get him out.'

'What on earth was he doing?'

'I'm not entirely sure, but he said if things worked out, there was a chance he'd have funds for us tomorrow night.'

'I must admit I'm starting to run out of money,' confessed May. 'I am supposed to return home tomorrow.'

'You might still be able to do that. If we can find where Cora is, then you'll have done all you can.'

'What about you?'

Morgan shrugged. 'The Shrewsbury police have written to Superintendent Jones asking if I can stay here for a while to help their investigation. I don't know if he'll agree, but if he does, at least my lodgings will be paid for by the constabulary.'

'Why do they want you to help?'

'I don't think they really do. Inspector Warboys wants to keep an eye on me in case I try and help Inspector Chard. I think someone was following me last night, but I can't be sure.'

'Where did you go?' asked May.

'Just around the town trying to track down the bailiff who found the bodies.'

'Any luck?'

Morgan shook his head. 'Not really. The best I could get out of people was that he had started calling in at the Three Fishes for the occasional meal; but not last night. You'd think he'd be easy to find with the name Scratch Harper.'

Unexpectedly, May swung around, alerted by a sound in a nearby bush. She grabbed Morgan's arm as a rat shot out and headed for the river.

'Oh my!' she gasped. 'What a fright!'

'You've seen rats before,' scoffed Morgan.

'It had nothing to do with it being a rat. Because you said you might have been followed last night, I thought someone was spying on us. Are you sure no-one has followed us today?'

'Calm down,' assured Morgan, 'we aren't doing anything illegal, and in any case, I've been glancing behind to make sure there's no-one there. I'll just have to be very careful tomorrow night when I meet Inspector Chard.'

'Where are we meeting him?'

'I'm meeting him at a pub called the Prince of Wales in Bynner Street. He was very clear you are not to come,' emphasised Morgan.

'But I want to help,' argued May.

'You've done enough, and so have I. We can only do so much. As it is, we could still end up both losing our jobs, let alone getting a prison sentence. Once I've seen him tomorrow, that'll be it. I don't mind causing the Shrewsbury police a little bit of confusion with any advice I give them, but that's the full extent of it.'

'I can understand your reluctance, being a policeman; but I'm prepared to do more.'

Morgan looked at May curiously. When he'd first got to know her, May was quiet, reserved, vulnerable even. She'd been recovering from serious injury and the memory of it had turned her to laudanum. Recently her temperament had changed and he found it unsettling.

'We have to use common sense. There's a degree of risk that we cannot take.'

'You're saying we as if you speak for both of us. Well, you don't. I have a mind of my own.'

'And a very headstrong one at that,' retorted Morgan. 'Why have you changed? I've never known you like this.'

'I haven't. This is how I used to be, and don't you dare call me headstrong ever again!'

May pursed her lips and fell into a sullen silence, causing Morgan to respond in kind.

***

'Look! There he is,' whispered May, punching Morgan on the arm.

The wait had been a long one and the pair had hardly spoken for several hours.

'About bloody time!' cursed Morgan. 'It's early evening.'

'I'll ignore the bad language just this once,' murmured May. 'Just keep your voice down.'

The pair watched as Warren removed the cigarette he'd been smoking and stubbed it out underfoot, before entered the building. It was some time before he re-emerged, but when he did there was a giggling blonde-haired girl at his side.

'That's Betty,' confirmed May.

'Pretty little thing,' commented Morgan before getting a poke in the ribs.

May scowled. 'Come on, Idris. We must keep up with them.'

It was clear Betty was chatting excitedly; and Warren was too busy trying to fend off her questions to check if they were being followed. Initially heading for English Bridge, they unexpectedly went down a small set of steps leading to the path by the river. They then walked along the eastern side of the river loop before proceeding up the exceedingly steep Water's Lane that led back into the town.

'A clever route,' puffed May. 'They've cut out having to go

through most of the town centre. I think they're heading for the railway station.'

The prediction was correct and Morgan sighed as they watched the short man buy a pair of tickets.

'I can't get near. Betty would recognise me,' said May, pushing Morgan forward. 'Try and find out where they're going.'

'Warren would recognise either of us!' he complained.

'Just do it!' hissed May.

She watched as Morgan went within earshot of Warren's conversation with the ticket clerk, then frowned as she saw him search through his pockets, evidently trying to get together enough money to pay for a fare.

With Betty still chatting incessantly, Warren led the way towards the platforms, whilst Morgan talked to the ticket clerk before handing over some money. Looking exceedingly ill-tempered he returned to May's side holding a pair of tickets.

'Ever been to Birmingham?' he asked.

***

'This disguise is going all to hell,' muttered Chard, looking at his reflection in the washstand's mirror. The staining on the lower part of his face from the dark fruit, which had looked so effective, had faded. In addition, the bandage over the top half of his face was slipping, causing the gap that exposed his eyes to obscure his vision. At least his stubble gave him a suitably disreputable appearance. He grunted with a small degree of satisfaction as he patted the padding inside his shirt. It was still effective in making him look fatter and providing he kept his left arm hanging useless in its sling, he could move around the town in daylight.

'How on earth am I going to get to Foden like this?' he asked himself. A businessman, even a criminal one, would hardly accept a meeting with someone who looked like a crippled tramp.

Chard's thoughts were interrupted by a knock on the door of his room.

'Mr Smith? It's Mrs Donnelly. A man has left a parcel for you.'

'What man?' asked Chard, full of curiosity.

'Ginger-haired chap. He wouldn't stay. Shall I leave the parcel outside your door?'

'Yes please, Mrs Donnelly.'

After waiting to hear the landlady's footsteps go back down the stairs, Chard opened the door and took in the parcel. Frowning in puzzlement, he put it on the bed and started to undo the wrapping. Once he'd unfolded the contents, he beamed broadly. 'Good old George!' he exclaimed.

TWENTY-TWO

Warren and Betty left New Street station completely unaware that they were being followed.

'Look at the size of this station, it's huge. There must be over a dozen platforms,' exclaimed Morgan.

'Come on Idris, we mustn't lose them,' urged May as she tugged at his sleeve.

'Calm down, May. This isn't like you. Are you sure you are alright?'

'I don't think I've ever felt so alive. This is the first time I've been to a city.'

'I wouldn't expect too much of it,' cautioned Morgan. 'Don't forget it's Sunday and our last train back to Shrewsbury is in a couple of hours. We've just got to hope Warren isn't going very far.'

The couple watched as Warren and Betty left the station and approached a line of hansom cabs.

Morgan groaned. 'If they take a cab we might lose them.'

Fortunately, Warren led the girl beyond the vehicles, out onto the street.

May gave a sigh of relief. 'It looks like luck is with us. I'm sure this is going to work out alright. We just need to keep them in sight.'

'I can't believe it's so busy for a Sunday evening,' commented Morgan as they walked along the noisy, busy street. 'It must be because the English are allowed to drink on a Sunday. Bloody heathens.'

'Stop cursing! Oh dear! I think we've lost them,' exclaimed May.

'No! I can see them. Warren has stopped to light a cigarette,' said Morgan triumphantly.

They watched as Warren took Betty by the arm and led her down another street, changing direction about a hundred yards further ahead.

'Where are we?' asked May.

'A sign up there says Dale End,' answered Morgan. 'They can't be going much further or they would have taken a cab.'

'Look, you're right. They're going into that building,' said May excitedly.

'Yes, and there's something going on. The girl seems to be arguing,' commented Morgan as they watched a woman in a bright red dress come out of the premises, grab Betty and drag her inside. Warren looked around the street nervously then also entered the building.

'Shall I go in after her?'

'No, Idris. Not until we know what 's going on and if Cora is in there.' May pointed to a sign across the road which read The Star Wine Vaults. 'Let's go in there. It should give us a good view of the building'

Morgan went through the doorway of the public house, and after a quick look inside to ensure it was reasonably respectable, signalled for May to follow.

'I cannot believe there are so many people drinking on the Sabbath,' she whispered. 'I'll go to that free table by the window whilst you fetch us some lemonade.'

Morgan went to the bar, returning a couple of minutes later with a glass of lemonade and a pint of bitter. 'What can you see?' he asked, putting the drinks on the table.

May scowled as she saw the beer. 'It looks like some kind of restaurant, but the curtains are closed. It's difficult to see with it being so dark outside, but there's a small sign next to the door, I think it's showing some kind of flower. There's a streetlamp close by so when it's lit up, we may be able to make it out.'

'I reckon we've got about an hour before we have to head back for the train,' said Morgan, sipping his pint and leaving a coat of foam on his moustache. 'All we can do is hope Warren comes out before then. If he does, I'll challenge him on the spot.'

May shook her head. 'When the streetlight comes on and I can see the sign properly we can describe the place to Inspector Chard. He'll know what to do for the best. If necessary, we can come back again.'

'No!' argued Morgan. 'We're too involved as it is. Let's just find out what we can and that's an end to it,' he said firmly. 'Wait here,' he ordered, before downing his pint in three gulps.

Wiping his whiskers with his forearm, Morgan went up to the bar and ordered a fresh pint of beer, unaware that he had caught the attention of a rat-faced man with an arm in a sling, standing on the far side of the room.

Waiting for his beer, Morgan nodded in a friendly manner to the next man at the bar, who was busily eating a cheese roll. He looked a genial old fellow, so Morgan felt it was safe to strike up a conversation.

'Good evening to you. I'm a stranger to the city. Could you tell me a bit about this street?'

The man took another mouthful of his roll, before replying. 'As long as yer don't mind me chobbling on this cob. It's bostin' fittle.'

Morgan had to concentrate hard on trying to understand his broad accent and strange words, and didn't notice the rat-faced man leave the pub in a hurry.

'What's the place across the road? It looks like some sort of restaurant,' said Morgan, reaching for the fresh beer that the barman had placed on the counter.

The local man laughed, sending bits of cheese from his mouth. 'You must be yampy,' he declared. 'It's the Crimson Orchid. Wenches aplenty, but only if you've got the ackers.' He rubbed his thumb against his fingers indicating he was talking about money.

Morgan realised the implication and nodded his thanks, before returning to his companion.

'What was that all about?' asked May.

'It's a knocking shop. I mean a brothel,' added Morgan.

'I know the term. You don't work in a workhouse infirmary without picking up these things. But surely it's a bit conspicuous?'

'I was thinking the same,' agreed Morgan. 'I know you can't really tell from outside for certain, and the name, which is The Crimson Orchid by the way, could be some kind of club or restaurant; but if a random man at the bar knows about it, then it's hardly a secret.'

'Whoever owns it must have some kind of influence with the authorities,' said May.

'If that's the case then we need to be cautious. Perhaps you're right and I'd better not challenge Warren.'

'I suggest that once we've finished our drinks, we should go back to New Street station,' agreed May.

By the time the couple were ready to leave, the streetlights had been lit, leaving Dale End with pools of dim gaslight illuminating the occasional stretch of pavement. As they headed back in the direction of the station Morgan stopped abruptly. Up ahead, under a streetlight were three young men. His experience as a police constable, patrolling the streets of Pontypridd on a Saturday night, instinctively told him they were looking for trouble.

'I think we'd better go a different way,' he said to May in a low voice.

Turning around, they set off in the opposite direction, with the intention of taking a turn at the next junction and finding an alternative route.

As they entered a dark patch of pavement there was a whistle from behind them, followed by an answering whistle from ahead. To May's alarm she noticed the shapes of two other men headed directly towards them.

'Quickly, we'll try this alley,' said Morgan, breaking into a run and dragging May with him.

It was dark, lit only by the glow from the nearby chemical factory, whose acrid fumes produced an eerie yellow haze.

'Shit! It's a dead end,' cursed Morgan. They were trapped.

The five men had followed them into the alley, and four stepped forward whilst the fifth, his arm in a sling, stayed back. The largest spoke. His voice a dull monotone that marked him as a local man.

'Now what would you be doing here?'

'What do you mean?' asked Morgan, glancing around anxiously for something to use as a weapon.

'How is it that someone who works for Harbury in Shrewsbury, happens to turn up on our patch the day after he won the wager?'

'Who's Harbury and what wager?' asked Morgan, pushing May behind him.

'Are you sure it's him?' The words were addressed to the man with an injured arm.

'Yes, Pitt. He chased me off and with the state of my arm I couldn't defend myself.'

'I don't know what he's talking about,' lied Morgan.

'Yes. Let us go,' added May.

Pitt hesitated for a moment, then shrugged and took a step forward.

Realising they were both in real danger, May gave an ear-piercing scream, hoping to draw attention to their plight. The man with the broken arm immediately ran off, and Pitt halted, momentarily distracted.

Seeing his chance, Morgan swung a boot at him, which failed to connect. Luckily, the narrowness of the alley made it difficult for the peaky blinders to make their numbers count. May screamed again, then hid behind a wooden barrel.

'Have this you bastard,' shouted Pitt as he sent a punch towards Morgan's stomach, a blow which the constable, used to fighting drunk miners on a Saturday night, easily blocked. One of Pitt's men tried to kick him in the leg, but to no effect, whilst the other two were still unable to give blows in the confined space.

May screamed again.

Morgan backed off in her direction, allowing his attackers more space. Desperately fending off several blows, Morgan was unable to prevent Pitt grabbing him by the throat and pushing him to the back of the dead end. He clawed at Pitt's face but couldn't break his grip.

'No!' cried May, coming from behind her cover to grab Pitt's arm.

One of the peaky blinders tried to push her away, but she pulled at one of Pitt's arms, giving Morgan enough leverage to put his forehead into his attacker's face.

Pitt cursed as he felt blood run down his face from a cut above his eye. At the end of the alley, the space was again compressed and Morgan realised that Pitt couldn't move back due to his men pressing from behind. Roaring with anger, he swung a fist at the side of Pitt's head. Unluckily it missed, which was his undoing. Pitt grabbed Morgan's arm and twisted it, forcing the constable towards the ground. There was a sickening crack as another thug sent his hobnailed boot into the constable's ribs. Morgan gave a groan and dropped prostrate as a flurry of kicks followed. May screamed again and flailed helplessly at their attackers.

'Drag him out of the way,' ordered Pitt.

His three accomplices pulled Morgan's inert form back up the alley, before returning and standing behind Pitt as he faced the helpless, tearful May.

'Now it's your turn,' he said cruelly, unbuckling the belt of his trousers.

Before May could scream again, there was a sudden burst of light and a female voice cut through the night.

'Stop right there, John Pitt.'

A young woman appeared as if from nowhere. She carried a small oil lamp in one hand and there was something in the other directed at Pitt's face.

'My hat pin is about an inch from your eyeball, and you know I'll use it,' she threatened.

From the light of the lamp May could see a dark-haired woman, of slender build, wearing a dress decorated with pearl buttons. There was a gleam of silver as the lamp picked out the eight-inch needle-sharp hatpin.

'Calm down Tilly, it's none of your business,' said Pitt, his hands still at his trouser belt.

'There'll be coppers here in no time. Everybody will have heard the screams and they'll have sent someone to the station for help, so you'd best be away,' she answered. 'You'll get off of course, but they'll have to arrest you for a night in the cells.'

Very slowly, Pitt backed away. 'I've not finished with you,' he snarled, pointing at May. 'If I see you around here again, you'll get what you deserve.'

The woman called Tilly kept her hatpin at eye level and stood next to the weeping May.

'Come on lads, we'd better go,' said Pitt, gesturing that they should leave.

The men turned to go and May gave a sigh of relief.

'Just one more thing though,' said Pitt. He reached inside his pocket, took out a small knife then bent over the unconscious Morgan.

'What's he doing? Stop him!' screamed May.

Pitt stood up, holding a fleshy object. In the flickering lamplight, May saw blood trickling down his hand; then she fainted.

***

May opened her eyes and looked at the ceiling. She was laying on something soft in a dimly-lit room.

'Awake at last,' said a soft voice.

Images of the alley and Morgan lying helpless flooded back into her memory, and she sat up in panic. 'Idris. How's Idris? Where is he? What did they do to him?'

'Calm down and drink this. I'm Tilly and I'll look after you.'

May looked at the woman who sat next to her, holding out a glass of something which smelled strongly of alcohol. She wore a colourful scarf around her neck and her fringe hung down to her eyes.

May took the drink and swallowed it in one gulp, which made her splutter uncontrollably for what seemed an eternity.

'Don't worry about your man. He's going to be alright. I had friends take him to the infirmary.'

'But what did they do to him? I saw the knife, and blood,' demanded May.

'I'm afraid John took his ear, but at least he'll live.'

May looked at Tilly with suspicion. 'John? You know the beast who attacked us? Why did he listen to you so quickly?'

Tilly waved a placatory hand. 'For one thing because he knew I would have put my hatpin through his eye; and for another, he's my husband.'

May jumped to her feet, immediately felt nauseous, then sat down again.

'Calm yourself. I came up from London full of daft ideas and wed him without knowing what I was letting myself in for. Our marriage lasted all of two months before I left him.'

May took several deep breaths, trying to regain her composure. 'I've got to see Idris.'

Tilly shook her head. 'No point. The infirmary wouldn't let you see him at this late hour, and it's too dangerous for you to be out and about on these streets at night. One of my neighbours is friends with one of the nurses. I'll ask him if he can have a word with whoever is on duty. They might tell him how your man is doing. Wait here whilst I'm gone.'

Tilly poured May another drink then left the room.

Instinctively May reached inside her dress and removed the small bottle of laudanum from its hiding place. For the first time in days she felt a real need to calm her nerves, which were causing her heart to race madly. Just a sip felt comforting and May realised it was the familiarity of putting the bottle to her lips that relaxed her, more than the drug.

A short while later, feeling the need to relieve herself, May looked at her surroundings. It seemed that Tilly lived in this single room, and it didn't appear as if there was an indoor privy. Desperately, she felt beneath the bed for the usual facility. Her searching hand grabbed what she assumed was the chamber pot, though it was exceedingly heavy.

'What…?' she exclaimed as she pulled the object into the light.

***

'I'm sorry I was so long. I decided to go with my neighbour to the infirmary,' announced Tilly.

'How is he?' asked May anxiously.

'Two broken ribs, a nasty blow to the head and of course the loss of his ear. He'll have to stay in the infirmary for a week. He'd been asking after you, so I told the nurse to pass on the message that you are safe.'

'Thank you. I'll return in the morning and visit him, but what time is it? I need to get back to Shrewsbury.'

'You won't get a train now. You'll have to stay here tonight. I can make a bed up for you on the floor and there's a pot under my bed if you need one, but let me get it out.'

May felt her cheeks redden at the offer and averted her eyes.

'Oh, my Gawd!' she exclaimed Tilly, the colour draining from her face. 'You found it didn't you? I just didn't think. It's been there so long.'

'I'm sorry. I was looking for a chamber pot and pulled it out instead. It must be worth a fortune,' confessed May

'I took it from a shop window last year after a row with John. Now I'm stuck with it,' replied Tilly, removing the long, sharp hatpin from her hair. 'If I try and sell it on, it'll be recognised and no-one will want to touch it, so it just sits there.' She stared for a long time at May, as if trying to make up her mind about something. 'You realise that I can't let you tell anyone.'

'I won't, I promise,' swore May, feeling a sense of panic. 'You probably saved my life this evening.'

'You'll go to the law,' replied Tilly, shaking her head sadly and moving closer.

'Wait! Look, I can't tell anyone because I'm in trouble with the law myself.'

Tilly looked at May dubiously. 'You?'

'Yes. I swear it. I'm helping an escaped convict. Someone in prison for a murder he didn't commit. As God is my judge. It's a long story and complicated, but I swear it's true.'

'You've got all night to tell me about it. Then I'll decide what's to be done.'

TWENTY-THREE

Chard stepped off the mid-morning train at New Street station, put down the parcel he carried and adjusted the brim of his hat. It was unlikely anyone would be able to identify him in Birmingham, and with his bandage firmly in place tilting his hat forward was pointless; but it increased his confidence. There had been a nervous moment outside Shrewsbury station when a police constable had eyed him suspiciously; but with a glance at his infirm arm, the officer turned away.

Chard had visited Birmingham several years before and as he left the station, he had the impression it was much busier. There was a cacophony of noise from street sellers and shoppers; the clatter of hooves from the carts, omnibuses and carriages that clogged the streets; and the hammering of building work; which assaulted his senses. Low cloud gave a claustrophobic feel and the odour of horse manure seemed to permeate everything.

'Right then, Mr Foden. Time to find you,' Chard said to himself.

Taking care to hunch forward slightly and affect a slight limp, Chard walked along Corporation Street, glancing at the brass plates of any building which might contain an office. He passed the turning for Fore Street, then the larger intersection with Cherry Street and Union Street. At the next junction he stopped to stare at the Cobden Hotel, where he had stayed as a child when his father had taken him on a business trip. A building close to Bradford Passage drew his attention, but the name of the occupant of the first-floor offices had been defaced and was illegible. Keeping the possibility at the back of his mind, he carried on beyond Bull Street to the Old Square. As he watched the horse-drawn trams thunder past, he doubted the sense of going any further. Up ahead was the County Court. Would a villain like Foden really want to be so close to an institution representing the power of law and order? Chard shook his head. Crossing to the other side of Corporation Street, dodging a fast-moving tram as he did so, he retraced his route along the opposite pavement.

Just beyond the junction with Bull Street he stopped to speak to a skinny boy in a white apron, who was cleaning the front door of a pub.

'Good morning lad.'

The boy turned and jumped back involuntarily at the sight of the bandaged apparition.

'Er…,' he responded, rendered temporarily speechless.

'Don't worry. I just want some information,' Chard said reassuringly, whilst holding up a coin. 'Do you by any chance know a businessman by the name of Mr Foden. I believe he has an office on Corporation Street.'

The boy blanched. 'It's none of my business, mister. I can't tell you anything.'

Chard smiled inwardly. The lad did know Foden. He put down his parcel and produced more money. 'You haven't got to say anything. All you have to do is nod or shake your head. Do you understand?'

The boy glanced around nervously, looked at the money, then gave a slight nod.

'Good lad. Is his office on this side of the road?'

There was an almost imperceptible shake of the head.

'The other side then. Is it between here and New Street?'

The boy nodded.

'Between here and the Cobden Hotel?'

There was another quick nod, then the lad snatched the money and went inside.

Chard grinned. It must almost certainly be the place which had initially drawn his attention, close to Bradford Passage. His problem was that he didn't know what Foden looked like. They had both been at Lord Berwick's party, but that was some time ago and Chard's memory of the guests was hazy. There were two options, he could change into the clothes concealed in his parcel and call on the office immediately; or he could spend another hour or so waiting close by, in case anything useful developed. He chose the latter, and took up a position just inside Bradford Passage, looking like a vagrant, and waited.

***

May left Shrewsbury station and headed for the town centre and her room at the YWCA. It had been a long, stressful night and a busy guilt-laden morning. The discussion with Tilly had taken an age; and it was only after confiding every detail of her involvement with Inspector Chard and the situation regarding Freda Lamb's missing sister, that Tilly finally accepted her own secret was safe. May had slept fitfully and rose early to visit Idris in the infirmary. He looked pitiful with his head bandaged over his missing ear and bruising covering half his face. The doctor confirmed he would need to stay in the infirmary for up to a week to recover from his beating, and to ensure there was no infection from his wound.

I'll have to meet the inspector tonight. How on earth am I going to be able to tell him I've given everything away to Tilly? May asked herself continually. He'll be furious.

Walking into the YWCA building in Princess Street, May was brought up short by a shrill voice.

'Miss Roper!'

May looked up to stare at a tall grim-faced woman standing behind the reception desk. She wore a black unadorned dress which matched her severe expression.

'Yes?' replied May rather sharply.

'It has come to my attention that you have not stayed in your room for the last two nights.'

'I have paid for the room,' snapped May, more concerned with her own problems than maintaining proper manners.

'Only until this morning.'

May cursed herself for forgetting she should have been returning to Pontypridd that morning. What would she tell her parents; and Doctor Henderson for that matter?

'I'll have to stay for a while longer,' she said, starting to walk towards the stairs.

'I am not sure if it would be quite appropriate,' responded the YWCA receptionist. 'This is a facility for respectable young ladies.

Not for those who stay out all night and return in the morning looking unkempt.'

May suddenly realised that apart from not having arranged her hair tidily, the back of her dress was covered in stains from the assault in the alley. Her temper then sparked at the frustration of not being able to tell the truth. Walking back to stand in front of the reception desk she rounded at her accuser.

'What are you trying to suggest?'

'I think that is self-evident,' sniffed the woman haughtily.

May felt duty bound to respond but could only think of a lie. 'I will have you know I have been at the bedside of my dying aunt. She passed away in the early hours of this morning, and I felt so distraught on my way back here that I slipped and fell in the gutter.'

The woman's face fell, her indignant expression replaced by one of guilt. 'I'm sorry,' she apologised, just as someone entered.

'Good morning. I've just come to leave a collection tin for our charity,' came a familiar voice.

May glanced at the newcomer then swiftly turned her head away. Not fast enough.

'What is *she* doing here?' demanded Mrs Hill from the Salop Home.

'That's Miss May Roper, one of our residents. I'm afraid he has just suffered a bereavement after being out all night, caring for her aunt.'

'May Roper indeed! That's May Feather! She's a drug-taking street girl who I had to remove from our premises.'

Without stopping to defend herself, May ran up the stairs to her room to pack her things.

Five minutes later she re-appeared, red with embarrassment as the two women in the foyer stood, stern faced and arms folded, as they watched her depart.

Now what do I do? May asked herself. There was no option other than to try and stay on. She had to meet Chard in Idris's place that evening which meant one more night at least. Hopefully the inspector would have some funds which she might be able to borrow. It seemed fate was determining that she should see this through to the end, whatever the cost.

***

'The man you found apparently had a broken arm and probably the pain made him stumble and fall into the canal. Your witness didn't see young Mr Pitt push him in. They were probably drunk and made a mistake, don't you think?'

'I think we can come to an arrangement, Harry.'

Chard tilted up the brim of his hat. One of the men speaking wore the uniform of a police superintendent, but it was his companion who drew Chard's attention. Respectably dressed, but with an air of unpleasantness.

'Good. I have a meeting shortly, but perhaps we can meet later to finalise the details. Somewhere discreet. Perhaps behind the cathedral? Say three o'clock?'

The policeman nodded and walked away in the direction of the county court, whilst Harry Foden entered the building which housed his office.

'Lucky me,' Chard muttered. He had wondered how best to approach Foden, but now the overheard conversation and his planned disguise would work in his favour. Picking up his parcel, Chard headed back towards the station, then turned into New Street to purchase a hold-all and a cut-throat razor. Then he headed for the city's market where he obtained a pair of second hand, thick-rimmed spectacles. Happy with his purchases, the fugitive inspector used the public convenience in New Street Station to transform himself.

'Ha!' he exclaimed, pleased with the reflection in the washroom mirror.

The bandage, padding, coat, and other old clothes were crammed in the hold-all. Nathaniel Smith the crippled vagrant had become Reverend Nathaniel Smith who presumably, given the rough beard that was developing, was a returning missionary.

'Pity about the trousers,' Chard thought. Evidently the vicar of St Chads was shorter than himself, for the bottom of the trousers flapped around his ankles. The spectacles were impossible to see through, thick lenses having been required by the previous owner, but Chard found he could balance them low on his nose, enabling him to see over the top of the frame.

After depositing the hold-all with a porter for storage, Chard set off for Foden's office, loitering on the opposite pavement until he saw someone appear at the entrance. Crossing the road between the busy traffic, he saw the person leaving was a smartly dressed man of dark complexion

'Mr Foden would prefer you did not come to his office again, Mr Cole,' said a young man in waistcoat and shirtsleeves who had followed the visitor to the doorstep.

Chard pretended to be just passing by and just gave a glance at the man who was leaving. For a brief moment their eyes met, and there was a mutual flicker of recognition. Neither said a word. Chard carried on to his previous vantage spot at Bradford Passage, and when he turned, Cole had disappeared from sight.

At a quarter to three, Foden emerged and Chard followed him as he went to a nearby bank. Five minutes later he emerged with a large envelope under his arm and headed for the cathedral.

'Clever!' thought Chard. It hadn't been difficult to come to the conclusion that Foden was going to bribe the superintendent over the crime they had discussed. But it would have been easy to assume that the transfer of money would take place at night, perhaps in a dark alley. It was a mistake many criminals made. Such clandestine meetings were nearly always observed by someone, and their very manner drew suspicion. The cathedral was discreet for the very reason that the grounds were busy. Nobody paid any attention to people passing by and exchanging the odd word or pleasantry. If the superintendent had gone into Foden's office in the middle of the day and come out with a large envelope someone might comment, but a casual brush-pass and nod to an acquaintance? Who would notice whether the policeman carried an envelope before or after, amidst the general goings-on? In this instance, Chard would.

As anticipated, whilst passing a group of schoolchildren being taken into the cathedral, the superintendent made as if to stumble. Foden came forward to lend the officer a steadying hand, and the transaction discreetly took place.

Foden stood for a while, looking pleased with himself, until the superintendent was out of sight.

'Good afternoon. Mr Foden isn't it? I've heard so much about you.'

Confusion crossed Foden's face as he saw a scruffy vicar, wearing thick-rimmed spectacles which slipped down his nose, approach with arm outstretched.

'God bless you my son,' Chard said with a beatific smile as he laid his arm on Foden's shoulder, his hand resting against the man's neck.

Flustered, Foden made to respond. 'I don't know what...' His words faltered as he felt a sharp pain, the feel of cold steel, and the sensation of something warm trickling down his neck. The vicar's smile had disappeared replaced by a look of steely determination.

'Don't make a move,' warned Chard. 'Just smile, whilst we have a little chat.'

'What do you want?' demanded Foden, obeying the instruction to smile. The question was asked calmly, out of curiosity rather than fear.

Chard moved the blade of the cut-throat razor concealed in the palm of his hand a fraction off Foden's flesh. 'I want to talk about Charles Landell. I want to know why you killed him.'

There was not a hint of concern in Foden's eyes, just a glimmer of amusement.

'You think I killed him? Now why would you be interested?' he mused.

'Answer the question,' demanded Chard, pressing the blade once more to Foden's neck. Confronting Foden directly was hardly subtle, but he had hoped to see in the man's eyes some degree of guilt, if not a confession.

'You must be the escaped prisoner. Chard isn't it? Interesting. I assumed it was you who'd killed him. If you think I murdered him, you're sadly mistaken. All you've managed to achieve is to make an enemy of me.'

'If you didn't kill him then who did? He owed you money, didn't he?'

'Damn right he did. He was going to pay his debts off when he disappeared without warning. I thought he'd double-crossed me. So, you don't have it then?'

'I don't have what?'

'Sabrina's Teardrop, the stolen sapphire.'

Chard frowned, angry at his incomprehension. 'Explain!' he demanded.

Foden's smile broadened. 'You don't have a clue, do you? Landell told me he was going to steal the sapphire and give it to me to clear his debts. I half suspect Lady Deansmoor put him up to it in order to claim on the insurance, expecting him to return it to her afterwards. Perhaps it was she who killed him,' he scoffed. 'Until his body turned up, I assumed he'd duped everybody. Instead, someone is sitting on a very valuable jewel.'

'Turn around,' ordered Chard, 'keep smiling, and walk towards New Street.'

Foden obeyed once more and Chard moved his arm as if he was just resting it on a friend's shoulder as they strolled through the city. The pavement became more crowded as they reached the main shopping thoroughfare and Chard was forced to move directly behind his captive.

'My blade is still only an inch away. Just one cut at the jugular is all it'll take,' he whispered in Foden's ear.'

'If our paths ever cross again, you're a dead man…' threatened Foden, just as he felt a heavy push in the back which sent him sprawling into a grocer's cart. Fury etched on his face, he got up and looked around, but Chard was nowhere to be seen.

TWENTY-FOUR

The Prince of Wales was one of those pubs that was easy to find if you knew where it was. Situated down a narrow residential side street, it wasn't visible from the end of the road. Chard hadn't been there for several years, and didn't know the current owners, but he understood it had respectable reputation. He approached the bar with a degree of trepidation, concerned his appearance might result in him being turned away.

After his encounter with Foden, Chard had rushed back to New Street Station, collected his hold-all, and changed into his previous disguise before catching the next train to Shrewsbury. After a visit to the town's library, he'd returned to his room at the Plough and Harrow to consider his next move, before falling fast asleep for several hours.

'Excuse my appearance, but I've had a hard time of it lately and a relative suggested we should meet here. I have money,' Chard said hopefully.

The landlord of the Prince of Wales looked at Chard warily, and raised an eyebrow at his wife.

'He speaks politely enough,' she commented, giving a nod.

Chard ordered a pint of bitter, then took his drink to a small table in the corner. There were several other customers in the room, and they eyed him suspiciously until they lost interest.

The beer tasted exceptionally good and Chard felt it helped him to concentrate on what he needed to do next. The revelation about the theft of the jewel complicated matters to a certain degree, but in other ways it didn't. The motive for murder was now more than revenge for unpaid debts, it was now possibly, or rather more likely, for possession of the sapphire. What hadn't changed was that there had apparently not been a forced entry into Landell's house, so whoever did it, knew either him or Sofia. If the motive was the theft of the sapphire, who would have known

Landell had it? Either someone else was complicit in the theft or they saw him take it.

Glancing at the clock over the bar, Chard saw that it was past nine o'clock. Morgan was late. Before he could dwell too long on the reason, the door of the bar opened and in walked May, carrying a case and a carpet bag.

'Good God!' exclaimed Chard, nearly spilling his beer. He quickly got to his feet, and went to take her arm, causing her to leap back in alarm.

Catching her breath, May apologised for her reaction. 'Sorry, Insp…'

'Call me Nathaniel,' Chard urged quietly.

'Sorry… Nathaniel. Idris told me about your disguise, but I wasn't quite ready for it,' May whispered.

Chard became aware of a degree of muttering coming from the other customers. 'You'd better come across to my table. Then you can explain what you're doing here.'

May went with Chard across to his table, trying to ignore the stares which followed her.

'Haven't they seen a woman before?' she asked Chard.

'Don't worry about it. From what I've observed, they look a bit peculiar but they seem decent enough. Now where is Morgan? Why are you here instead of him?'

May looked upset. 'I'm afraid he's in the infirmary.'

'What? In Shrewsbury you mean? What happened?'

'No. In Birmingham. I'm afraid something unfortunate happened.'

'Birmingham? How is he?' demanded Chard.

'It's a long story. It started with me going to the Salop Home…'

Before May could tell her tale, she was interrupted by a polite cough from the landlord who now stood next to them.

'You didn't explain that the relative coming to meet you was a young lady. We do not, as a rule, allow unaccompanied young ladies into the bar.'

'She's my cousin,' replied Chard, 'and she is no longer unaccompanied. She's with me.'

The landlord looked dubiously at the very attractive redhead and the scruffy, bandaged man with the unkempt beard, before gesturing to his wife. She came to stand alongside as May spoke up.

'I am indeed Nathaniel's cousin. He wandered away from home after an accident and we've been searching for him ever since. We had word he was in Shrewsbury and managed to get a message to him, asking to meet here.'

'Why here?' asked the landlady, as sharp as a knife.

May smiled sweetly. 'Because it is known to be very respectable, and I knew I would have to find somewhere to stay. Do you have rooms?'

The landlord and his wife exchanged questioning looks, whilst May prayed Chard had obtained some money as promised.

'There's one room we can rent out, for the right sort of guest,' the landlord finally decided. 'I'll take your bags up, whilst you continue your conversation.'

As soon as they were left alone, Chard congratulated May on her quick thinking. 'I'm impressed. It was very convincing.'

'I just hope you've got the money to pay for the room because I've run out of funds and I've got nowhere else to go.'

'I've got money which I was going to give to Morgan, but why are you still here? I thought you would be back in Pontypridd by now.'

May sighed. 'So did I. As things stand, my Idris is in the infirmary, my parents are no doubt furious, I've probably lost my job, I've become an accomplished liar and there are people in Shrewsbury who think I'm a prostitute. Oh! I nearly forgot. I pinched the vicar's clothes for you, so I'm also a thief. Things can't get much worse.'

'You could get caught helping me and go to prison,' said Chard ruefully. 'Now what happened to Idris?'

'As I started to tell you, I went to the Salop Home...'

Chard listened in silence as May recounted her tale, shaking his head sadly as she described Morgan's injuries.

'It's my fault. I should never have allowed you both to get involved.'

'It was our choice,' argued May, 'and now we have to see it through. I sent telegrams to my parents and to Doctor Henderson today saying I would send a fuller explanation in a letter tomorrow.'

'As long as you don't tell them you've been involved in helping me. Not a soul must know, for your own safety. Do you promise?'

May bit her lower lip guiltily. 'I'm afraid there's something I haven't told you.'

'What's that?' Chard asked apprehensively.

'I told you how Tilly rescued me. What I haven't told you is that I accidentally discovered she had stolen property in her room. It was a large solid silver item worth a lot of money. I didn't know exactly what it was, but Tilly said she stole it on impulse and anyone else would easily recognise it. She's had it since last year, but can't sell it for fear of being turned in.'

'Why doesn't she just return it or throw it in the canal?'

'Because she needs money to get out of the area and even a fraction of its worth would enable her to start a new life.'

'What was her reaction when you found it?' asked Chard, taking a sip from his drink.

'I thought she was going to kill me to prevent me from talking. My only way out was to convince her I wouldn't go to the police, which meant...'

'You told her you were helping an escaped prisoner,' sighed Chard.

'That's right,' she admitted. 'The only good thing to come out of it is that Tilly promised to find out what she can about Cora. She knows all sorts who live in the area, and if she discovers anything in the next few days, she'll leave a message with Idris at the infirmary.'

Chard nodded. 'I'll give you enough money to cover your costs in returning to Birmingham to visit Idris, and for your stay here. That should just leave me enough for the next three or four days. Let me get the money out for you.'

'No!' said May hurriedly. 'Some people already think I'm a prostitute. How would it look if you passed me money across the table?'

Chard gave an embarrassed cough. 'I'll slip the money under the table, but it's not easy using one arm.'

After some shuffling of chairs, and glances at the other customers, the transaction was successful, much to May's relief.

'I've said what's happened to me. How have you got on?'

Chard frowned. 'Not as much as I would have liked, but I think I've eliminated one suspect. I also visited Birmingham. I was there earlier today so we may have passed each, though possibly I was wearing the vicar's clothes,' he added, smiling. 'I confronted someone to whom Landell owed money. He wasn't a very pleasant man, but my gut instinct is that he told me the truth, and that he's not the murderer.'

'What are you going to do next?'

'There is possibly a connection between the murders and the theft of Sabrina's Teardrop, the sapphire I told you about. I want to speak to its former owner, Lady Deansmoor.'

'Do you know where to find her?' asked May.

'I called at the library earlier and found out the address of the Deansmoor Estate. It's near Stafford, so I'll be taking the first train there tomorrow morning. After that I want to try and find the bailiff who found the bodies of Sofia and Landell.'

'Idris had been trying to find him for you. He said the bailiff has been seen in the Three Fishes pub recently. I'm sure Idris would have found him by now if I hadn't persuaded him to help me follow Warren,' said May guiltily. 'Where is the Three Fishes? I could go there for you.'

'Next to Newman's Vaults in the High Street, there's a shut.'

'A what?'

'It's what we call an alley,' explained Chard. 'At the top of the shut you're at Bear Steps and to the right is Fish Street where you'll find the pub. The shut's name is Grope Lane.'

'I don't like the sound of that,' said May, looking appalled.

Chard laughed. 'Believe me, the old name for it was much worse. Anyway, there's no need for you to go there. I need you to listen to me very carefully.' Taking May's hand in his, Chard stared into her eyes. 'I can understand your wish to stay in the area to be nearer to your sweetheart; but please do not get yourself involved any further. If fortune favours me, I will solve this myself and clear my name. Then I'll do whatever I can to put things right for you. I promise. Just keep yourself safe.'

May nodded, taken aback by the sincerity in the inspector's voice.

'If you get any information about Cora, then send a message to me at the Plough and Harrow. Don't forget, I'm using the name Nathaniel Smith. Other than that, please don't get involved.'

'I won't,' promised May, knowing it was another lie. For there was one more thing she had to do, and the inspector wouldn't approve

TWENTY-FIVE

Reginald Ferguson strode purposefully across the town square, pushing to the ground an errand boy unfortunate enough to block his path. The lad looked ready to mouth an insult, but saw the anger in the man's face, and changed his mind.

'Major! Major Ferguson!'

The prison governor looked around to see who hailed him, and then composed himself, adjusting his top hat, as Jeremy Stanmore approached.

'How are you Major? I haven't seen you since our evening of sport. How's your great beast?'

'In fine condition as always. Just a few marks on him, but they'll soon heal. He's a reliable creature, unlike some people.'

'Someone appears to have upset you, Major,' commented Stanmore with an amused smile.

Ferguson grunted and shook his head. 'I cannot abide incompetence, Stanmore. If you want to find out the cause of my annoyance then follow me. You will be a valuable witness when I come to make a formal complaint.'

Ferguson lead the way across the square to the police station. Cursing the desk sergeant as a member of an ineffective police force, he blustered his way into Inspector Warboys's office, with Stanmore in tow.

'To what do I owe the pleasure?' asked Warboys sarcastically as the two men entered. He noticed that both men had a similar straight-backed imposing posture which no doubt intimidated their underlings. The blonde-haired Stanmore was by far the taller, but looked less threatening than the lean, hard figure of the prison governor.

'My escaped prisoner, Inspector. The fact that he is still at large is a personal affront. Why haven't you caught him yet?' demanded the major.

The heavily-jowled inspector gave an insincere smile. 'We are doing all we can, Governor. I want to catch him as much as you do. In fact, if you hadn't have let him escape, we wouldn't be having this problem.'

Ferguson looked as if he was going to explode, prompting Stanmore to put a hand on his shoulder. 'Let me assist, Major,' he offered, stepping forward.

'Could you perhaps be more specific as to what progress you have made?'

'We have alerted our colleagues in Manchester; in case he took a train to the north. I also sent one of my men, Constable Fugg, south to Pontypridd to make enquiries. Constable Morgan, who is from their constabulary suggested it was Chard's likely destination. Fugg has reported that he interviewed the regulars at the pub Chard used to frequent, and he was given a lead.'

'Good,' interjected Ferguson.

Warboys shook his head. 'Not really. They told him that Chard was using the name David Jones and living with a family called Williams somewhere in the Rhondda valleys.'

Stanmore smiled cynically. 'Wild goose chase then. You could search for years for a Jones or Williams down there. There would be thousands of them.'

'Exactly,' confirmed Warboys. 'I've ordered Fugg to return and in the meantime Constable Morgan seems to have disappeared from the town.'

'Incompetence after incompetence,' ranted Ferguson.

'However,' interrupted Warboys, not the least bit concerned by Ferguson's temper, 'I have received some information this very morning.' He paused, waiting for the major to calm down and start paying attention. 'Our fugitive has been spotted in the city of Birmingham. He assaulted a member of the public near the cathedral and was proclaiming his innocence. Apparently, he has adopted a disguise and is posing as a man of the cloth.'

'Disgraceful!' exclaimed Ferguson, thumping the inspector's desk.

'I assume you will be sending officers to Birmingham?' added Stanmore.

'Not our jurisdiction, but I am assured they will be looking for him as keenly as ourselves. The witness has given a description of his current appearance and we'll have his likeness in every newspaper across the Midlands by this evening.'

'Do you think he'll return to Shrewsbury?' asked Ferguson.

'Although a sensible man would make for the ports and safety abroad, it is possible that Chard is insane and really believes he is innocent. If that's the case, he might return to the scene of his crime as killers often do. He could also go to his home town in North Shropshire, but the Shropshire County Constabulary are also looking for him.'

'Do you think there's the slightest possibility he's innocent?' demanded Stanmore.

'None whatsoever. He's guilty, and I am never wrong.

***

'At last!' Chard said as he approached Wisteria Lodge. The morning had been extremely tiresome. Having risen early he had caught the first train to Wolverhampton in his guise as the disfigured man. There he had changed into his Reverend Smith persona in the public convenience, leaving his hold-all at the station. The connecting train to Stafford was on time but then came the difficulty of finding Lady Deansmoor. He had asked the cab driver outside the station to take him to Deansmoor Hall which was a considerable distance, only to find that the stately home had been sold. An act of kindness by the new owners meant that he had been taken in their carriage to the correct residence.

Wisteria Lodge was a very attractive property, but somehow not quite what Chard had expected for someone of Lady Deansmoor's standing. Brushing the dust from his clerical jacket, he tugged on the bell-pull and hoped that he looked sufficiently presentable. Having shaved, tidied his hair and retained the spectacles he looked more like a village priest than the unkempt missionary of yesterday.

To Chard's surprise, the door was not answered by a butler but by a nervous-looking woman with a twitch in one eye.

'I am sorry to disturb you, would it be possible to speak to Lady Deansmoor?' asked Chard politely.

'Finnick! Who is at the door?' came a demand from within.

'My name is Reverend Smith,' said Chard to the lady's maid.

'Wait here,' she replied.

Chard waited as the woman disappeared, overhearing 'I don't care who he is. Send him away.'

The servant returned but Chard interrupted her before she could speak.

'Could you tell her ladyship that it is about her relative, Charles Landell. It is most urgent.'

Finnick disappeared once more and Chard could make out murmurings from within, before finally being granted an audience with the grand dame.

'It is my great pleasure…' Chard began as he approached the elderly, but spry noblewoman.

'Yes, yes, just sit down,' she commanded. 'Now what is all this about young Charles? Have you seen him?'

As he turned to take a seat, Chard adjusted the spectacles on his nose in order get a clearer view of the room. There were some lovely antiques and furniture of the finest quality, with even a nod to the modern era in the shape of a telephone on a corner table. Yet there was something that didn't seem quite right.

'Has your ladyship not heard?'

'Heard? What do you mean heard? Heard what? I have been out of the country for some time and only returned last week. I am not particularly close to Charles, but I would like to see him again. I understood he had gone away, without leaving a forwarding address.'

'I believe you last saw him at a party thrown by Lord Berwick?' Chard tensed as he spoke, hoping that the mention of the only other time she might have seen him would not register.

'Indeed. How did you know?'

'It was the night Sabrina's Teardrop was stolen. I have heard a rumour that it was Charles who stole it.'

Lady Deansmoor blanched. 'What? Never!' she blustered. 'The police said a criminal gang was responsible. Now who are you and why are you here?'

'I am afraid I am the first to tell you that Charles Landell was discovered dead some weeks ago.'

Confusion spread over Lady Deansmoor's face. 'Dead? How?'

'It appears he was a victim of foul play. I won't go into the details, but he was found at his house. Do you know anyone who might have wished him harm?'

Lady Deansmoor sat silent for a while before responding. 'Shouldn't the police be asking me that question?'

'No doubt they may do so at some point. In the meantime, I am asking on behalf of a well-wisher.'

'I am afraid I must ask you to leave,' insisted the dame, getting to her feet. 'Finnick!' she yelled. 'See the reverend out.'

As a sop to politeness, she held out her hand to Chard. 'A pleasure to meet you, Reverend. Perhaps we will meet again. I regret I am unable to be of assistance.'

Chard took her hand and bowed, before leaving the lodge with a smile on his face. No doubt it would be a long walk before he could get someone to give him a lift, but the trip had been worthwhile. Lady Deansmoor's reaction to the rumour of Charles having stolen the sapphire had told him a lot. She also appeared genuinely shocked at the news of his death. Then there was her financial situation. The pay-out from the insurance company would have been substantial, yet despite the comfortable lifestyle and having spent time abroad, the hall had been sold and there was a distinct lack of servants.

'I think we'll have to meet each other again, your ladyship,' he promised himself.

***

After Chard had left, Lady Deansmoor sat back in her chair, tapping her fingertips together in thought. After a while, she smiled slyly.

'Finnick!' she yelled.

'Yes, your ladyship.'

'Fetch me the telephone, then make yourself scarce.'

With the phone in her hand, and Finnick in the kitchen, Lady Deansmoor smiled broadly. 'I think the boot is now on the other foot,' she muttered, before making her call.

TWENTY-SIX

May frowned as she posted the letters. The one to her parents had been fairly simple to compose. It stated simply that she had made such good progress in defeating her craving of laudanum, and that she had resolved to stay for a further week. She would return completely cured and fully restored to her old self. There was no lie in the statement, because the desire for the drug seemed to have disappeared. She counted herself fortunate that her addiction had not been as bad as many poor wretches, and been caught before it could destroy her life. Thanks to Inspector Chard's discretion and the charity of Doctor Henderson she had retained her job, which made the second letter so difficult to write. In it she apologised profusely to the doctor for her failure to return. Rather than revisit her earlier lie of visiting an ailing relative, she offered her resignation from her post as she had failed him. Promising to return to the infirmary on the following Monday in order to collect her personal items, May asked if he might provide her with a reference for future employment.

Wiping a tear from her eye, May went to the post office counter and enquired about a local address. Inspector Chard would be so cross if he found out, but it was something which was nagging at her and it had to be investigated. May walked out into the busy town centre and, after asking for directions, made her way in the direction of St Chad's church, which overlooked The Quarry. It was a misleading name, because instead of an ugly rock-strewn landscape, she found a beautiful public park that sloped down towards the river. Tempting as it was to explore, May walked along the road in front of the church until she reached the Kingsland Bridge. Once over the river, it took some time before she found the grand house of Major and Mrs Ferguson.

'I have come to call on Mrs Ferguson. I am Miss May Roper and you might mention that we have a mutual friend,' May informed the butler who answered the door.

He looked disparagingly at her dress, but nodded and went inside for a moment.

May felt self-conscious. Her dress from the previous day, soiled from the events in Birmingham, had been given to a washerwoman used by the Prince of Wales pub. All she had to wear was the spare dress from her case which hadn't been pressed. It was decent enough, but not of the quality expected for someone calling on a lady of Mrs Ferguson's standing.

'Mrs Ferguson will see you, Miss Roper, though it would be appreciated if in future you might make an appointment.'

May considered adopting the demeanour she had used when pretending to be Lady Fetheringham, but decided not. If she was to get anything out of this meeting, there could be no falsehood.

The butler showed May through to a room off the main hall where Mrs Ferguson sat in a comfortable armchair, waiting for her unexpected guest. She wore a dress of the deepest crimson and her jet-black hair was worn in the latest Gibson style.

'Miss Roper, I understand. You say we have a mutual friend?' The tone was cautious.

May stared at Mrs Ferguson's eyes, ready for any reaction. 'Yes, Mr Thomas Chard.' The shock was noted, despite the almost immediate recovery.

'You had best take a seat. Would you care to take tea?' offered the hostess.

'That's very kind, thank you.'

A silver bell summoned the butler, and soon a tea service was produced and tea poured, before Mrs Ferguson dismissed her servant, leaving the two women alone.

'Now then, why have you come to see me?' asked Mrs Ferguson finally.

'I understand you and Mr Chard were once very close.'

'You have the advantage of me, Miss Roper. May I ask how you know Thomas Chard?'

'He is … a friend,' answered May. 'We met when he came to Pontypridd last year.'

'Ah, I see,' responded Mrs Ferguson, with an edge to her voice. 'You're rather younger than I would have expected,'

May felt herself blush slightly, but kept her expression straight. 'Mr Chard is somewhat older than myself, that's true. However, I believe you are under a misapprehension. Our friendship is not one of romance, it is of debt. He once saved my life.'

'I appear to have been mistaken in my assumption. Thomas is a very handsome man, and it was natural for me to think…'

'There's no need to explain,' responded May. 'As I was saying, you were once close to Mr Chard?'

'Yes, but it wasn't to be. I didn't stand by him over a stupid family argument and then he met that foreign witch.'

'They say he murdered her, and her lover. Do you think he did?' May asked bluntly.

'He may have done. His escape from prison points to his guilt.'

'Yet other people had more to gain by the death of Charles Landell, her lover.'

'Such as?' demanded Mrs Ferguson.

'His partners. Mr Stanmore or Mr Warren for example. He also owed money to people. Then again, perhaps it was someone who hated Mrs Chard.' There was no response to the intended barb so May pressed on.

'You last saw Thomas at a party I understand.'

Mrs Ferguson's brow furrowed in anger. 'Who told you that?'

'He was on duty, supposedly protecting a jewel, but instead he was with you.'

'It is not a matter for discussion. I think you should leave.'

'Did anyone ask you to keep Thomas occupied?'

Mrs Ferguson made no reply, but rang the bell to call the butler.

'I will go, but if you decide you want to tell me anything, you can find me at the Prince of Wales in Bynner Street,' said May firmly, as the butler entered.

'Miss Roper is leaving. See her to the door, and do not allow her to enter again.'

Having been quickly hustled outside, May stood on the drive and realised that it was possibly the first time she had referred to the inspector as Thomas.

***

Chard knew he should really have gone to look for the bailiff who discovered his wife's body, yet he was tired from his journey to visit Lady Deansmoor. Eventually he got a lift on a passing waggonette, then took a cab to Stafford station, where his train to Wolverhampton was delayed for two hours. Chard had considered staying in his vicar's disguise until Shrewsbury, but then news of yet another delay at Wolverhampton prompted him to assume the identity of the disfigured man. He realised how fortunate that was when he saw the posters displayed around Shrewsbury station and the town centre. The rough sketch portrayed him as he had appeared to Harry Foden in Birmingham: in his clerical outfit, wearing thick-rimmed spectacles and sporting a beard. His beard was already gone, Chard resolved to dump his clerical clothes as soon as possible.

In addition to feeling weary, Chard was aware that George Lamb would seek him out for news of Cora and would call at the Plough and Harrow. In fact he was already there.

'There you are!' called George as Chard stepped into the bar.

'*Shwmae* George.'

'What's that mon?'

'Sorry George. Force of habit. It's a greeting down in Wales. I bet if you spent a year down there, you'd be calling everybody "butty" instead of "mon". You've got a drink I see. Mind my bag and I'll get myself one.'

Although Chard had been staying in the pub, he had avoided the bar, which had a reputation for being a rough sort of place, frequented by Irish labourers working on the railway.

'I'll have a pint of bitter and something stronger as a chaser please Liz,' he asked as he got to the bar.

A large man in a torn shirt and a dented bowler hat, was leaning alongside as he ordered. Prodding Chard on the shoulder he spoke in a heavy Irish accent, 'I haven't seen you before here now. I'm not sure I like what I see. What would the chaser be then? Scotch I suppose?' he asked, raising an eyebrow.

'Of course not,' scoffed Chard, 'Make it a Jamesons, and one for my friend here,' he added; making sure to pronounce the brand as "Jemison's", as a former colleague who hailed from Dublin had taught him.

'Good man yerself,' thanked the man, slapping him on the back. 'You're welcome in here anytime, and just let me know if anyone gives you any trouble.'

Chard nodded his thanks and took his drinks to George Lamb in two journeys, cursing the fact that he couldn't use his left arm.

'I'm getting fed up with this disguise, George. I need to gather some berries to restain my skin. I'm used to putting on the bandage with the gap for my eyes, but it keeps slipping, and as for this bloody arm…' Before he could continue complaining Chard felt something heavy on his foot. He looked down and groaned.

'Oh bugger. You've brought Barney.'

'Aye, mon and you'll have to have him here. He's chewing everything in sight. Now stop moaning about your disguise and tell me what you've found out about Cora.'

'We have some progress George, and at a cost. It is almost certain Warren took her to Birmingham. We think we know where she is and have an informant looking into it.'

George ran a hand through his copper-coloured hair. 'Is that all? Almost certain? It's not enough,' he complained.

'I said that the information came at a cost. Constable Morgan is in Birmingham infirmary. We're dealing with some very violent people,' countered Chard earnestly.

'All the more reason to move heaven and earth to save her.'

'Just give me a couple more days, three at the most. Our informant said a message will be left with Morgan and Miss Roper will be visiting him soon. Let's see what comes of it.'

George grunted, clearly dissatisfied, and finished off his drink in one gulp.

'Alright, but you're taking the bloody dog,' he said with finality, before walking out.

TWENTY-SEVEN

'Now clear off, Finnick. Meet me outside the Theatre Royal in an hour. You can have the time to yourself, but try not to be frivolous,' warned Lady Deansmoor.

The downtrodden maid gave a nervous smile before walking off as quickly as she could, in case her mistress changed her mind.

Lady Deansmoor gave a relieved sigh. Her meeting was one to be kept confidential at all costs. The previous day's visit from the Reverend Smith had been unexpected and, to a degree, unsettling. Even more so since she had arrived in Shrewsbury that morning and seen the posters of the escaped prisoner, Thomas Chard. The poster showed him bearded, but otherwise it was the same man. Not that she had been in any danger when he called, for he wasn't the murderer of young Charles; he couldn't be. What had been unsettling was the news that Charles was dead. She felt no grief; he was, or rather had been, thoroughly dishonest. It meant, however, that there was more at stake than she had originally bargained for. The whole business had to end, which meant bold action. When she made the telephone call after Nathaniel Smith departed, she had expected a strong reaction at the other end of the line. To her surprise, there had been silence as she spoke, then a calm instruction to meet in Shrewsbury the following day.

Entering The Quarry through the wrought iron gates opposite St Chad's church, Lady Deansmoor walked grandly down the central path dividing the grassed areas, until she was level with the hedges that marked her destination. This was The Dingle, the magnificently landscaped sunken garden in the centre of the park, complete with large ornamental pond. Although there were a number of visitors, it was not warm enough for the summer picnickers of earlier weeks, and a little too early for anyone to be taking a midday break. Lady Deansmoor found The Dingle even quieter; a haven of peace. She descended the pathway to stand, as instructed, close to the ornamental pond, facing a statue of a goddess.

The sudden touch on her shoulder was almost imperceptible. 'Don't turn around,' came the whispered warning. 'It is best we are not seen conversing. What do you think of the statue?'

'Sabrina, goddess of the Severn. Very droll,' she commented with a sardonic grin.

'Ironic, I would have said. Now make your way to your left. There's a bench conveniently placed where we can talk in private.'

'You must have known I would have eventually found out about Charles.'

'Yes, but letting you believe I had made an arrangement with him, and facilitated his trip to America, was more beneficial in the short term.'

'I would have still thought that, if I hadn't had my caller yesterday. You realise it must have been the escaped prisoner, Chard?'

'I said to move on. I'll stand here a while, then follow you to the bench in a few minutes. We'll discuss matters then.'

'Indeed, we will,' agreed Lady Deansmoor, walking away. 'There needs to be a rebalancing of our account. You've got a lot more to lose than I have.'

The elderly noblewoman made her way around the pathway within The Dingle until she found the bench, hidden from view by a hedge and a large rhododendron bush. There she waited, looking over her shoulder at a gap in the foliage, through which she could observe the wildfowl on the ornamental pond.

The sudden stab behind the ear was painful, though it was impossible to scream due to the hand covering her mouth. There was a sensation of intense cold flowing into the top of her neck and she felt her arms jerk spasmodically. Then darkness.

***

'Come on Barney, help me think.'

It had been an intensely frustrating day for Chard, the only thing he'd achieved, was to get a dog collar for Barney and to build a makeshift kennel in the yard of the Plough and Harrow. Neither was a priority in the circumstances, but he there was nothing else to be done until evening fell.

'You're not much help, are you?' he complained to the dog which had paused once more to relieve itself. It seemed the whole of the Shrewsbury constabulary had been ordered to search the town centre, looking for someone impersonating a vicar. Rather than chance his luck, Chard took Barney for a walk upstream of the Rea Brook, to find some wild berries. It would take him away from the town centre for a couple of hours and hopefully clear his head. Normally he avoided talking to himself, but having Barney there made it feel less abnormal.

'We're now convinced the murders are connected to the theft of the jewel, aren't we?'

Barney looked up at his master with a blank expression, before being tugged along by the lead.

'If that's the case, we're looking at people who were at the party when the jewel went missing, correct?'

By now Barney had caught up and had started padding on ahead, his muscular body pulling the lead taut.

'We're also sticking with the assumption that Landell knew his killer, because the murderer didn't have to force his way in. And we know he owed money to Harry Foden.'

Barney stopped and relieved himself again.

'That's right Barney. We believe Foden was telling the truth and it wasn't him. On the other hand, we know Landell had embezzled money from his business partners and that they've benefitted from his demise.'

Chard had stopped walking whilst waiting for Barney. The dog finished, then looked questioningly at his master.

'No. You're right to ask, but I'm confident this has nothing to do with Sofia.'

Immediately, the act of saying his wife's name filled him with sadness and a wave of grief, despite the unhappy marriage, threatened to swallow him.

There was a tug on the lead as Barney surged forward again, and Chard shook his head clear.

'Tonight, we'll find the man who found the bodies. If that doesn't bring any benefits, I'll approach Warren and Stanmore directly and try to shake the truth out of them. The money Harbury gave me is nearly gone and if we don't find Cora Lamb soon, I'm not sure that George won't turn me in. We're running out of time.'

***

It was nine o'clock in the evening when Chard walked along the cobblestones of Fish Street towards the Three Fishes, with Barney in tow. He was concerned on a number of fronts. The information that the bailiff had taken to drinking there might be wrong; there was a risk when going somewhere different that he might somehow give himself away; and he couldn't ignore the gut feeling that someone was following him. Not just that evening either. It was just a sense someone or something was observing from a distance. It was unnerving.

Chard let Barney off his leash, watched him disappear towards the graveyard of St Alkmund's church, and entered the old timber-framed pub.

He had last been inside the pub only two years previously, on duty as a police officer, which raised the risk of being recognised. He kept the brim of his hat down and spoke in a low voice.

'Good evening,' he said as he approached the bar.

'You look as if you've been in the wars,' answered the landlord, a jovial man in shirtsleeves and a mustard-coloured waistcoat.

'Mining accident up north,' answered Chard, disguising his voice as best he could. 'A pint of bitter please; and could you point out a man called Scratch Harris if he's in? I was given his name by a mutual friend.'

'Really?' asked the landlord, looking doubtful. 'He's the chap over there with the bad skin, talking to the coachman; but I'd call him Mister Harris if I were you.'

Chard looked across the small, but crowded, room and easily picked out a man suffering from some sort of skin disease, dry scales covering his forehead and cheeks. He was talking with a tall man wearing the long boots of a coach driver. As Chard made his way in their direction, he picked up snippets of their conversation.

'I don't mind saying... he's a hard man to work for...'

'... decently paid though... and I hear his wife ...'

'... bloody great beast of a thing...'

'... hate animals, me ...'

'... furious when he escaped...'

'... still, as I say, his wife...'

'... I'm off for a piss...'

Chard watched the coachman disappear to the toilets through a door at the end of the room, then sidled up to Harris, who scratched the skin behind his ear absent-mindedly, causing a shower of flakes to fall on his shoulder.

'Mr Harris? I wonder if I can have a moment of your time?'

Harris looked at Chard's bandaged face and made as if to comment on it, but then changed his mind. 'If you're quick. I'm in conversation with my friend, but you've got my ear until he comes back.'

'I'll get to the point then. I heard you found the two bodies in the house over at Kingsland last year.'

Harris gave an involuntary shiver. 'Bad it was. Still gives me nightmares. A terrible way to go.'

'Tell me, did you notice anything unusual?'

'Apart from the bodies you mean?' responded Harris sarcastically. 'What's your interest?'

'It's just a curious tale and I wanted to hear it first-hand. I'll put a whisky behind the bar for you,' offered Chard.

'Fair enough,' agreed the bailiff. 'It was straightforward by and large. We got there and had to break in ...'

'It definitely hadn't been broken into before?' interrupted Chard. 'No damage to the locks or anything?'

'No. I would have said,' answered Harris, irritated at Chard's interjection. 'Anyway, we wanted to be thorough so I said to search the cellar. We found the door had been barred shut and it was a bugger to open. Then we found the bodies, just inside. There were scratch marks on the inside of the door where they had tried to open it.'

Chard wanted to close his ears, but steeled himself to listen.

'There'd been a few bottles of wine left in the cellar and they clearly had drunk those to sustain themselves, but I reckon it was hunger that saw them off. The poor fellow had been so desperate he'd even tried eating…' Harris paused to take a drink of his beer, his hand visibly shaking at the memory. '…his cigarettes.'

Chard, who had been bracing himself for different details, seized on the bailiff's words.

'His cigarettes? Are you sure?'

'Of course, I'm sure,' snapped Harris.

'But he couldn't have smoked,' Chard told himself aloud.

'He bloody did mon,' argued Harris. 'There was a packet of them disgusting Turkish things in the room and another unopened pack outside the cellar door.' The bailiff glanced over his shoulder at the creak of the door to the toilet. 'Anyway, my friend is returning, so just make sure you leave that whisky behind the bar for me.'

'Thank you,' replied Chard. 'I'll do that. If you remember anything else unusual, leave a message for Nathaniel Smith at the Plough and Harrow. I'll see it'll be worth your while.'

His mind racing, Chard went to the bar and paid for the bailiff's whisky, before rushing outside to find Barney.

'Who was that?' asked the coachman.

'Curious really. I'll tell you later, but only after we finish talking about your Major Ferguson and that delicious wife of his.'

TWENTY-EIGHT

'Inspector Warboys!'

The policeman groaned when he saw Major Ferguson hailing him. It was sheer bad luck that he had gone into the square just at the wrong moment.

The major broke away from his discussion with Jeremy Stanmore and Leonard Warren and strode purposefully towards Warboys.

'Have you made any progress in catching the fugitive Chard?'

'Major Ferguson, I am on my way this very morning to speak to my opposite number in the County Constabulary. In addition, there are some formalities to deal with in relation to yesterday's incident.'

'What incident?'

'Have you not read this morning's paper, Major? Lady Deansmoor was found dead in The Quarry yesterday.'

'Oh, that? I was just discussing it with my friends. Died in her sleep. Hardly unexpected at her age according to the paper,' scoffed the Major.

'I agree, but nevertheless, due to her position I do need to cover all possibilities, such as why she was in Shrewsbury and who might have been with her. I don't suppose you noticed her yesterday?'

'I did leave the prison to run a private errand for an hour in the morning, but I wouldn't have a clue what Lady Deansmoor looked like. My wife met her once, and she was in town yesterday. I'll ask her if she noticed anything.'

'Thank you, Major. That would be most helpful,' thanked Warboys, turning to walk away.

'Wait a minute, Inspector,' interrupted Ferguson, gesticulating with his arm for his two associates to join them.

'I want to know what you are doing about the murderer, Chard. Mr Stanmore and Mr Warren here, also have an interest in recapturing the killer of their former partner.'

'We are doing all we can,' growled Warboys, irritably.

'We understand there's a man with a crippled arm asking questions about the murders,' said the major.

'Perhaps he is helping Chard,' suggested Warren. 'What are you going to do about it?' he added sharply.

'Mind your manners, sir!' responded Warboys, losing his temper.

'I apologise,' responded Warren. 'I've picked up a damnable itchy rash, and it's made me quite irritable,' he explained.

The inspector calmed down. 'I'm sure this man asking questions is a wild goose chase. How would he be helping Chard? We know he's guilty, so the only help he needs is to get out of the county. Why he went to Birmingham and then came back is a mystery. In fact, the more I think about it, the less I believe it really was him in Birmingham. Now what I will share with you, if you allow me to then get on with my business, is my primary suspicion.'

'Which is?' asked Stanmore, with interest.

'That he is being aided by the two people who came up from South Wales to visit him. Namely, Constable Morgan, who has gone missing; and a Miss Roper who has been seen around the town, most recently in the Coleham area.'

'What do they look like?' asked Warren.

'Constable Morgan is a physically fit man of medium height sporting mutton-chop whiskers; whereas Miss Roper is I suspect, in her early twenties, of pleasing appearance and has auburn hair.'

The two business partners exchanged glances before Warren spoke up. 'We think they paid us a visit under false pretences last week.'

Warboys raised an eyebrow. 'I don't know exactly what they're up to, and I've got no cause to arrest them; but I've told my constables to keep an eye out and hopefully they'll lead us to our man.'

***

When Chard went out through the back entrance of the Plough and Harrow into the yard, he was surprised to find May Roper waiting for him.

'I thought you'd come out eventually, Insp… I mean Nathaniel. Have you heard the news?'

'What are you doing here? Have you had news from the infirmary? Why didn't you just send a message? What's happened?' demanded Chard, shunting May around a fence and out of sight.

'I needed to warn you and I didn't want to trust a messenger, or leave something in writing.'

'You could have been spotted,' scolded Chard.

'I've been very careful. I noticed that a police constable saw me in the town about half an hour ago, and started following me at a distance. I lost him in the market hall. To answer your remaining questions, no I haven't been to the infirmary yet, and Lady Deansmoor is dead.'

The shock was clear on Chard's face. 'She can't be. I saw her only the day before yesterday.'

'She was found in The Quarry on a bench. They say she died in her sleep.'

'Why was she in Shrewsbury?'

'The newspaper article didn't give a reason.'

Chard stroked his chin. 'It can't be a coincidence. I go there and ask her about the stolen jewel and the murders, then the following day she turns up in Shrewsbury for no obvious reason. Then for her to be found dead when she seemed fit and well when I saw her? I must be getting closer and someone is becoming nervous.'

'I thought you should know about her death as soon as possible, because although they say she died in her sleep...'

'You did right. Thank you. In return I'll share with you what I discovered last night. It was something which didn't make any sense,' said Chard ruefully.

'What's that?'

'I'll spare you all the details, but suffice it to say Charles Landell was found with cigarettes on his person.'

'Why doesn't that make sense?'

'Sofia hated the smell of tobacco, almost religiously so. The thought of her getting involved with any man who smoked, however rich or handsome, is unthinkable.'

'You mean the cigarettes couldn't have been his,' said May, with a smile of realisation. 'It doesn't help us with the killer's identity though, many men smoke.'

Chard nodded, 'But it narrows down the suspects. The cigarettes were Turkish, quite popular I know, but fewer men smoke them than the regular brands.'

May gave a soft clap of delight. 'Warren smokes them, I'm sure. Dreadful smelling things.'

Chard smiled grimly. 'Knowing he's the likely culprit is a great step forward, but it's not proof. No doubt the cigarettes in question are long gone and unless he wrote his name on the packet for some reason, it still wouldn't be proof. I can't see any way of clearing my name other than to make him confess.'

'Be careful! He might have killed Lady Deansmoor so perhaps you've worried him enough to come after you as well.'

'He'd have to find me first. In any case, if Warren is sufficiently worried, he might make a mistake, which is what I want.'

'Won't it put more pressure on him if we can rescue Cora? She can testify that he took her to the brothel,' suggested May.

'Indeed, it will,' agreed Chard. 'I've promised George Lamb some progress by the end of the week, so it seems that must be the priority for all our sakes. Can you go to the infirmary this afternoon?'

'That was my intention,' replied May.

'Good. I'll come round to the Prince of Wales tomorrow morning to see how you've got on.'

***

It was early evening, and Chard had just returned from taking Barney for his second walk of the day, when the landlady passed him an envelope containing a message.

The note was brief. "HAVE INFORMATION. ROMAN RUINS MIDNIGHT TONIGHT. COME ALONE – HARPER".

'What do you think then, Barney?' he asked the dog as it wandered obediently into its makeshift kennel. 'I couldn't help but feel someone was watching us on our walk just now, and then we get this note.'

Barney looked up with doleful eyes as the kennel door was closed.

'I share your concerns Barney, I really do. Perhaps we've smoked out Warren good and proper, in which case I'll be prepared.'

***

Chard had prepared the pony and trap in good time for his night time excursion. Its hire was paid for until the weekend, when his funds would run out.

'Come on then, Barney. Up you come.'

Chard lifted the muscular dog onto the trap, then took his seat at the front, placing a lit oil lamp alongside.

Once clear of the town, he took his left hand out of its sling and removed the bandage from his head. If it really was Scratch Harris at Viriconium, then he would just pull the brim of his hat down and quickly stuff his left arm back into its sling. Due to the late hour Chard did not encounter any other vehicles, though once or twice he thought he heard a horse's hooves somewhere in the distance. Crossing Atcham Bridge and passing by the gates to Lord Berwick's Estate, Chard wondered what might have happened if he hadn't been assigned to protect Sabrina's Teardrop. Then he scolded himself. The jewel would still have been stolen, Sofia would still have been killed, and he would still have been blamed.

Chard turned off the old Roman road, and headed south east along the road to Ironbridge. After a few hundred yards, he turned right at a crossroads and took a narrow country lane past some isolated farm buildings before arriving at his destination.

Viriconium, once the fourth largest city in Roman Britain, was located a few miles east of Shrewsbury, near the village of Wroxeter. Having been deserted by the last of its inhabitants around the seventh century A.D. most of the stonework had been taken for use elsewhere, or had sunk into the ground. A wall of the basilica still stood though, and excavations had revealed the foundations of the bath house.

Standing on the driver's seat, Chard surveyed his surroundings as best he could. From what little moonlight broke through the clouds, he could discern the outline of the basilica wall. Beyond it, he could just about identify the hedge which marked the Ironbridge Road, curving its way south east. Chard knew that if he crossed the low fence into the field, the ground would be uneven and he could fall into an excavation pit; but the lamp would help if he made his way slowly.

'Down you get Barney. See if you can sniff out anyone here.'

Unwilling to attempt the jump, Chard had to lift the dog off the back of the cart. Once firmly on the ground, Barney started to sniff his way about, squeezing through the fence, and disappearing into the darkness.

Chard fingered the handle of the sharp carving knife in his belt. The only useful weapons he could find at the pub were an old axe and the knife, which at least had a keen blade. Climbing the fence into the excavation field, he held his lamp out to make his way across the site, nearly losing his balance as he crossed over an exposed section of the roman baths. Reaching the huge basilica wall, he was about to extinguish the lamp to await his mysterious contact, when he was nearly knocked over by Barney; who came barrelling from the direction of the far hedge, heading back towards the pony and trap.

'What the hell?' exclaimed Chard, turning around to see where his terrified dog had gone.

'Do not move an inch, if you value your life,' warned a voice from the darkness.

Disobeying the command, Chard raised his lamp, to see that he was staring into the mouth of a long-barrelled pistol.

A terrifying, bestial growl came from somewhere behind, causing Chard to turn. There was an ear-shattering noise as the pistol fired; an excruciating pain in the side of his head; followed by the impact of something heavy thumping into his back, forcing him to the ground. The ground felt cold and hard beneath his cheek, then he lost consciousness.

TWENTY-NINE

'I told you not to move. You must be the luckiest man alive.' Chard sat up, dazed. Immediately he felt giddy and lay back again.

'You've been out cold for a few minutes. Just rest there for a short time, then I'll get you back to town.'

'Who the hell are you?' Chard demanded, unsure whether or not the man was a threat.

'Let me introduce myself Mr Chard. I haven't had the opportunity until now. The name's Cole, Elijah Cole.'

Chard tried to sit up once more, this time with a degree of success. He was aware that the side of his head ached furiously and he put a hand out to feel it. A warm stickiness clung to his fingers as they came away.

'Ironically enough, your head's going to need a bandage,' chuckled Cole, holding Chard's lamp between them, so that they could see each other's faces. 'Don't worry too much about the blood, most of it isn't yours.'

'I recognise you! I saw you at the dogfight at Haughmond, then again leaving Harry Foden's office in Birmingham.'

Cole stroked his Van Dyke beard and smiled, the light from the lamp casting shadows across his dark features. 'He was rather insulting about my ancestry. I do hold grudges and I will ensure that I pay him back.'

'Why did you shoot me? Are you working for the police?'

'God forbid to the latter, and I wasn't shooting at you. I was shooting at that,' Cole replied pointing behind Chard. 'He landed on you as it was, and it wasn't easy to roll the damn thing off.'

Chard recalled something hitting him in the back, and turning, saw the cause. Lying on the ground, just a few feet away, was the corpse of an enormous dog.

Slowly, he got to his feet and (after a nod of reassurance from

Cole) walked across to take a closer look at the creature. Half its head had been blown away, leaving what was left of the shattered skull exposed.

'I thought something like this would happen, so I brought this. It was my grandfather's,' said Cole, holding out his weapon for Chard to examine. Taking it, he was surprised by the weight and the calibre of the pistol.

'Ever seen one before?' asked Cole.

'Not one like this,' Chard answered, all the time trying to figure out who his rescuer was, and why he should be prepared to hand over the weapon.

'It's called a howdah pistol. Very popular with officers who served in India. Huge stopping power on them because they were designed to be taken on tiger hunts; just in case one of the beasts managed to climb onto an elephant's back. The bullet must have just grazed you on the way past. Your brief unconsciousness was more down to the dog landing on you.'

'You said you thought something like this would happen. How? For that matter, how did you know I would be here and why are you interested?'

Cole gave a disarming smile. 'So many questions!' He laughed. 'I suppose I should start at the beginning. I am a man with a reputation for getting things done. I work only for myself, taking on assignments as I please. I promise results, and if I make a little profit on the side then no questions are to be asked.'

'I take it you've taken on an assignment to return me to prison.'

Cole smiled broadly, and shook his head. 'No. When Sabrina's Teardrop was stolen, I was asked to recover it by the insurers, due to its immense value. Unfortunately, they were too late in contacting me. The trail had gone cold, and the police were hardly thorough. My investigations revealed the disappearance of Charles Landell, a relative of Lady Deansmoor. It seemed too much of a coincidence so soon after the theft. I then looked into Lady Deansmoor's financial situation, through various contacts, and found it was not terribly good. I came to the conclusion Landell had taken it, possibly with Lady Deansmoor's knowledge. The intention may have been for Landell to hand back the jewel secretly to Lady Deansmoor for a cut of the insurance proceeds. However, given Landell's disappearance, it was more likely he'd double-crossed her and fled to live a new life, rumoured to be in America.'

Chard nodded. 'All reasonable assumptions.'

'Given the circumstances, yes. But not provable without finding the jewel. Nor would it have been wise to slander someone of Lady Deansmoor's standing without strong evidence. I did offer to make further enquiries in the United States, but the insurers declined, and agreed to pay.'

'Then the bodies were discovered,' said Chard.

'Exactly! As soon as the insurers heard, they asked for my assistance once more. I remained convinced Landell had taken the sapphire. That meant his murderer, and of course that of your wife, probably had it.'

'So, you were after me?'

'Not unless you were the murderer. You aren't, are you?' joked Cole. 'I mean, if you want to confess...'

Chard started to react, but Cole just smiled.

'No. Of course I wasn't after you. If you'd stolen a fabulous jewel, why would you take up a post as a policeman in the valleys of South Wales?'

'I wish Inspector Warboys had been of the same mind,' reflected Chard.

'He wasn't because you had two police forces, County and Town, which don't like each other; dealing with two different crimes and not wanting to see the link.'

'Has the jewel not turned up anywhere? Sold to a foreign museum, or a private collector perhaps?'

'That's the puzzling thing,' answered Cole. 'I have many contacts, some of whom are rather disreputable, but there's not been a whisper. I have come to the conclusion that it must be in the possession of someone who already has a more than comfortable lifestyle. Someone who can afford to keep it hidden away for a few years; when it can perhaps be disposed of more easily, without risk of capture.'

'I suppose I could have been doing the same. Keeping my head low as a policeman in South Wales for a couple of years,' suggested Chard.

'I didn't discount that entirely. I wanted to speak to you when you were in prison, but I was refused entry. Then when you escaped, I did consider it very seriously indeed, whilst continuing my other investigations.'

'What changed your mind about me?'

'It was when I was dismissed from Foden's premises. I saw you looking at me when I came out. You were in disguise of course, but it was the intensity of your stare that made me curious. I went to the end of the street, turned back, and from then on I've been following you.'

'Why not turn me in?'

Cole scoffed. 'Because you are clearly a man of ingenuity. I accepted your innocence when I could see that you were staying around, evidently covering the same ground as myself. You want to clear your name. I was hoping you might draw out the man who we're both after, particularly after Lady Deansmoor's demise. Rather successfully, I'd say.'

'Did he get away?' asked Chard.

'For the moment. He must have had his vehicle on the Ironbridge Road beyond the far hedge.

I doubt he saw me though, from that distance. He probably thinks it was you who fired the shot. I left my horse a quarter of a mile back, so couldn't have caught him; not in the dark and with so many country lanes. You perhaps recognise what's left of the dog?'

Chard nodded. 'A Boerboel. Either Stanmore's or Major Ferguson's.'

'Ferguson's?' queried Cole.

'The prison governor. His wife was with me at the party when the sapphire was stolen, and he wanted me dead, which is why I broke out of the prison.'

'We still have two suspects then. Damn!'

'Make that three,' added Chard. 'I was expecting a trap tonight, but I thought it would be Leonard Warren. It could be two of them, or indeed all three, are acting together.'

Cole looked discomfited. 'Nevertheless, the clear lead we have is the dog. Tomorrow I'll visit Ferguson's and Stanmore's houses and try to find out which beast is missing.'

'As we appear to be working towards the same ends, you might wish to join me tomorrow morning,' suggested Chard. 'There's a possibility of putting pressure on Warren, who might still be our man; and I will know more then. Call for me around nine.'

Cole nodded. 'Agreed, but for now, we'd best get you back to the Plough and Harrow.'

CHAPTER THIRTY

Chard splashed his face with water and reflected on the events of the previous night. Cole had helped him back to the pony and trap where Barney greeted him guiltily with a slobbery lick. They collected Cole's horse, and returned to Shrewsbury.

Chard had managed three hours of sleep before he was awoken by the sound of an early morning beer delivery.

'Damn and blast!' he cursed as he pulled his bandage too tightly across his head. The right-hand side, just above the temple, was badly swollen.

He'd just finished tying the bandage when Mrs Donnelly knocked on the door of his room. 'There's a gentleman outside wanting to see you, Mister Smith; and if I could have a word with you later about your room rent? The arrangement with Mr Harbury was that you would be leaving tomorrow.'

'Tell my visitor I'll see him outside presently. As for my stay, I'll be on my way in the morning,' Chard replied, more than a little concerned. He'd virtually run out of the money Harbury had given him; but it was a predicament that would have to be left for the time being.

When Chard walked into the street, he was aware of the contrast in apparel between himself and his rescuer from the previous evening. He wore his floppy, wide-brimmed hat and the same large overcoat; beneath which was his now grimy shirt. In comparison, Elijah Cole wore a tailored dark grey suit, with a faint pinstripe. His red silk tie was fastened with a silver tie-pin and a silver watch chain dangled from his waistcoat. To top off his appearance, Cole wore the latest homburg hat and carried a silver-topped cane.

'I congratulate on your appearance Mr Cole,' greeted Chard. 'Smart without being vulgar.'

'I wish I could say the same,' replied Cole, with a chuckle. 'How is your head?'

'Swollen, but only painful if I touch it, or put this damn bandage on too tight,' grimaced Chard.

'As we are allies on this venture, for I need you just as much as you need me, you may call me Eli.'

Chard shook his outstretched hand. 'Thomas; but for now, I'm using the name Nathaniel,' he explained. 'Follow me, we're going to the Prince of Wales.'

The two men walked the short distance to May's lodgings, Chard leading the way and Cole following about twenty yards behind. At the pub, Chard waited for Cole, then indicated that he should be the one to knock on the door. 'You look more respectable than me,' Chard explained. 'They've seen me with Miss Roper, but I don't think they were happy about it. Ask to have a word with her, then I'll gesture from out here.'

Cole straightened his tie, then went to the door and knocked hard with his cane. Chard watched from around the corner as the landlord answered and exchanged words, before disappearing inside. When May eventually came to the door, Cole gestured over his shoulder; then she spotted Chard and went back inside.

'She'll be with us in a minute,' informed Cole on his return.

'Good. I'll go on to the end of the street and wait around the corner. We should be free enough to talk there for a few minutes,' said Chard.

'How's Morgan?' Chard asked May when the three were finally together.

'Before we start, who is this gentleman?'

'A friend, who wants, more or less, the same thing we do,' answered Chard.

'If you may permit me to introduce myself, my name is Elijah Cole. I understand you are Miss Roper. I am at your service.' The words were spoken almost sensuously, with a dazzling smile.

Chard scowled unintentionally. 'We can't be seen together so let's be brief. How is Morgan, and was there any message left for you at the infirmary yesterday?'

May nodded, with a serious expression. 'Idris has to leave the infirmary. They need the bed and they think he is recovered enough to travel. As for the message, Tilly wrote that she should have an answer by today, but it might be too late. I need to go to her address. I would have gone by now, but I thought I should check with you first.'

'I can't have you risking yourself again,' said Chard earnestly. 'I'll have to go.'

'But then you'll be at risk. The train station had town constables on the platform yesterday when I got back. One started to follow me after I left and it was hard to lose him. It's too dangerous for you.'

'I'm sorry,' apologised Cole, 'but I am still not fully informed about this. I understand this is something to do with putting pressure on Leonard Warren?'

'Warren abducted a girl and took her to a brothel in Birmingham,' explained Chard. 'She's the sister-in-law of a good friend. If we can rescue her, we can hopefully get Warren arrested or at least force him into a foolish move.'

'Then I wish you good luck,' responded Cole, 'but I don't think he's our man, and I don't want to waste time in getting whoever has the jewel.'

'I understand, Eli. It's my problem alone and I've given my word to rescue the girl, so I have to do it. It'll be good to cause Harry Foden some trouble as well.'

'Foden?' queried Cole, intrigued.

'He owns the brothel in question.'

'Then why didn't you say so?' exclaimed Cole. 'I need to pay him back for some of the things he called me at his office. I'll come with you.'

'I hate to ask, but I'm out of funds and can't even afford another train fare,' explained Chard.

'Say no more. If I am successful in my assignment then my fee will easily cover costs; and in any case, this is about my reputation. It would be better though, if we set off from a different station. We'll hire a growler to take us to Wellington and catch a train from there,' suggested Cole.

'What do you want me to do?' asked May. 'I can't just sit here worrying.'

Chard thought for a moment. 'First, write down directions to Tilly's. After we've gone, go into town and send a telegram to

Constable Matthews, explaining that his cousin has been injured. Say he'll be on the 9 p.m. train to Cardiff and will need to be met and assisted back to Pontypridd. Eli and I will fetch Morgan from Birmingham and put him on that train. Afterwards, go and visit the Lambs and assure them we are going to get Cora back.'

'I have a pencil and notebook if you need it for the directions,' offered Cole.

May took them and drew a neat map, adding written instructions. When she finished, she looked at Chard's bandaged face and stared into his eyes. 'Do you think Cora can be saved?'

'I'm sure of it,' replied Chard with confidence; but May could see the lie.

***

It was drizzling when Chard and Cole left New Street Station for Dale End; and although it was mid-afternoon the weather, combined with the dirt and smoke of the city made it seem later. Within the privacy of a toilet cubicle at the station, Chard had removed his bandage and freed his arm; happy to rely on the broad-brimmed hat to conceal his identity. As the two men made their way along the pavement, Cole decided to raise something which particularly interested him.

'This woman Tilly, wants to escape her sordid existence here, but cannot because she is unable to pass on some valuable stolen property?'

'That's correct,' replied Chard as they made their way in the direction of the chemical works marked on May's map.

'You don't feel conflicted? After all, as a policeman you would want to arrest her, wouldn't you?' probed Cole.

'I've had to be conflicted about a lot of things recently,' grimaced Chard. 'She is possibly risking her life to help me, a fugitive from the law; and possibly saving Cora Lamb from God knows what fate.'

'I could possibly help with her little problem,' suggested Cole. 'Though I would have to take a commission, to make it worth my while.'

'Are you suggesting…?'

'All I'm saying is that, depending on the item, I could either return it to the owners for a fee or, perhaps find a buyer?' explained Cole, raising an eyebrow.

'I don't want to know,' said Chard firmly. 'We must be close, let's take another look at Miss Roper's map.

The two men consulted May's directions and took several turns down narrow, stinking alleys until they stood before a converted storehouse which had been divided into three dwellings.

Before they could enter, they were startled by a broad Birmingham accent.

'What yer want?' demanded an old toothless crone standing behind them, who seemed to have appeared from nowhere.

'Just checking who lives here, old woman,' snapped Chard.

'No need to be like that,' she replied sharply.

Eli Cole stepped forward and offered her a silver sixpence.

'Excuse my friend, mother. He's got a cob on,' he explained, whilst Chard looked on, surprised that Cole seemed to know the local way of speaking.

'Aye, a face as long as Livery Street,' the crone replied, taking the coin.

'Can you tell us who lives here?' asked Cole politely.

'That one's empty, the one at the back belongs to Old Joe, but he's out at the factory; and this one is young Tilly's. I wouldn't go in though.'

'Why not?' asked Chard.

'Best keep out of it. There was some blarting went on about an hour ago. Someone was in there and I reckon must have lamped her yampy. I don't want no trouble with that sort.'

'Someone's been in there, and beaten her? Who was it?' asked Cole urgently.

'I didn't see nothing. I'm off. Ta-ra a bit,' said the old woman, scurrying off.

Chard opened the door and entered.

'Tilly?' Chard called out softly.

Directed by sobs, the two men found her curled in a ball, in the corner of her room, next to the bed.

Chard knelt down beside her and gently touched her arm. Immediately, she shivered and curled up even tighter.

'Who are you?' she asked weakly.

'Friends of May. She couldn't come today so we came instead,' answered Chard. 'I'm Thomas Chard, the man she's been helping. 'Who beat you?'

'Foden,' she muttered through bloodied, swollen lips.

'You're safe now. Let me help you up.'

Putting his arm gently around her shoulder, Chard encouraged Tilly to turn her head towards him. Suddenly he froze.

'What's the matter,' asked Cole, moving nearer.

Slowly, Chard turned towards him, moving Tilly's body as he did, and revealing her ravaged face. 'He's taken her eye.'

THIRTY-ONE

'He swore that if I interfered any more, he'd come for the other one. I've got information, but unless you can get me away from this city, I daren't tell you,' groaned Tilly.

'We can keep you safe,' said Chard.

'I hate to contradict you, but you probably can't, whereas I definitely can,' interjected Cole. 'The important thing at the moment is to get this young lady to a doctor. You carry her, Thomas, whilst I go ahead and find a cab.'

Chard nodded his agreement and made to lift Tilly into his arms.

'Wait!' she cried. 'There's an item under my bed. If you're going to take me away from here, then I'll need it.'

'May told us about it,' explained Chard. 'Mr Cole here can be trusted. He will make whatever arrangements are necessary.'

Cole reached under the bed and pulled out a bag containing something heavy. He looked inside, then gave a whistle. 'A rather large silver trophy. Yes, I believe we can set you up nicely with the proceeds. Perhaps London?'

Tilly gave a painful nod, and let herself be carried out into the alley whilst Cole ran ahead.

As they made their way, ignoring the stares of passers-by, Tilly spoke.

'They took the girl you're after, and another, to the canal this morning.'

Chard slowed his pace, his concern evident. 'Why?' he asked, fearing the worst.

'Because they're being taken to France. They're going by narrow-boat as far as London on the Black Slipper, then to London Docks. Foden will be following later, by train. It's all I know.'

'Thank you, Tilly. You're a brave young woman,' answered Chard gently.

***

'What is it Fugg? Can't you see I'm busy?' snarled Inspector Warboys.

Fugg, eager to get into his superior's good books after the wasted journey to South Wales, snapped smartly to attention.

'Good news sir. The red-headed girl that you believe might be helping Chard was apparently seen earlier this morning. One of the constables was asking around, and someone said she'd been talking to two men. One was a dark-featured, well-dressed individual; whereas the other was dressed shabbily and had a bandaged face.'

'Where was this?' demanded Warboys, putting his paperwork to one side.

'Near the railway footbridge in Belle Vue.'

Warboys growled. 'I've had enough of playing cat-and-mouse. Speak to the duty sergeant and pass on my instructions. He's to send every available man to Belle Vue. Wait! Better send a few to Coleham, just to be on the safe side. If any of those three are spotted, then I want them arrested on suspicion of helping an escaped felon, and brought here.'

'Yes sir. Anything else?'

Warboys paused for a moment. 'Yes. Go and tell Major Ferguson that I'm taking some direct action. It might appease him for a while.'

***

Chard and Cole sat in the waiting room of the doctor's surgery, on the outskirts of Birmingham.

'They say he's the best,' consoled Cole.

'He can't give her sight back though. If it wasn't for me dragging Miss Roper and Constable Morgan into all this, she wouldn't have lost her eye.'

Cole shrugged. 'We can't change the past. All we can do is to make the best of the current situation. I will ask something though. After all you've been through, why do you usually refer to your friends only by their surnames? You are content enough to call me Eli.'

'I don't know,' answered Chard. 'It just seems to make things easier. Miss Roper has always been Miss Roper and Constable Morgan has always been Morgan.' Shifting in his seat uncomfortably, he returned to the subject of Tilly.

'Can you really keep her safe in London and make sure she's provided for?'

'Yes,' answered Cole confidently. 'I have property there, and she can be cared for by my maid until she's well enough to find somewhere else. I have enough contacts to ensure some form of employment that will keep a roof over her head, and there'll be the proceeds from the disposal of her silver. I, on the other hand, am going to be out-of-pocket if I don't recover the stolen jewel. This doctor is damned expensive. I've asked him to patch her up and provide enough opiates for me to take her by train to London tonight. The sooner she's away from this damnable city the better. I can return to Shrewsbury tomorrow, then we'll turn our attention to Stanmore and Ferguson again.'

'Don't forget the reason why we came here,' reminded Chard. 'We need to rescue Cora Lamb, and they've got a head start. It stands to reason why they decided to use a narrowboat. If they wanted to move them by road, there would have to be stops on the way where the girls might be spotted. Going by rail would be quickest, but with many opportunities for their captives to draw attention to themselves. Narrowboats are slow, but they can keep the girls out of sight.'

'How long do you think it'll take them to get there?'

Chard shrugged. 'Perhaps five days. It's slow, but the safest method.'

'I'll make some enquiries in London. I have someone I can rely on to look out for the boat passing through Brentford on its way to the Thames. From that, I can work out when and where they are liable to join a ship. If Foden is arriving later by train, the chances are they'll meet on the dockside.'

'A lot can happen in five days. I just pray we can be there to stop them,' said Chard. 'In the meantime, I had better get going. I can pick up Morgan from the infirmary, take him back to Shrewsbury, and put him on the train to South Wales. If I don't leave now, I won't get him to the station on time.'

'Then off you go, Thomas, take some funds with you,' insisted Cole, passing over some money. 'And don't forget to put that bandage back on. I'll see you tomorrow.'

***

It was early evening when the policeman came. May had been staring out of her room window, when she saw him come down Bynner Street, knocking on the door of every house. Something within warned her that it would be prudent to take her coat and move downstairs. She ran down to the ground floor then out through the back door unnoticed. Moving around the side of the pub, she stopped and sneaked a look around the corner, just as the policeman approached the front door.

'Good evening Constable,' greeted an old man who was leaving the premises, having had his daily pint of stout. 'Not going in for a few pints in your uniform, are you?'

'No, you cheeky old bugger. We're looking for a red-headed young woman; a stranger to the town, with a Welsh accent.'

'Oh, she's in there,' said the old man helpfully. 'Got a room upstairs. Not in any trouble, is she?'

The policeman grinned. 'Just go home, old man,' he said, walking into the pub.

Panicking, May ran to the end of the street; but everywhere she looked, there seemed to be a policeman knocking on doors. Changing direction or ducking for cover whenever she might be spotted, May fled through Coleham and across Greyfriars Bridge, then past the Salop Home. Once in the town, the sudden absence of policemen was noticeable. They had targeted the area across the river deliberately. Someone must have given her away. In her mind, the best thing would be to head for the railway station. If Thomas was going to put Idris on the nine o'clock train, then it would make sense for her to accompany him. She would feel guilty at not staying to help clear Thomas's name, but with the police chasing her, she would be more of a hindrance. Walking down the High Street, May sensed someone was watching her, though it couldn't be the police. They would no doubt just chase and arrest her. She shrugged the thought away and walked up Pride Hill, past the shops closed and shuttered for the day.

Ahead, smoking a cigarette and heading in her direction, was Constable Fugg. The fair-haired policeman took a long draw on his cigarette, and exhaled a cloud of blue tobacco smoke, before coughing harshly. Then a quizzical look came over his face as he saw May, still backing away, in the distance. May noticed his hesitation, and as the detective moved closer, she instinctively turned and ran.

'Oi! Stop!' Fugg pulled out his police whistle and went to blow it, but then realised it was pointless, as every other man on duty was over the other side of the town. He himself would also have been there, had he not been trying to find Major Ferguson. His call at the Major's house had been fruitless, with the butler saying neither the master nor mistress was at home. Having eventually been to the prison, he'd been informed that the Governor was out of town attending a regimental reunion. Throwing his cigarette to the ground, Fugg set off in pursuit, almost immediately slipping on a dog turd. Getting back to his feet and cursing loudly, he saw May disappearing around a corner, heading for Mardol.

'Out of my way!' yelled May, as she pushed past two youths, heading as fast as she could down the Mardol Hill. Although the top of the street was empty, further down towards the river, May could hear the sound of drunken revelry. If she could only lose her pursuer, she could turn right at the bottom of the hill onto Smithfield Road, which circled back towards the railway station. On she hurried, oblivious to the difference in the area in daylight hours, when families and respectable citizens shopped safely on the busy street.

'What do we have here then lads?' said a soldier, grabbing her arm. Three of his drunken comrades laughed, until she kicked her assailant hard between the legs, and pulled herself free. Glancing behind, she could see Fugg was gaining, so she rushed on, ignoring the foul insults shouted by the injured soldier. Ahead two men in shirtsleeves were engaged in a fist fight whilst several onlookers cheered their favourite.

'Stop that woman!' yelled Fugg.

May turned and saw the policeman was only ten yards behind. 'That's the bastard who arrested us last week!' screeched a woman's voice.

'Yes, the little shit!' shouted another.

The shouts had come from an alley, which was signed Masons Passage; and May looked on as two women, their blouses hardly containing their breasts, shouted obscenities at Fugg. Then they picked up stones and started to throw them at the unfortunate policeman, who tried to fend them off. Others joined in the fun, causing him to retreat as fast as he could.

Breathing a sigh of relief, May ran on and turned the corner on to Smithfield Road, heading parallel with the river, back towards the northern end of town. Despite having lost her pursuer, May was only too aware that Smithfield Road was a busy thoroughfare on which she might easily be spotted. As it was, she still felt as if someone was watching her.

Taking a small detour from the main road, she tried to take a short cut by the cattle market. It was dark here, and there was only one carriage that overtook her before pulling up; stopping no doubt to check on the horses.

May passed it without a thought, thinking of how good it was going to be to see Idris again and return to Wales. Moments later she felt something being clamped over her face and, overwhelmed by a noxious vapour which flooded her senses, she passed out.

***

Constable Morgan was in a weakened state when Chard collected him from Birmingham infirmary, but able to stand on his own feet and walk unaided, albeit slowly. The fact that some of his belongings would have to remain at his lodgings in Frankwell, and might not be recovered, didn't cause him concern. All Morgan wanted to do was to get back to Pontypridd.

Conversation on the journey to Shrewsbury was stilted and awkward, for Chard in particular; the guilt of having dragged the young constable into danger weighed heavily on his mind. At least he was pleased to find no police on duty at Shrewsbury railway station. Morgan was put on the intended train without incident and Chard felt relieved. It lasted only as far as the Plough and Harrow.

As Chard approached the pub, he was greeted by a deep Irish accent.

'Don't go in!' the voice warned.

On turning towards the sound, Chard was surprised to see the Irishman with the dented bowler hat he'd met earlier in the week. 'Why not?'

'There's a constable inside. The area's been crawling with the coppers, so it has. They're looking for a man with a bandaged face. They reckon he's been helping a man on the run. Nobody's given you away though.'

'Thank you for the warning.'

'I'm no friend of the police, and I don't forget a man who's bought me a drink neither,' replied the man, tapping the side of his nose. 'There's something else. A lad came running up when I was standing by the door, looking out for you. He had an envelope which he'd been told to give to the bandaged man. I gave him a clip across the ear and took it.'

'Did he say who the envelope came from?' asked Chard.

'No, but here it is. I haven't opened it.'

Chard took it with his free hand, opening it with his teeth, pulling out the contents and letting the envelope fall to the ground. As he read it, he felt a cold anger rise within himself. It was in the same writing as the note which had lured him to the Roman ruins. This time it read:

'I HAVE THE REDHEAD. COME ALONE AT MIDNIGHT TO MORETON CORBET CASTLE OR SHE DIES.'

'What does it say?' asked the Irishman.

'Something I have to deal with. Here's some money for a few drinks. Try and keep everyone occupied inside for the next ten minutes, particularly the constable.'

'That I will,' agreed the man, tapping the side of his nose again.

Chard ran to the stables, freeing his left arm from its sling as he did so. Hitching up the pony and trap as quickly as he could, he jumped onto the driving seat, only to hesitate when he heard a whining. Cursing himself, he jumped back down and opened Barney's kennel.

'Come on then, you stupid animal. I've got a feeling this could be the last time I'll get to take you anywhere. If I'm going into "the valley of death" you might as well come with me.'

THIRTY-TWO

The ruins of Moreton Corbet's castle and mansion house, about ten miles or so north east of Shrewsbury, was just off the country road between the village of Shawbury and Chard's home town of Wem. Chard could see why the kidnapper had chosen it: the place would be deserted at night. At least there was little cloud in the sky, allowing some measure of moonlight for which Chard was grateful.

'Why the hell didn't I make sure there was an oil lamp?' Chard demanded of Barney, who was laying quietly at his feet.

To Chard it felt as if the journey as far as Shawbury took an eternity, but fortunately he'd made good time.

'There's a coaching inn, so we'll stop there. If I arrive at the ruins too early it might endanger May. I'll leave you here to mind the trap,' Chard explained to the dog. He expected no response and got none, but somehow talking to the animal made him feel more in control.

There was plenty of room in the inn's yard, and knowing the stop would not be a long one, he hitched the pony's reins to a nearby fence whilst he went inside.

before he entered, he removed the bandage. No point in any pretence, he told himself. By the end of tonight I will either have got my man, or I'll be lying dead in a ditch alongside Miss Roper.

When he entered the bar, several locals turned to look at him. It was possible that someone might recognise him from years gone by, or from the wanted posters in Shrewsbury, but he didn't care. Even if someone went to get a constable, they wouldn't return in time, and people in small villages like this generally tended towards a quiet life. Going to the bar, Chard ordered a whiskey. He glanced at the clock on the wall, then went to sit by the fire. Really, he shouldn't have been served, rural areas having tighter licensing restrictions than the towns; but Chard knew that opening hours weren't enforced with vigour. Gradually, the other customers started to leave, and Chard, with another glance at the clock, realised it was also time for him to go. Bending down as if to adjust his shoe, he grabbed the iron poker from the fire stand, and slid it inside his coat.

When he got back to the cart, he patted Barney and placed the poker alongside him.

'You mind that, Barney. It might not be much, but it's all I've got,' Chard muttered, wishing he had Cole's howdah pistol.

'Time for this to end, one way or the other,' he muttered, as he set off on the dark, lonely road.

***

The ghostly ruins of Moreton Corbet castle were approached via a narrow lane, off the Wem Road, past some farm outbuildings. As he came to the end of the lane, Chard pulled to a halt. He knew there were two sets of ruins here. To his left, somewhere in the darkness, were the remains of a thirteenth century castle. However, his attention was fully drawn directly ahead, to the magnificent Elizabethan mansion house; the outline of its ruined southern range majestic, yet somehow terrifying, framed in the moonlight.

Chard took a deep breath, picked up the iron poker, and jumped down. Barney stood up, shook his body, yawned, then leapt to the ground to follow his master.

'Good boy,' said Chard warmly. 'I could do with the company.'

Barney looked up in response to the kind words, then wandered off into the long grass, sniffing as he went.

Shaking his head, gripping his makeshift weapon tightly, Chard walked forward towards the ruins, unsure exactly which part to head for. Deciding it was pointless waiting for a sudden bullet, or an attack by a savage dog, he decided to call out.

'I'm here! Show yourself!'

Chard knew the shout would alert no-one other than the kidnapper. The nearest villages were too far away and the farm outbuildings unoccupied. In the distance, beyond the castle ruins, was the remote Saint Bartholomew's church; but his voice would not carry as far as the vicarage.

Seconds later, a light appeared by the Elizabethan structure. It was a figure, carrying a lamp. Chard stepped forward, his limbs heavy and his chest tight, as he prepared himself for what might be his death. The iron poker, less than two feet long, was slipped up the sleeve of his coat, concealed from sight. As he got closer, it was possible to make out that the holder of the lamp was a woman. When he was within ten paces, she held the lamp up to her face.

'Dear God! Della!' exclaimed Chard.

Without saying a word, Mrs Ferguson turned and walked through a narrow doorway into the ruined building. Chard followed silently. They were now inside the roofless structure of the southern range.

'That will do, Mrs Ferguson.'

The voice, coming from the shadows, made Chard jump. He turned to the side as a tall figure stepped forward, holding a pistol.

'So glad you came,' said Jeremy Stanmore, moving his aim from the woman to point at Chard's chest. 'I had no guarantee you would. I feared the police might have picked you up. Not that it would have been a disaster, but this makes things so much neater.' He waved the gun briefly towards Mrs Ferguson. 'Lead on, or I'll put a bullet in you right here.'

Reluctantly, Della moved to Chard's left, and stepped over a low wall into what would have been a small ante-room. It had high walls, but the roof was also open to the night sky.

'You have a sense of the dramatic. Why here, and why did you choose the Roman ruins last time?' asked Chard, to give himself time to think.

'Here, because it's the sort of place a fugitive who used to live in Wem would know about. Also, it's because it comes under the County Police, not under that idiot Warboys. It suited me to have him blundering around until now. A neat ending to this little scenario needs to be fed to someone more intelligent. As for Wroxeter, at the time I wasn't absolutely sure it was you, Mr Chard, or how much you knew. I thought inviting you to the site where Sabrina's Teardrop was said to have been found would be enticing. I haven't forgiven you for killing my animal by the way. Talking of which, where is your gun?'

Chard smiled, realising that Stanmore was unaware of Cole's involvement in the shooting of his dog. It had been a dark night and perhaps he had been too far away to see what had happened before making his escape.

'I don't have one,' he answered, holding up his arms, and opening his hands; sending the poker sliding further up his sleeve.

Stanmore turned his attention back to his other captive. 'You know where to go,' he ordered.

Chard guessed where they were headed, for he had taken a sweetheart to the ruins once when he was a youth. Within the room was a small flight of steps leading into a cellar. It had a very low entrance and was dark inside, even in daylight.

'Mind your head,' warned Stanmore sarcastically as Chard followed Mrs Ferguson, ducking through the cellar entrance to stand beneath the low barrel-vaulted ceiling.

'Where is Miss Roper? She's the reason I came,' asked Chard, fearful that Stanmore had already disposed of her.

It was Mrs Ferguson who replied. She held the lamp so that the light carried to the corner of the small cellar. 'She's over there, Thomas. I was taken this morning, and then he took this girl earlier tonight.'

'May!' exclaimed Chard, moving towards where she lay bound and gagged on the cold stone floor.

'Stay where you are!' ordered Stanmore. 'And you, Mrs Ferguson, put the lamp on the floor.'

'Are you going to lock us in, like you did to Landell and my wife?' asked Chard.

'A bit difficult when there's no door. I do apologise for what happened to your wife by the way. She was in the wrong place at the wrong time. For that matter, I didn't originally intend for you to be blamed.'

'No, it was meant to be Warren wasn't it? That's why you left the cigarettes he was known to smoke.'

'Very good, Mr Chard. I knew that eventually the bodies would be discovered, though I was expecting it to take a lot longer. I knew Landell had dismissed his staff, ready for his departure to America; but what I didn't know was that he had re-mortgaged the property and bailiffs would call. In any case, I thought why not frame my only remaining partner and draw attention away from myself? If Warboys had been more intelligent, then he might have picked up the clue; but as it was, he decided you were to blame so I was happy enough with that. Now please be so kind as to pick up those ropes on the floor and bind Mrs Ferguson.'

Chard turned his back on Stanmore whilst he picked up the ropes, finding it difficult to bend his right arm, with the poker up the sleeve of his coat.

'Why kill Landell though? Had he stolen the sapphire?'

Stanmore laughed. 'Stolen it? It was given to him! I saw Lady Deansmoor secretly hand it over. The theft had been arranged to take place at a social gathering, just to ensure there were witnesses to confirm it had been taken.'

'All an act in order to claim the insurance. I had that impression having visited Lady Deansmoor,' said Chard standing before Mrs Ferguson and taking her hands. 'So, the temptation of taking Sabrina's Teardrop was too much for you,' he added accusingly.

'I believed killing Landell and stealing the jewel would give me huge wealth,' responded Stanmore, 'and as a bonus, if Warren was eventually blamed, I would also have sole control of our business.' He gave a sigh of regret. 'Unfortunately, things didn't quite work out as anticipated.'

'Kelly?' asked Chard, whilst tying Mrs Ferguson's hands.

'That's right. He recalled seeing me on the night Landell went missing, so when the bodies were found he thought it would be worth blackmailing me. His mistake,' grunted Stanmore. 'Get on the floor, Mrs Ferguson,' he added.

Her face pale with fear, Della knelt down, then lay next to May; whose eyes betrayed her terror.

'I take it that you can't have sold the sapphire yet. Where is it?' asked Chard, to distract his captor.

'It's been in the safest place in the world, until recently. Not that it's worth anything. Now tie her feet.'

Chard stopped, his back still to Stanmore. 'Not worth anything?'

'It never was,' came the reply, accompanied by a mirthless laugh. 'It's a fake. The valuation was done by a crony of the old bitch's husband. They insured it heavily and used it as collateral against borrowing. She only wanted Landell to steal it in order to defraud the insurance company. He would have got a percentage of the proceeds. The thing was that he didn't know it was a fake. If he had known and told me, then I wouldn't have killed him, or your wife. I only found out after I took it to an unscrupulous but reliable jeweller of my acquaintance. I said tie her feet!'

'You're quite the killer, aren't you? I assume Lady Deansmoor died at your hands?' suggested Chard, binding Mrs Ferguson's feet.

'I'd been blackmailing her after I discovered the jewel was fake. She would go to prison for the rest of her life if it was shown she had defrauded her insurers of such a large amount. That's why I kept the sapphire, as proof of her crime. Of course at the time she was unaware I had killed Charles, I just said he had gone to America to flee his creditors. I knew when the bodies were eventually found I would need to deal with her, and that was the case. She thought she could switch our positions and blackmail me instead. More fool her.'

Mrs Ferguson panicked and started to struggle as Chard attempted to tie the final knot around her ankles.

'Keep still!' ordered Stanmore. 'Unfortunately, this stupid woman, her mind turned by the visit of your young red-headed friend there, had started to consider your innocence. Then by chance she noticed me in The Quarry and saw me enter The Dingle on the day Lady Deansmoor died. Rather foolishly she confronted me about it. I had planned to just use her as bait; but I got out of her that this other one could be contacted at the Prince of Wales.

She was hard to follow around the town in my carriage, especially with the police after her, and it was by chance that I finally took her by the cattle market. Now keep facing away from me and kneel down,' he ordered.

Chard searched for a way to buy time. At some point he was going to have to swing around and strike with the poker, but he needed to catch Stanmore off guard. 'You explained how you knew where May was, but how did you know I was at the Plough and Harrow, the first time I mean.'

'You told the bailiff who found the bodies. He told his friend, Major Ferguson's coachman who told his master; then Ferguson told me when we were talking in the square. Of course, no-one knew at the time who you were, I just thought you were a nuisance. I only put two and two together when you turned up armed at Wroxeter and killed my dog.'

'What's your plan now? Why didn't you just turn me over to the police?' Chard asked.

'I didn't know how much you had found out. You might have told them your suspicions about Lady Deansmoor being involved in the theft of her own jewel; which could have started awkward questions. With that fool Warboys in charge, it was unlikely the murder charge would have stuck anyway, enabling your continued interference in my affairs. Of course, dear Major Ferguson would have wanted his revenge. He loves her you know,' added Stanmore, 'even though he beats her.'

Slowly, Chard started to ease the poker down from his sleeve, into his hand, whilst Stanmore continued to speak.

'You will be found, having taken your own life after killing the two women before you. The one who deserted you and married the governor, and the other with whom you were having a torrid affair.'

'But I...'

'I know it's not true, but the papers love a scandal. You killed Lady Deansmoor after having visited her home disguised as a man of God, then luring her to Shrewsbury. Your entire rampage will be put down as the act of a madman, determined to go on a killing spree of helpless women before taking his own life. I was very fortunate that the police didn't catch you tonight. It saved me a lot of trouble.'

Muscles tensed, Chard prepared to spring. The one thing in his favour was that Stanmore would need to take a clear shot for it to look like suicide. If it took two bullets to kill him it would prove his own innocence.

'You see how clever it is?' Stanmore bragged. 'I would have had to have disposed of Mrs Ferguson anyway, but now I can put the blame on you. Naturally, I'll kill you first.'

Chard heard the hammer of the pistol being cocked, and swiftly swung around from his kneeling position with arm outstretched. By luck, rather than judgement, the tip of the poker hit Stanmore's thumb just as he fired, causing him to drop the weapon in pain. The sound was deafening within the enclosed space as the bullet smashed into the brickwork of the vaulted ceiling, sending a cloud of dust down on the occupants. Unfortunately for Chard, the wild swipe had caused the poker to slip out of his grasp, and it clattered across the stone floor. Landell looked for the pistol, but before he could grasp it, Chard kicked it away towards the bound women in the corner. With a roar, Stanmore bent down and picked up the poker. Aware that his opponent was bigger than him and also had a weapon, Chard turned his back to dash towards the pistol. He was too slow, and grunted as a blow across his shoulders made him lose balance and fall to the floor, landing on Mrs Ferguson.

'Damn you! You cur!' yelled Stanmore, unaware of the faintest of noises behind him.

He rained down several blows, landing on both Chard and Mrs Ferguson, when to their surprise, he gave an horrific scream of pain. Chard moved his hands which had been trying to protect his head from the blows, to see that Barney had clamped his enormous vice-like jaws around Stanmore's lower leg. There was a tearing of flesh and sinew as the dog shook his prize vigorously from side to side. Stanmore lost his balance and fell to the floor, trying to swipe at the dog's head with the poker.

Despite hurting like fury from what felt like a broken arm and an injured back, Chard got up and threw himself at Stanmore, snatching the weapon from his hand.

'Get the dog off!' screamed the savaged figure, writhing on the floor, desperately trying to tear the animal away to relieve the pain.

Chard shrugged, then hit Stanmore hard across the head with the poker, hoping it wouldn't kill him, but not too bothered if it did. The man stopped struggling and lay still, whilst Barney still gnawed at his leg.

'That's enough. Good boy!' said Chard, stroking Barney and slowly persuading him to let go. A quick search inside the prostrate man's pockets found a small pocket knife.

Stepping across to the two bound captives, Chard untied Mrs Ferguson first because she had accidentally taken some of the blows when Stanmore had been hitting him. There was a nasty cut over her eye, causing a stream of blood to run down her face, and he feared her collar bone might be broken.

'Thank you,' she moaned, but Chard had already moved to free her fellow prisoner.

'You're safe now,' he whispered, kissing May on the forehead, before untying her bonds.

'Oh, Thomas,' she replied, hugging him as if she never wanted to let go.

Chard let her hold him for a few seconds, but then broke the embrace.

'I need to tie him up, if he's still breathing. Once I've done that, I need you to take the lamp and head past the castle ruins. You'll see the tower of St Bartholomew's church not too far away. Bang on the door of the vicarage and get help. I'll stay here with Mrs Ferguson. With a bit of luck, my dear May, this nightmare is over.'

THIRTY-THREE

Chard sat in the locked room, waiting to be seen by Inspector Miller of the Shropshire County Constabulary. May had eventually woken the vicar of St Bartholomew's from his slumbers. On seeing her distressed state, he'd ridden his bicycle to Shawbury to get medical help. The rest of the night had been spent in the vicarage, with Stanmore left in the cellar under the watchful eye of a local farmer. When the county police were fetched in the morning, they insisted on putting both Stanmore and Chard in handcuffs. Given the unusual circumstances of the case, the police took the two captives to their headquarters offices in Shrewsbury; where, in the absence of cells, they were secured in separate locked rooms.

Regardless of his situation, Chard felt refreshed, having slept better than he had for many nights, despite his injuries. The thing now concerning him was the angry conversation echoing down the corridor.

'I say they are both our prisoners, so hand them over without delay!' insisted a voice which was unmistakeably Inspector Warboys.

'I agree. I want Chard back in my prison, where he belongs,' said Major Ferguson.

'The man is recovering from injuries. In addition, he is *our* prisoner, as the crime of kidnapping took place outside of Shrewsbury,' argued Inspector Miller, almost shouting to get himself heard.

'My wife was kidnapped inside Shrewsbury and taken outside the town; so the place of the crime is inside Shrewsbury.'

'I would have thought you would be grateful Chard saved your wife's life,' retorted Miller.

'To a degree, I am,' replied Ferguson. 'On the other hand, he injured one of my men and escaped from my prison, so I want him back there. Also, I find it hard to believe Stanmore took my wife. I haven't been able to speak to her properly yet. The doctor at the infirmary insisted she should rest for the day; but I'll get the truth out of her.'

'Your wife has already given a full statement and she was unequivocal about Chard's innocence and Stanmore's guilt.'

'Nevertheless, the murders took place in my jurisdiction,' interrupted Warboys. 'I shall take this matter up with your superintendent and the Chief Constable for Shropshire if necessary.'

'That is your prerogative,' agreed Miller. 'However, they will not be available until Monday afternoon. By all means come back then.'

Chard heard further mutterings and then a door slammed. The possibility of returning to the prison concerned him, and he was eager to discuss the matter with Inspector Miller. As the time dragged on, Chard ran through every possibility. Would Stanmore somehow get off? Would Major Ferguson persuade Della to withdraw her evidence? Where was Sabrina's Teardrop? Stanmore said he hadn't got rid of it, so where could it be?'

Eventually the door opened. 'Follow me,' ordered a cheery constable.

'Constable Godfrey! What are you doing here?'

'Changed over to the County Police along with a few of the lads after you left for South Wales. We didn't like the way things were going in the town force, and the county was eager to have us, so here we are. Glad things seem to be working out for you Mr Chard. We knew you couldn't have done those murders, so we weren't looking too hard for you.'

Godfrey led Chard to another room, where Inspector Miller was waiting.

'Take a seat. How are your injuries?'

'The doctor you kindly sent for assures me there's nothing broken. I've got a badly bruised hip, upper arm and back. He said I was very fortunate,' replied Chard.

'Good,' said Miller, frowning. 'I admit I'm not entirely sure what to do with you,' he confessed.

'I couldn't help but overhear your visitors,' said Chard.

'Unfortunately, this isn't the largest of stations,' shrugged Miller. 'The point is, they're right about the murders being in their jurisdiction. Even the kidnapping technically took place in Shrewsbury town.'

'Has Stanmore confessed?'

Miller gave a rueful smile. 'Yes and no. He admits to taking Mrs Ferguson, but denies everything else.'

'But he confessed in front of us all...' objected Chard.

'I don't disagree. I am holding him on the evidence of Mrs Ferguson's statement. If she withdraws it however...' Miller left the statement dangling in the air.

'Miss Roper heard it! What about her evidence, and mine for that matter?'

'The evidence of a fugitive from prison and his accomplice? The defence would tear it to shreds. No, everything depends on Mrs Ferguson. Though I do happen to believe you. If I had my way, I would put you in front of a magistrate on Monday morning and get you released. However, if there is any possibility of the evidence against Stanmore being inadequate, then I'm afraid I'll have to turn you over to Inspector Warboys. In fact, I should do that right away in any case, as technically all of the offences are outside my jurisdiction.'

Neither man spoke for a moment or two, until inspiration came suddenly to Chard.

'Sabrina's Teardrop,' he said, smiling.

'What?'

'The jewellery theft. It was one of your cases, outside of the town.'

'Yes, I've read the statements and I'm aware of your claims, but Stanmore has denied it.'

'What if I can prove he had the sapphire?' asked Chard.

'If you could prove that, then it would back up the statements. It would also relate directly to a County Constabulary case, and I could get you in front of a magistrate on Monday morning.'

'I feel I can prove it, but it would require some assistance from yourself. There's a gentleman by the name of Elijah Cole who is returning from London today. He mentioned he'd been staying at the Raven Hotel when last in Shrewsbury, so that's where you'll find him. Could you ask him to come and see me?'

***

It was mid-afternoon when Chard received the first of two visitors.

'How are you Thomas?' May asked, as soon as she entered the room.

'Never mind me. How are you after such an ordeal?'

'They aren't going to charge me for helping you. They say there's not enough evidence. Inspector Miller was very kind.'

'So, what are you going to do now?'

'I'm going to collect my things from the Prince of Wales, and catch the first train home,' May replied sadly. 'I have no choice. I've no money left other than my train fare, and my parents will be worried.'

'So will Doctor Henderson,' added Chard.

'I doubt he'll have me back, after my deceit. Everything will be bound to come out.'

Chard gave her a hug. 'Never mind. It'll all blow over.'

'But what about you? Why haven't they let you go?'

'Don't worry, May. They will. I'll be back in Pontypridd before you know it.'

'Then I'll say goodbye, for now. Thank you for saving me, once more.' May gave a smile, though tears were starting to form, then left.

An hour later the second visitor arrived, to Chard's delight.

'Eli, I'm glad they found you.'

Cole returned the greeting with a smile. 'I understand you got your man.'

'Yes, but I'm not out of the woods yet. The final nail in his coffin will be the jewel. It's a fake. The sapphire is just a very convincing imitation.'

'Tell me more,' insisted Cole.

Chard recounted the events of the previous evening, whilst Cole listened without interrupting.

'He didn't tell you where Sabrina's Teardrop was hidden though, did he?' he asked, when Chard finished his tale.

'Actually, I've realised that he did,' said Chard. 'To be frank, I could have asked Inspector Miller to take me to Stanmore's house and picked it up straight away; but that would have denied you the claim to have recovered it. After all you've done, you deserve to get your fee from the insurers. I'll tell you exactly where to find it; but I'd be obliged if you went with a policeman as a witness, and insist on taking Barney with you. I wouldn't be alive if it wasn't for him; and at the moment they've got him penned up and liable to be destroyed as a dangerous dog. You can pass him onto George Lamb at Brougham Square afterwards.'

'What if he doesn't want to take him?' asked Cole dubiously.

'Tell him it's just for a couple of days; assuming I'm going to be freed. Talking of George, any progress on finding Cora?'

Cole nodded. 'I've made arrangements for the narrowboat's progress to be monitored as it approaches London. We've got at least until Tuesday before it arrives. I've also asked a contact at the docks to check shipping lists, to narrow down the likely vessel.

We'll catch them Thomas, don't you worry.'

'Should we involve the local police?' asked Chard.

Cole shook his head. 'I think not. With a man like Foden, you never know who's in his pocket. I think it's safer to handle this ourselves. However, if you're still in custody by then, I might have to change my mind.'

'I agree,' said Chard. 'How is Tilly?'

'Safe. She's at property I own in London, being looked after by a retired nurse. I dare say she'll be content if we give Foden his just desserts. In the meantime, tell me where to find Sabrina's Teardrop…'

***

As Chard walked out of the courthouse alongside Elijah Cole on Monday morning. He heard raised voices from across the town square.

'Arrest that man! He's escaping!'

Cole looked in the direction of the shouting and gave a broad smile. 'It looks like some people are going to get upset.'

Rushing towards them were Inspector Warboys and Major Ferguson; the latter red with anger.

Chard held up a placatory hand before they got too close.

'Wait, gentlemen please. I have been released by the magistrate.'

'Why?' demanded Warboys. 'We were just on our way to see the Chief Constable of the County Constabulary to have you returned to the prison.'

'Because irrefutable evidence has been found linking Stanmore to the murders of Mr Landell and my wife. My name is cleared.'

Warboys spluttered with anger, whilst Ferguson continued to argue. 'What about assaulting my prison guard and escaping from custody?'

'Ah yes,' grimaced Chard. 'I have to admit my release is temporary as such. I have been bailed for the assault on the prison guard, with Mr Cole here providing surety.'

'This is most irregular,' interrupted Warboys.

'The magistrate has rather rushed things through, given the circumstances of my wrongful arrest,' admitted Chard. 'Nevertheless, there's nothing you can do about it. Good day, gentlemen.'

Leaving the policeman and prison governor speechless with indignation, Cole and Chard set off for George Lamb's house.

'How did you know we'd find Sabrina's Teardrop there? You still haven't told me,' said Cole.

'When we were in the cellar at Moreton Corbet, Stanmore mentioned it was *"in the safest place in the world, until recently"*. Earlier he'd said that he still had it, so logically he had either moved its location, or the place was no longer the safest. I reasoned that if you owned a fighting dog capable of tearing someone apart, then the safest place to keep anything would be where you also kept the beast.'

'As it transpired, in a metal cage at his house. I found Sabrina's Teardrop under the dog's bedding,' added Cole.

Chard nodded. 'When the dog was killed, he still kept the jewel there, but of course it was no longer *"the safest place in the world"*.'

'Brilliantly thought out, Thomas. Now all we've got to do is rescue Miss Lamb.'

THIRTY-FOUR

'Are you sure this is the right quay and the right berth?' whispered Chard.

'Undoubtedly,' assured Cole. 'Le Papillon Noir, French owned, out of Le Havre. The crew unloaded its cargo of wine before you turned up. Most of them have gone ashore, for a night on the town, leaving just a handful on board. It's the ideal time for Foden to put the girls on board and lock them in a cabin.'

'They'd better not have harmed our Cora,' grunted George Lamb, tapping a crowbar across the palm of his hand.

The three men were huddled behind a stack of crates, outside a large warehouse. A thick fog had descended and they could barely see beyond ten yards. There was the distant blast of foghorns further along the Thames, and the occasional shout from workers unloading on other quays; but other than the intermittent slap of water against the dockside, it was quiet in the immediate vicinity. The polluted air felt heavy and cloying, with a foetid stench of damp and decay.

'What if we miss them in this fog?' asked George anxiously.

'The shipping lists have been checked and I'm confident it's the right vessel,' replied Cole. 'They'll have to pass this way to get to it. It sails in the morning, so they'll be boarding tonight. Do you have your revolver ready, Thomas?'

'I do, but I would rather not use it.' Chard checked the chamber of the gun lent to him by Cole, for the third or fourth time.

Cole patted his howdah pistol. 'Hopefully we won't need to. Gunfire would rouse the skeleton crew from the ship, which won't help the situation.'

'The main thing is to keep our Cora safe,' interrupted George.

'I agree,' responded Cole, 'but…'

'Quiet!' whispered Chard sharply. 'I can hear footsteps.'

The three men fell silent, tense with anticipation, as a figure came through the fog.

'Foden!' muttered Chard.

Harry Foden stopped just within sight, and lit a cigarette. He was dressed in a dark suit, with a raincape and top hat.

The three observers looked at each other, the desire to confront the man obvious in their expressions; but they knew it was imperative that they waited. Fifteen minutes passed, with Foden in view, impatiently tapping his foot, before the others arrived.

It was the high-pitched squeal of indignation that alerted them.

'Shut up or I'll cut you,' admonished a voice Chard seemed to recognise. It had an unmistakeable Birmingham monotone, but without the very broad accent of some of the peaky blinders.

Chard's assumption was correct, as Pitt came into view, holding a knife at the throat of a pretty blonde-haired girl. He was followed closely by another blonde, accompanied by another man, holding a pistol against her ribs.

'It's Cora!' breathed George, excitedly.

Chard placed a calming hand on his friend's shoulder. 'Not yet!'

'What was that?' exclaimed Cora's captor, turning around. 'I thought I heard voices.'

Cole moved silently to the end of the stack of crates, intending to approach from behind, under cover of the fog.

'It was nothing. You're just jumpy,' snapped Pitt, unaware of Cole moving cat-like towards his companion.

'I'm going too,' whispered George eagerly, and before Chard could restrain him, his friend set off, following Cole's example.

'Blast this damn weather!' cursed Pitt, as a thick patch of fog drifted across, obscuring him from the others. Walking forward cautiously he caught a glimpse of Foden a few yards ahead. Instinctively, his captive tried to pull away, receiving a slap for her pains. The terrified girl started to sob.

'Betty, are you alright?' called Cora, unable to see her through the fog.

'Keep her quiet!' snapped Pitt, whilst trying to control his own prisoner, who was weeping even louder.

Eager to obey, the man with the pistol tucked the weapon in his belt, then put one hand over Cora's mouth, whilst using the other to twist her arm behind her back. Then in just one moment, his expression froze and his body went rigid as he felt the muzzle of a gun pressed against the back of his head. Releasing Cora, and turning slowly, he came face to face with a man whose large-bore handgun was now pointing directly at his nose. Cole pressed a finger to his lips, ordering silence, then gestured for Cora to move back in the direction of the warehouse; where she found the welcoming arms of her brother-in-law.

'About time!' grunted Foden, moving through the fog to greet Pitt. 'Any problems on the way here?'

'None. These bitches have been as good as gold until this one started sobbing just now.'

Foden leaned forward and lifted Betty's crestfallen chin with his index finger. 'You can cry all you want. No-one will come to your rescue. I own you. It is something you will have to accept, until I pass you on to your new owner.'

Absorbed in his conversation, and enjoying the girl's distress, Foden was unaware of the movement of Chard. Despite the pain in his bruised hip, he had moved stealthily forward, keeping to the shadows of the warehouse wall, and was now positioned behind Foden, blocking access to the ship's gangway.

In the distance, there was a loud splash as if something had fallen off the quayside, causing Pitt to look back into the fog, to where he assumed his accomplice and Cora were standing.

'What's going on back there? Bring her here!' he demanded, but no response came.

'There's something wrong,' exclaimed Foden, aware of the sound of footsteps coming from the direction of the ship's gangway.

Pitt instinctively grabbed Betty closer, holding his knife to the girl's throat.

'There's no escape,' came a voice from somewhere behind Foden.

'None at all,' came the answering voice from behind Pitt, as Cole stepped through the mist into view. The howdah pistol was held with a rock-steady hand, pointed at Pitt's head.

'Move a step closer and I'll slit her throat,' Pitt threatened; but there was panic in his voice.

'If you do, my friend here will blow your head clean off your shoulders,' interjected Chard, stepping into view. 'And I'll happily do the same to Mr Foden here, after what he did to Tilly.'

'What? What did he do to Tilly?' demanded Pitt, eyes darting wildly, looking for a way out.

'Foden here, took her eye. We found her on the floor of her room,' answered Cole.

'She was your wife, wasn't she?' added Chard, seeking to stoke the confusion forming on Pitt's face. 'I assumed you knew he was going to do it. Surely he told you before you set off on the canal?'

'Mr Foden, they're lying, aren't they?' asked Pitt. When no denial came, he moved the knife away from Betty's throat and pointed it accusingly at Foden. 'She might have run out on me, and she might be a pain in the arse, but she's still my wife. You had no right, Mr Foden. No right at all!'

'I had every damn right. She was snooping into our affairs. It's probably her fault this has happened tonight. I'll happily take her other eye, the next time I see her.'

Pitt dropped the knife and released Betty, who ran into Cole's arms.

'You have no escape Foden, I assume you will come with us quietly. Not to Birmingham though. I'll have you charged with abduction here in London, where hopefully your influence hasn't spread,' said Chard sternly.

No sooner had the words left his mouth than another thick bank of fog rolled in, enveloping them all. Seizing his chance, Foden ran.

'Bugger!' exclaimed Chard as he heard Foden's footsteps run off somewhere to his right. Ignoring the aches from his bruised body, he set off in pursuit.

There was a loud splash somewhere behind him, followed by a shout from Cole. 'Pitt's got away!' A crash and a curse up ahead indicated that somewhere ahead Foden had tripped and fallen, and indeed, when Chard passed into a patch of lighter mist, he could see his quarry regaining his feet. Running as fast as he could, Chard caught Foden around the legs in a rugby tackle which sent him crashing to the ground; but in doing so he dropped his pistol. Grabbing his opponent's body, he heaved him over so that he had Foden pinned on his back.

'Got you, you bastard!' he snarled triumphantly, leaning forward until their faces were just inches apart.

Unnoticed, Foden's right hand slid into his pocket and pulled out a small object. At the press of a small button a four-inch blade flicked out; and his arm made ready to plunge it between Chard's ribs.

'Look out! Knife!' yelled Cole, who had just caught up.

With a look of alarm, but lightning quick reflexes, Chard rolled to one side, grabbed Foden's wrist with his left hand; and with the aid of his other hand, drove the blade into the villain's own chest.

Foden spasmed, coughed up blood, then lay still.

'Well done, Thomas. Let's drop him in the water and get away,' congratulated Cole.

Chard lay, exhausted, on his back. 'You do the honours Eli, then let's all go home.'

EPILOGUE

Elijah Cole looked on at the solitary figure standing over the unmarked grave. Eventually the mourner turned and walked back in his direction, an expression of regret etched into his features.

'I'll get her a headstone, Eli. It's one of many things I need to do. My solicitor will sort out the financial matters, as Sofia had some investments of her own; but I'll need to contact her relatives in Italy. Superintendent Jones has authorised special leave of absence for me to deal with my affairs, but I'm going to have to provide a full account of everything that's happened. For all I know he'll end up dismissing me. My temporary replacement has apparently been doing a good job.'

Cole smiled benevolently. 'Come now, Thomas. I'm sure it will work out for the best. At least you are finally a free man.'

The two men left the churchyard and walked towards the centre of town in silence.

Despite his sombre mood, a recollection of an earlier incident brought a slight smile to Chard's face. 'You should have seen Major Ferguson's expression when I walked into the Dana to deliver a gift to my former cell-mate. He just went bright red and walked away. It's a damn shame Della ended up with him. She deserves better. At least my fate didn't have to wholly depend on her witness statement. I had feared Ferguson would have taken it out on her.'

'With Stanmore eventually confessing in the face of so much evidence, there was no murder case for you to answer.'

Chard nodded. 'Kelly refused to press charges for assault, because I'd found his brother's killer. I'm sure they could have thrown something else at me for having escaped custody; but given the rescue of two women from white slavery, the magistrate was happy to quash all charges.'

Heading up Pride Hill, a police van pulled by two black horses went past.

'That reminds me, have they caught Warren yet?' enquired Cole.
'They picked him up yesterday, so that's something for Warboys
to be happy about. I dare say he'll need to have something positive,
because when Superintendent Edge returns and finds out about his
ineptitude, he'll be lucky to keep his job.'

'It's a pity we couldn't have brought all of the kidnappers to
justice,' said Cole ruefully. 'I pushed the one with the pistol off the
quay, then Pitt went and jumped in of his own accord. I'd like to
think they drowned, but I fear not. At least we know Foden won't
cause any trouble in future.'

Chard frowned. 'I've never taken a life before. It prays on my
mind,' he confessed, stroking his neatly-trimmed sideburns in
thought.

Cole put a hand on his shoulder. 'Foden deserved it and if you
hadn't acted, then he would have done for you instead.' Seeing the
brooding look in Chard's eyes, he changed the subject.

'What about that dog of yours? Is it still with the Lambs?'

'Only for the time being. It keeps chewing George's shoes. I was
going to give it away, but the damn thing seems to know it saved my
life. I suppose I'll end up keeping it.'

'How is Cora Lamb?' asked Cole.

'In good spirits, considering the ordeal she's been through; and
of course, George and Freda are delighted. They asked me to pass
on their thanks. She couldn't have been rescued without your
help.'

'Think nothing of it. If you hadn't worked out the location of
Sabrina's Teardrop I would have been seriously out of pocket. As it
is, the insurance company will be paying my fee and suing Lady
Deansmoor's estate. There won't be much left of it by the time
they've finished,' replied Cole.

'What about Tilly? Have you found her employment?'

'I shall. She seems to be a bright young woman and obviously
very brave. She's coming to terms with her new disability and wears
a silk eye-patch. The doctor says there's no sign of any infection. I've
disposed of her illicit nest-egg and the proceeds, less my commission,
will keep her solvent for quite a while. On the subject of young
women, do you have any news from May?'

Chard gave a disappointed sigh. 'I received a letter from Miss Roper this morning. Unfortunately, she's been dismissed from her post at the infirmary.'

'I'm sorry to hear that,' responded Cole sympathetically. 'Any news on her suitor?'

'Constable Morgan seems to be making a good recovery from his injuries and she intends to accept his proposal of marriage,' answered Chard, but with no enthusiasm. 'She reasoned that eventually it will come out that Morgan was in Shrewsbury at the same time as herself, and the wrong assumption would be made. Probably better to take the plunge and get engaged, rather than have her father force it upon them.'

The two friends stood outside the Raven Hotel and Cole offered his hand. 'Please pass on my best wishes. I have a meeting with another prospective client to attend back in London; but I had to come and see you today, in case I didn't get another chance before you returned to South Wales.'

'Much appreciated, Eli,' thanked Chard, shaking his hand warmly. 'I couldn't have cleared my name without you.'

'A word of advice, Thomas. You've been through a lot in a very short time. Once you've settled your affairs here, take a rest.'

'I would if I could, Eli; but I'm obliged to return to duty. I'll soon be back in South Wales, and it'll be a relief after all I've been through. A quieter time of things is what I need right now, and surely nothing else can go wrong …'

AUTHOR'S NOTES

It is always a temptation when writing an historical novel to overwhelm the reader with too much detail. As a result, things that some readers would find interesting have to be left out. As with my previous two books, my preference is just to add some short notes here, at the end. Other additional information can often be found on my Facebook page.

a) Lord Berwick's mansion

This is Attingham Park, a National Trust property and a very popular tourist attraction. The 7th Lord Berwick had not expected his inheritance and spent little time at the property, preferring the warmth of the Mediterranean. Lady Berwick had obtained a legal separation from her husband for mistreatment, which was a relative rarity. The house was very unusual in that it did have full electric lighting. The description of the house is as accurate as I could make it, having spent a day 'casing the joint' as it were.

b) The plight of the Pennels

Sadly, this scenario is quite realistic. Infant calmatives were not regulated and often contained opium by-products. As to whether Mrs Pennel was charged – that will have to wait until the next Chard mystery

c) Shrewsbury Town

It still nestles within the loop of the River Severn, with more or less the same street plan as in Victorian Times. The nature of the town itself, has inevitably changed, having now become heavily focussed on tourism; and expanded its outer limits to include many large housing estates on former green field sites. Although there is a plethora of very good hostelries in the town, there are far fewer than in Inspector Chard's time. Several still exist, though may have changed their name. Of the ones mentioned in the book, the Three Fishes is still there, and so is the Prince of Wales. The Plough and Harrow is long gone, but was located in the area known as Coleham. The police objected to the renewal of its licence in September 1896 when it was run by Liz Donnelly. It was described as 'frequented by Irish navvies of the poorer sort' and had stabling at the rear.

The Raven Hotel, the Theatre Royal and the cattle market have all gone. I am grateful to the books of David Trumper (particularly *Shrewsbury in Old Photographs* ISBN 0-7509-0704-5) for photographs of the old council offices in the town square, the old market hall, and many of the timber-framed medieval buildings which were torn down in what appears to have been acts of civic vandalism by town planners in the last century.

On the plus side, the current indoor market hall has in recent times won 'Britain's Favourite Market', many other historic buildings still remain, and of course the Quarry Park remains as beautiful as ever.

d) Policing

Readers of my previous books will know there really was a Superintendent Jones in Pontypridd (Evan Jones, an outstanding policeman who was much-loved and respected), but I will add that there was also a Superintendent Edge at Shrewsbury.

I was very lucky to come across:
Policing Shropshire 1836-1967 by Douglas J Elliott – Brewin Books
which gave some fascinating information about policing during the period, and although I might have used a little artistic license, I've tried to keep things as accurate as possible.

There does appear to have been a bit of rivalry between the town police and their county counterparts. The Shropshire County Constabulary did have their administrative headquarters in the council offices across the town square from Shrewsbury Borough Police Force's station.

Incidentally, it was just a few years later, in 1900, that the town's police station was moved around the corner to Swan Hill, where 'Police Station' remains carved into the brickwork.

e) The Dana

At the time of writing, it is still possible to take tours of the prison. Rumoured to be haunted, having been the site of a number of executions, it was decommissioned not many years ago, having been around since the eighteenth century. I personally found the main A block incredibly claustrophobic although there was plenty of natural light; and the hanging room was chilling.

f) Charitable institutions.

The YWCA opened in 1896

There was a children's home at Montague Place (now a modern NHS health centre).

The Salop Home did exist and was a wonderful charitable institution which did a great deal of good. It closed in 1901 after its principal supporters had passed away.

g) Haughmond Abbey

This is an English Heritage property and open to the public. I have visited it a number of times in its wonderfully peaceful location on Haughmond Hill.

h) Dogfighting

A despicable activity, quite rightly illegal, but still practised. The South African Boerboel is a terrifying creature.

i) Peaky Blinders

They were not a single gang, despite the popularity of the TV series set some decades later. It was more a fashion trend for local gangs, in the same way as we refer to punks, skinheads and mods etc. The peaky blinders 'style' in the late Victorian period, included bell-bottom trousers, bright scarves, a distinctive haircut and a bowler hat with a misshapen peak which came down over one eye. Gangs of trouble makers in other parts of the country were known as sloggers or hooligans; and in Manchester as scuttlers.

I have researched a number of articles on the subject but would mention *The Gangs of Birmingham* by Philip Gooderson – Milo Books - ISBN9781903854884

j) Birmingham

Corporation Street and Dale End are still busy city streets, but look nothing like they were in the 1890s, when there were numerous small side streets and a chemical works in the area. The Star Wine Vaults did exist, although the Crimson Orchid is entirely fictional.

k) Chard's disguise

I think it worth mentioning that the head bandage described is very easily tied. The staining of the skin with berry juice, if done carefully, is quite effective (yes, I tried it). Regarding his arm: if anyone is offended by my use of the terms cripple or crippled; I was using contemporary language. I was surprised to discover that the terms disability and disabled in Victorian times meant mental illness. It wasn't used in relation to physical issues until the mid-twentieth century.

l) The football match

A mixture of fact and fiction, but mainly fact. Such a match did take place in the Birmingham and District League. Details of the pitch location and original team colours are correct, as was the rule on substitutes i.e. there were none.

It was indeed Shrewsbury's first season as a professional club, and the previous year they had lost 14-1 against their opponents, so Harbury would indeed have been given very good odds. I have recounted what happened on the pitch accurately, including Morris turning up late, leaving Shrewsbury to start the game a man short. The scorers and eventual result, as well as the injury to the goalkeeper are factual. The key bit I changed is that Shrewsbury's real opponents were Wolverhampton Wanderers Reserves; but it was a fine result nonetheless.

m) Wroxeter Roman ruins

Viriconium was once the fourth largest Roman city in Britain. Most of it remains unexcavated. Today it is an English Heritage site open to the public. It has a very interesting visitor centre and small museum. Some of the items found on the site are also displayed in Shrewsbury Museum, which is located in the town square.

n) Howdah pistol

Such a weapon did exist. The four-barrelled version is particularly impressive. Apparently, some officers in the First World War preferred to use them rather than their official sidearm.

o) Moreton Corbet castle

A lovely peaceful English Heritage site. A bit of a hidden gem. Very atmospheric in the fading sunlight. The house saw violent action during the English Civil War. The cellar is still there, exactly as described.

p) The abduction

I have read several accounts of young women abducted and taken to France during the period. Notable is the case of Mary Jane Kelly, Jack the Ripper's final victim, who escaped and returned to England; only to suffer a worse fate years later. I highly recommend *The Five* by Hallie Rubenhold ISBN 9780857524485 which describes admirably the lives of the Ripper's victims.

q) Tilly's stolen item

I've deliberately left this vague, and hopefully some readers will have picked up the possible implication. The 1895 FA Cup was won by Aston Villa. It was subsequently stolen from a shop window in Birmingham, and nobody knows what happened to it. Decades later an old man claimed to have been the culprit and said he'd melted it down, but no-one knows for sure.

Last, but certainly not least, I would like to thank my wife Janet and also my publishers, Seren, particularly Mick Felton, Sarah Johnson and Simon Hicks; who have been so supportive.

Leslie Scase